KT-153-554

'Can I tempt you to a boat trip, my lady?'

Lucy became aware of a man in a rowing boat pulling towards her, but she was so mesmerised that she felt no fear. A few more deft strokes with the oars and he had drawn up by the bank beside her. She knew who he was, of course, had known almost from the beginning, and the strange thing was that she wasn't at all surprised.

'How did you know I would be here?'

'I didn't. I simply hoped you would be.'

His hand was outstretched. She could reach out and take it and seal her own fate, or she could turn and run and her fate would still be sealed—in another way. The choice was hers. She took the hand.

Born in Singapore, **Mary Nichols** came to England when she was three, and has spent most of her life in different parts of East Anglia. She has been a radiographer, school secretary, information officer and industrial editor, as well as a writer. She has three grown-up children, and four grandchildren.

Recent novels by the same author:

THE HONOURABLE EARL
THE INCOMPARABLE COUNTESS
LADY LAVINIA'S MATCH
A LADY OF CONSEQUENCE
THE HEMINGFORD SCANDAL
MARRYING MISS HEMINGFORD
BACHELOR DUKE
AN UNUSUAL BEQUEST
TALK OF THE TON

WORKING MAN, SOCIETY BRIDE

Mary Nichols

MILLS & BOON®

DID YOU PURCHASE THIS BOOK WITHOUT A COVER?

If you did, you should be aware it is **stolen property** as it was reported *unsold and destroyed* by a retailer. Neither the author nor the publisher has received any payment for this book.

All the characters in this book have no existence outside the imagination of the author, and have no relation whatsoever to anyone bearing the same name or names. They are not even distantly inspired by any individual known or unknown to the author, and all the incidents are pure invention.

All Rights Reserved including the right of reproduction in whole or in part in any form. This edition is published by arrangement with Harlequin Enterprises II BV/S.à.r.l. The text of this publication or any part thereof may not be reproduced or transmitted in any form or by any means, electronic or mechanical, including photocopying, recording, storage in an information retrieval system, or otherwise, without the written permission of the publisher.

This book is sold subject to the condition that it shall not, by way of trade or otherwise, be lent, resold, hired out or otherwise circulated without the prior consent of the publisher in any form of binding or cover other than that in which it is published and without a similar condition including this condition being imposed on the subsequent purchaser.

MILLS & BOON and MILLS & BOON with the Rose Device are registered trademarks of the publisher.

First published in Great Britain 2007
Harlequin Mills & Boon Limited,
Eton House, 18-24 Paradise Road, Richmond, Surrey TW9 1SR

© Mary Nichols 2007

ISBN-13: 978 0 263 85173 1
ISBN-10:   0 263 85173 7

Set in Times Roman 10½ on 12½ pt.
04-0507-92142

Printed and bound in Spain
by Litografia Rosés S.A., Barcelona

WORKING MAN, SOCIETY BRIDE

Chapter One

July 1844

After waiting outside the station for twenty minutes while a train from another line passed through, the train from London drew into Leicester and hissed to a halt. The Countess of Luffenham and her daughter, Lady Lucinda Vernley, waited until a porter came along to open the door before stepping down on to the platform.

Lucy was glad to leave the sticky heat of the carriage and breathe fresh air again. She would have liked to open the window as soon as they left London, but her mother forbade it on the grounds that they would be choked on the smoke and covered in black smuts, which they would never be able to clean off their clothes. And as their clothes had cost the Earl a pretty penny, they would have to put up with the heat. And so, for six interminable hours, they had sat and cooked.

Mama did not like travelling by train and would have much preferred to go by coach, but that would have taken even longer and necessitated changing the horses every dozen or so miles and staying at least one night somewhere on the road. The Earl, for all his apparent wealth, was a careful man and begrudged the cost when they could travel first class by rail and reach London inside a day. When his wife had mildly pointed out that they still had to be taken to the railhead by carriage and fetched again on their return, he had given her a lecture on the economics of using his own horses for a short ride and railways for a longer trip, and she had fallen silent. Arguing with the Earl was something she was not prepared to do.

'Good afternoon, my lady,' the porter said, touching his cap and taking her small valise from her to carry it out to the waiting carriage. 'Shall the wagon be coming for your luggage?'

'Yes. You will find everything labelled. See that it is all loaded properly. The last time we travelled a hatbox was lost and it took days for it to be found and returned to me.'

'I was very sorry about that, my lady. I'll make sure it doesn't happen again.'

They swept past the luggage van where two porters were busy disgorging boxes, trunks, portmanteaux and hatboxes on to the platform. They looked up from their task to watch the ladies go. The Countess, who did not deign to notice them, walked past, looking straight ahead, her back ramrod straight. She was dressed in a gown of some silky, striped material in three shades of brown: chocolate, amber and coffee. Her hat, trimmed with feathers, flowers and loops of ribbon, echoed these colours. Her daughter was in deep pink, the bodice of her gown closely fitting, its voluminous skirt arranged in tiers each trimmed with matching lace. She wore a short cape and a tiny bonnet set on the back of her pretty head. They were followed by a maid in dove grey. When all three disappeared from sight, the men shrugged their shoulders and returned to their task.

The carriage was waiting with the hood down and they

were soon on their way through the familiar countryside of Leicestershire. This was rolling terrain, with hills and dales, some quite steep, good hunting-and-shooting country. Cattle and sheep grazed in the meadows and cut hay lay on the fields to dry. Field workers, who were turning the hay with rakes, looked up as they passed; some who recognised the carriage touched their caps or gave a little bob of a curtsy. The Countess graciously acknowledged this with a tiny inclination of her head.

At the halfway point the carriage drew into the yard of a posting inn where Mr Downham, the Earl's steward, had arranged for fresh horses to be brought to complete the journey. The ones that had met them at the station would be taken on to Luffenham the next morning after they had been rested. While the change was being made, the Countess and her daughter went inside the inn for refreshment. It was a time-honoured practice that was rapidly dying out as the new railways spread their tentacles across the countryside. But there was still no line near enough to Luffenham Hall to obviate the need for a change of horses.

When they returned to their seats, the hood had been put up because they would not be home before late evening and by then it would be dusk and growing cooler.

'Well, Lucy,' the Countess said, when they were on their way once more, 'nearly home.'

'Yes, Mama.' In one way Lucy was glad to be going home after two months in London as a débutante; she loved the countryside and countryside pursuits, especially riding her mare, Midge. On the other hand she would miss the excitement of the balls, soirées, picnics and other outings, which had filled her days and evenings while she had been in the capital, not to mention the young men who had danced attendance on her. It would have been flattering if she hadn't known it was because she was the daughter of an earl and therefore a catch.

'It is to be hoped you have benefited from your season,' her mother went on. 'Your father was of a mind that something might come of it.'

'I know, Mama.'

'You did like Mr Gorridge, didn't you?'

Mr Edward Gorridge was the son of Viscount Gorridge, a neighbour and old acquaintance of her father, although Lucy had never met the young man before being introduced to him in London. He had been away at school and then university and after that had been on the Grand Tour and their paths had never crossed.

'Yes, Mama. But I am not at all sure that I should like to be married to him.'

'Why ever not?'

Lucy found it hard to explain. Edward Gorridge had been polite, fastidious in his dress and behaviour, but there was something about his pale eyes she found disturbing. 'I don't know, Mama. I think he is a cold fish.'

'Fish! Lucy, how can you say so? I thought he was charming.'

'Charming, yes—but was he sincere? And is charm a good basis for marriage?'

'It is a start.' Her mother had used every opportunity, every wile known to her, to throw her and Mr Gorridge together without breaching the bounds of propriety and Lucy had more than a suspicion that her parents had already decided he should be her husband. She did not know why they were in such a hurry to have her married—she had not yet reached her twenty-first birthday and, as far as she was concerned, there was plenty of time. She wanted to enjoy being a young lady a little longer, to find just the right man, and was convinced she would know him when she met him.

'Why him, Mama? Why not one of the others?'

'Did you find yourself attracted to one of the others? If so, you gave no indication of it. You said Mr Gorridge was a cold fish, but you did not appear to warm to anyone yourself.'

'I found them all a little shallow.'

'No doubt some of them were, but surely not all? I thought you would take to Mr Gorridge. He has a little more about him.'

Lucy laughed. 'More about him! You mean he's heir to Viscount Gorridge and will come into Linwood Park one day.'

'It is a consideration.'

'For you and Papa perhaps, but not for me. I want to be in love with the man I marry.'

'Love is not the only consideration, Lucy, nor yet the first. It grows as you learn to live together and accommodate each other. Papa has a great regard for me, you know he does, and I hold him in deep respect and affection, but that was not how it started.'

'How did it start?' Lucy would never have dared to ask such a question a few weeks before, but her mother seemed to be inviting it.

'We met at a ball, during my come-out Season. My papa had looked over all the eligibles—that's what we used to call them in those days—and decided your father was the best choice. He was already a Viscount, heir to the old Earl, whose country home was Luffenham Hall. The family, like my own, was a very old and respected one. I had nothing against the match and neither had he and we met frequently at balls and soirées and tea parties, and it was taken for granted he would propose....'

'Which he did.'

'Yes. Very properly, after our fathers had agreed a settlement.'

'Were you never carried away by passion?'

'I should think not! Ladies, Lucinda, do not speak of passion. I believe you have been reading too many novels, or perhaps Miss Bannister has been filling your head with nonsense. If that is the case, then we shall have to reconsider her position.' Lilian Bannister was governess to the family; though Lucy no longer needed her, she was still employed looking after Rosemary and Esme and young Johnny until he was old enough for a tutor.

'Oh, Mama, of course she has not. I'll swear Banny doesn't know the meaning of the word.'

In spite of herself, the maid smiled. She was not supposed to hear the conversations of her betters, much less react to them, but she could not help it. A more stiffly correct figure than Miss Bannister would be hard to imagine, but as Bert, the footman she was secretly walking out with, was fond of saying, 'Still waters run deep.'

'Perhaps not, but I beg you not to let your papa hear you say such things. You must conduct yourself with decorum, or you will find Mr Gorridge looking elsewhere.'

Lucy would not have minded if he did, but decided it would be unwise to say so. 'Is he looking at me for a future wife?' she asked innocently. 'If he is, he gave no sign of it.'

'Perhaps he was waiting for a little encouragement.'

Lucy doubted it. They had been carefully chaperoned the whole time, but on one occasion, when she had been strolling in the garden to cool down after a particularly strenuous dance at one of the balls they had attended, he had come upon her and flirted outrageously, even taking her hand and bending to kiss her cheek. She was sure that given the encouragement her mother was talking about he would have behaved even more disgracefully. She was glad when other dancers came out to join them and he returned to being the polite, courteous man he had been hitherto. 'I cannot dissemble, Mama, it is not in my nature. When I meet the man of my dreams, he will need no encouragement to know how I feel.'

'Oh, I am losing all patience with you, child. When we go to Linwood Park next month, it is to be hoped you will have come to your senses and realised you cannot let such a chance slip through your fingers.'

'I wonder if Mr Gorridge is being told the same thing,' Lucy mused.

'Very likely,' her mother said.

There didn't seem to be any answer to that and Lucy sat back and mused on what her mother had said. She did not think she was truly ready to commit herself to marriage and she was afraid of making a terrible mistake. It was all very well to talk of the man of her dreams, but who was he? How was she ever going to meet him? And what about Mr Gorridge? Why could she not oblige her mama and take to him? Was she doing him an injustice calling him a cold fish? Perhaps, in the surroundings of his own home, he might improve.

'It's been a long day—' the Countess broke in on her thoughts '—and not over yet. I would much rather have travelled in the old way and stopped for a night somewhere. We could have stayed at a good hotel or put up with Cousin Arabella in Hertfordshire and arrived home feeling fresh. I am exhausted.'

'You will be able to stay in bed until luncheon tomorrow if you want to.'

The Countess laughed. 'I might very well do so, seeing that

your father is not due back until tomorrow evening. I do not know why he could not have done his business days ago and returned with us.'

The Earl had escorted them to some of their social engagements, but much of the time was closeted with bankers and lawyers on business; as he did not consider it necessary or desirable to acquaint his wife with the nature of the business, she had no idea what it was all about.

They fell into silence as the heat of the day cooled and the shadows lengthened. The clip-clop of the horses' hooves and the rumble of the wheels were soporific and they were almost dozing when the carriage turned off the main road on to a lane that wound uphill. When they topped the rise, they could see down into the valley where Luffenham Hall nestled, shielded from the prevailing east wind by the hill down which they were descending and a small stand of trees.

Lucy roused herself to look out of the window as the carriage turned in at the wrought-iron gates. Ahead of her, at the end of a long drive, was the imposing façade of the house, with its redbrick walls covered in generations of creeper. At each corner of the building was a white stone turret with glazed slits for windows. Lucy always supposed her father's forebears had been undecided whether to build a warm country house or a castle. The result was an incongruous mix, which she was happy to call home.

Before the carriage came to a stop on the wide sweep of gravel at the front entrance, the door was flung open and a small figure in a nightshirt dashed down the steps to greet them. 'He should be in bed,' the Countess said, but she was smiling because Johnny had wrenched open the door before the coachman could do so and clambered inside to embrace his mother.

'Oh, Mama, I'm so glad to see you. You've been gone ages and ages and I wanted you to see me riding Peggy. I jumped him over a fence and Collins said I'd make a huntsman yet.' The little pony had optimistically been named Pegasus by Johnny, who was convinced he was a flyer, but the name had been shortened to Peggy.

'I'll see you ride tomorrow,' his mother said, pushing him off her lap. 'Do let us go indoors.'

They trooped into the house, the inside of which was an eclectic mix of old and new, some large airy rooms, but many smaller rooms that had, over the years, been designated for particular purposes, which in a more modern house would have been included in the overall plan. The hall itself was large and covered in black-and-white marble tiles. Here they were met by the butler and Miss Bannister, who had come looking for her charge. 'I'm sorry, my lady, but he would come down.'

'So I see, but take him to bed now.' And in answer to her son's wails of protests that he wanted to hear all about their trip to London, she said, 'Tomorrow will be time enough for that, Johnny. I am very tired after my journey, so run along, there's a good boy.'

He went reluctantly. Lucy could not help comparing the way he was treated by their mother with the way she and her sisters had been brought up. They would never have had the courage to defy Miss Bannister and come downstairs after they were supposed to be in bed and would certainly not have dared to argue with their parents about it. But it was understandable, she supposed. After having three daughters, her mother had given up hope of a son, and then Johnny had arrived, eight years after Esme, so was it any wonder he was the apple of his parents' eye and they could not bring themselves to punish him when he was naughty?

Annette, the maid, followed the governess and the boy upstairs to take off her bonnet and make sure there was hot water for her mistress in her room and her nightclothes were put out in readiness. Sarah, the most senior of chambermaids, would have done what was necessary for Lady Lucinda.

'Miss Rosemary and Miss Esme are in the small saloon,' the butler told them. 'They have waited supper for you.'

'Oh, dear, and I thought I would have supper in my room and go straight to bed,' her ladyship said, not to the butler, of course, but to Lucy, as they made their way past an anteroom that served as a cloakroom and, ignoring the doors that led to the large reception rooms, proceeded down a gallery lined with pictures to one of the smaller rooms towards the back of the building where they sat when they had no visitors. 'I really do not think I have the energy for their chatter.'

'Then go to bed, Mama. I am sure they will understand. I will tell them all they want to know.'

'I think I will,' she agreed, joining her other daughters.

Rosemary, at seventeen, was as tall as Lucy, but her hair was darker and piled up in loops and ringlets that had taken the maid who looked after her ages to produce. She was wearing a yellow-and-white striped dress with a cream lace bertha and tight sleeves ending in a fall of lace. Lucy, who was not so particular over her appearance, except when Annette was helping her to get ready for an important function at which she was expected to shine, had often thought that her sister was more in tune with what their mother expected of a daughter than she was. Lucy did not have the patience for elaborate hairstyles, preferring to tie her hair up and back and let the light-brown tresses fall in ringlets where they would. After her long journey, she yearned to brush it out.

Fourteen-year-old Esme's hair was lighter and was worn

very simply tied back with ribbon. She had not yet lost her puppy fat and had plump, rosy cheeks and blue eyes. Her dress was a pale cream colour with a wide green sash. She was sitting on a stool beside the window, but jumped up when her mother and sister entered.

The Countess stayed long enough to receive a dutiful peck on the cheek from each girl and a murmured, 'We are glad to have you home, Mama,' before leaving them.

As soon as she had gone the girls launched into quizzing their sister. 'What was it like travelling by train? Did you meet the Queen? Did you see Prince Albert? Is he as serious as they say he is? Did you go to many balls? What did you wear? Did you have all the beaux falling at your feet? Did you get a proposal?'

'Hold you horses, I can't answer all your questions at once, you know. I'll tell you all about it while we have supper.'

She hurried to her room, washed and changed into a light sprigged muslin and brushed out her hair. Feeling fresher, she rejoined her sisters in the smaller of the two dining rooms. Lucy was ravenous, having eaten only a light repast at the inn two hours before—and that had been the first food to pass her lips since they had set out from London before eight that morning. The meal was a cold collation and, once it was on the table, they were left to serve themselves.

'Now come on, Lucy, don't keep us in suspense,' Rosemary chided her as she filled her plate. 'We want to know everything, don't we, Esme?'

Lucy indulged them with a description of her first ride in a train, which had had her heart in her mouth until she became used to the speed, of tales of the balls she had attended, the picnics she had enjoyed, the rides in Hyde Park, the people she had met.

'Did you really meet the Queen?' Rosemary asked.

'I was presented in a long line, if you can call that meeting her. She's very tiny and quite pretty, but I could see she was determined to stand on her dignity. I imagine Prince Albert has his hands full, though she seems besotted by him. It's funny, isn't it? Mama was only telling me today that one could not expect to fall in love with the man one marries until after the wedding. It seems to have happened to Her Majesty.'

'What about you?' This from Esme. 'Did you fall in love?'

'No.'

'Why not? Did no one express undying love for you?'

'No.'

'Oh, how disappointing.'

'Not at all. There's plenty of time. I did meet one young man Mama and Papa seem quite keen on.'

'But are you?'

'I don't know what to think. He's pleasant enough, I suppose.'

'Pleasant? Is that all? Who is he?'

'Mr Edward Gorridge, heir to Viscount Gorridge.'

'Of Linwood Park!' Rosemary exclaimed. 'Oh, Lucy, that's a palace. Just think about being mistress of all that. Did he propose?'

'No, he did not. It's much too soon. We have to get to know each other better, so Mama says.'

'How are you going to do that?' Esme asked. 'Is he coming here?'

'No, Mama and Papa are taking me to Linwood Park at the invitation of the Viscount. We are going to visit for a few days next month.'

'Oh, how I envy you.'

Lucy smiled at her younger sister. At fourteen she was not yet out of the schoolroom. 'Your turn will come.'

'Not before I've had mine,' Rosemary said. 'And you can be sure I shall not turn my nose up at someone like Mr Gorridge, simply because he is merely pleasant. Pleasant will do for me if a place like Linwood Park comes with it.'

'Rosie, how can you say that?' Esme said. 'That would be asking to be miserable. Wealth is no guarantee of happiness.'

Rosemary laughed. 'No, but I could be miserable in comfort. Love is all very well, but it cannot survive in a garret. I certainly should not like it.'

'It's a good thing we are not all alike, Rosie,' Lucy said. 'Or no poor man would ever marry.'

'Like marries like,' Rosemary said flatly. 'It's the way it is. A lady cannot marry a labourer, any more than a princess would marry a pauper.'

'Well, I am determined not to wait until after I'm married to fall in love with my husband,' Esme put in. 'Supposing you married someone and then met someone else and fell in love with him, it would be too late, wouldn't it? I would rather not risk it.'

It was a sentiment with which Lucy concurred. She would give herself a chance to fall in love with Mr Gorridge and she hoped it would happen because, if she refused him, she did not know what her parents would say or do. Did the labouring classes have these problems? she wondered. Did their parents dangle prospective partners in front of them and expect them to marry on the slightest acquaintance? What incentive would there be to do that? They were not encumbered by titles and wealth and the need to marry well. Sometimes she regretted her father's rank and the need for her to conform. On the other hand, Rosie was right; she would not like living in a garret at all. If garrets were anything like the servants' rooms on the top floor of Luffenham Hall, they were too small to swing the proverbial cat and where would she keep all her clothes? There wasn't much chance of that happening, considering she was unlikely to meet a labourer socially. How else did couples meet and fall in love? She resolved to try very hard to love Mr Gorridge and the best way to do that was to concentrate on his good points and ignore those she found less attractive.

As soon as they had finished their meal she told her sisters she was tired after her journey and, dropping a kiss on the cheek of each, went up to bed.

She woke early next morning to the sound of birdsong and, without waiting for the chambermaid, hurried out of bed to draw the curtains. The window looked out on the stable yard; beyond that was a paddock and on the other side of that the park that made up the grounds of the Hall. The village of Luffenham could not be seen from the house because of the screening of trees, but the top of the steeple was visible against a clear blue sky. It was going to be another scorching day. She washed in the cold water left on the wash stand, scrambled into her habit, tied back her hair with a ribbon and pulled on her riding boots. Grabbing her hat, she hurried downstairs to the kitchen.

'My, you're about early, Miss Lucy,' Cook said. 'I've only just started preparing breakfast.'

'A glass of milk and a piece of toast will do, Mrs Lavender. I'll have it here, like I used to when I was little. I want to have a ride before it gets too hot.'

'Miss Lucinda, you are not little any longer. You are a young lady who is well and truly out, and I am not sure your mama would approve of you eating in the kitchen.'

'Oh, don't be so stuffy, Mrs L. Besides, Mama is still fast

asleep in bed.' It was said with an engaging smile. 'If I wait to have breakfast in the dining room, the morning will be half gone.' And with that she put her hat on the table and sat down, knowing she would have her way. The cook sighed and poured her a glass of creamy milk, just delivered from the cowshed, and pushed a toasting fork into a slice of bread. 'I'll do it,' Lucy said, taking it from her. 'You get on with whatever you were doing.' She sat on the fender in front of the range and opened its door to toast the bread.

'You'll spoil your complexion sitting so close to the fire,' Cook said. Her own cheeks were rosy from working in constant heat. 'Hold something in front of your face.'

Lucy laughed and ignored her. 'What has been going on while I've been away? Has Sally-Ann's young man proposed yet?' Sally-Ann was one of the maids who was walking out with a groom. 'Has your sister had her baby? Have they started haymaking on Home Farm?'

The cook laughed. 'You don't change, Miss Lucy. Still as full of questions as ever.'

'How can I learn if I don't question?'

'And that's another one. In answer to your first, yes, Andrew has proposed, but they've decided to wait a year before naming the day, and you are burning that toast.'

Lucy hastily pulled it off the fork and turned it over before holding it to the fire again. 'And the rest?'

'My sister has had a boy, but it was touch and go. It was a difficult birth and she lost a great deal of blood and the infant was weak—' She stopped suddenly, remembering her audience was an unmarried and carefully nurtured young lady. 'But I should not be telling you such things. Suffice to say he is beginning to put on a little weight now and is to be called Luke after his father. And I forget your last question.'

'Have they started the haymaking?'

'I heard they were going to make a start today. Why do you want to know that?'

'I like to watch the men at work.'

'Miss Lucy!' The cook was shocked, knowing, as Lucy did, that the men worked in shirtsleeves, many of them with their sleeves rolled up, displaying muscular arms and, in the absence of collars and ties, a certain amount of neck and chest.

Lucy, laughing, removed the toasted bread from the fork and returned to the table to spread it thickly with butter. 'There's no harm in seeing how the work is done. I admire the skill of the men, all working in unison. It must be back-breaking, but they are all so cheerful.'

'So they would be, considering the wet winter we had and everything so late. They are glad to be working again. Are you sure you won't have any more to eat? That's hardly enough to keep you going all morning.'

'It is quite enough, Cook. For the last two months I've had nothing but seven-course meals, tea parties and complicated picnics. I have had my fill of food.'

'You enjoyed yourself, then?'

'Oh, yes, it was wonderful, but I'm glad to be home.' She finished the milk. 'Now I'm off to have Midge saddled.' With that she picked up her hat and danced out of the kitchen door, munching the last of the toast as she went.

The outside staff were all busy. Some were working in the garden, others grooming the horses that had brought her and her mother home. Some were cleaning out the carriage; others were saddling up some of the riding horses to exercise them. The horse master had a young colt on a long lead and was training him to answer to the bit. She watched for a moment in admiration and then went into the stables where Midge put her head over one of the doors and snickered. She stroked her nose. 'Have you missed me, old thing? Well, let's go and have a good gallop, shall we?' She opened the door and slipped inside to saddle her.

'Miss Lucy, I'll do that for you.' It was young Andrew, Sally-Ann's intended.

'Thank you, Andrew, but, if you are busy, I can do it myself.'

'Not too busy, miss. I mean, my lady.' He hurriedly corrected himself, remembering she had just returned from her débutante season in London and that meant she was grown up and a proper lady now and must be treated as such. 'I must make sure the girth is properly tightened or his lordship will have my head on a plate.'

She laughed. 'Miss will do fine, Andrew.' She watched as he deftly saddled the mare. 'I believe congratulations are in order.' And, because he looked puzzled, added, 'I understand you have spoken for Sally-Ann.'

'Oh, yes, miss, thank you, miss.' He led the horse out into the yard and bent to clasp his hands for her to mount. 'Mind how you go. She hasn't had much exercise lately.'

'I will.' She accepted her crop from him and trotted out of the yard towards the drive. Halfway down she turned and cantered across the grass and on to the parkland that surrounded the Hall.

Midge was frisky and Lucy decided that the park was too restricting and made her way to a gate, which led on to a lane. From there, she found her way on to a wide, grassy track between a meadow and a field of growing wheat. Due to a cold, wet spring, the second year in succession, the wheat had struggled to grow and the harvest would be late. She had heard tell that there was new machinery being tried that would do the job of several men and wondered if they would accept that, or would they be afraid of being thrown out of work, as the cotton workers had been a few years before? Life was hard enough for them as it was, what with one poor harvest after another and the price of corn kept artificially high, but how would they fare if farmers began to mechanise jobs that until now had been done by men?

The haymakers were busy in one of the meadows and she reined in for a minute to watch. The men were moving steadily forward, their muscular arms, tanned from the sun, working to an age-old rhythm. Swathe after swathe fell to their scythes and behind them the women raked it out to dry in the sun. She rode on and up on to the heath, where she let the mare have her head and before long they left the cultivated fields behind. The heath was covered in scrub and a few trees, where sheep nibbled at the heather and sparse grass. Skylarks nested up here, and butterflies flitted from flower to flower. Overhead a kestrel hovered.

She drew the horse to a walk as they topped the rise and then stopped to sit, looking down on to a valley with a river snaking along the bottom. Down there were more cultivated fields, and a few farm buildings. Across the valley more sheep grazed on more meadows. It was all her father's land, acres and acres of it that had been in the family since the Reformation, as he was very fond of telling anyone who would listen. It was good hunting-and-shooting country, too, and later in the year her father would invite friends and relations to stay for a week's shooting and again just after Christmas for the hunt, as he did every year.

She put her hand up to her face to shade her eyes when she spotted three men in the valley. They were certainly not labourers, because two were dressed in top hats and tailcoats.

The third was more casually dressed. They appeared to be examining something on the ground and she spurred her horse down the steep slope towards them, crossed a narrow wooden bridge over the river and cantered up to them. She realised as she drew near that they were using a theodolite and one carried a notebook in which he was making notes. They looked towards her when they heard the horse and the youngest of the three, who had been squatting down examining the ground, stood up.

He was a hugely impressive specimen of manhood. Well over six feet tall, his shoulders were massive, straining the cloth of his tweed tailcoat. His chest was broad and his hips, clad in plain brown trousers, were slim. He wore a loosely tied neckcloth and, unlike the other two, he was hatless. His curly light brown hair was worn collar length. He had large hands that, at the moment she reined in and stopped, were crumbling the soil between his fingers.

He smiled, displaying even, white teeth. 'Good morning, miss.' His accent, while by no means uncouth and certainly not betraying the patois of the peasant, was not refined as a gentleman's would be. She found it difficult to take her eyes off him and, though she knew there were two others present, she was facing him and him alone.

'What are you doing?' she asked, without returning his greeting.

'Surveying, miss.'

'Surveying what?'

'The land, miss, for a railway.'

'Here?' She was astonished. She had heard her father say more than once that he abominated railways and would not have one on his land, which was inconsistent considering he used trains himself when it suited him.

'It looks as good a route as any, but we can't tell until we've walked the whole way.'

'From where to where?'

'Leicester to Peterborough, to join the Eastern Counties Railway to the Midland.'

'I find it difficult to believe my father has agreed to it.'

'And who is your father?'

He did not appear at all overawed, which made her all the more determined to stand on her dignity. 'The Earl of Luffenham and, before you ask, you are on his land, which, if you are surveying, you surely know already.'

The young man bowed, though it was more a formality than any show of respect. 'I am sorry—if I had known who you were, my lady, I would have addressed you correctly.'

He saw before him an arrogant child of wealth and class on a superb horse. Judging by the size of the horse and the easy way she sat on it, she was quite tall. Her riding habit, which was spread decorously over her feet, was of dark-blue taffeta with military-style frogging across the jacket. Her tiny riding hat, with its wisp of a veil, was perched on top of dark golden ringlets. Her eyes, looking fearlessly into his, were greeny-grey. He would have liked to despise her, but found himself admiring her spirit. She was evidently not afraid of approaching three men and telling them exactly what she thought of them.

'That doesn't answer my question. Has my father agreed?'

'We are not seeking the agreement of anyone at the moment, my lady. We have yet to establish the feasibility of such a line.'

'And to do that, it appears you must trespass.'

One of the others gave a little cough, which made her drag her eyes away from the young man towards him. 'My lady, I think you will find the Earl's land begins on the other side of the water.' And he pointed in the direction of the river behind her.

'It does not. It extends up to that ridge.' Her riding crop indicated where she meant. 'This whole area is Luffenham land.' She swept her arm in a wide arc.

'Until we see evidence we must beg to differ, my lady.'

'Then I suggest you apply to the Earl, who will no doubt supply it. In the meantime, desist whatever it is you are doing.'

The youngest man laughed and she swung round to face him again. 'It is not a laughing matter.'

His amber eyes were alight with amusement. 'I am sorry, my lady, but we have been given a job to do and we will not meekly leave it on the say-so of a young lady who can have no idea what she is talking about. I suggest you continue your ride and we will talk to your papa when the time is right.'

His condescension infuriated her; though she would have liked to go on arguing, she was not sure enough of her facts, and instead wheeled round and cantered off. Once back over the river, she slowed to a walk, though she did not look back. She was sure that if she did, she would see that they had resumed their inspection of the terrain. She ought to have asked their names so that she could tell her father who they were, but nothing on earth would persuade her to humiliate herself further by turning back to do so.

The man had been insufferably rude and the two others, who were older and should have tried to curb him, had said nothing, except to back him up. But my, he was a handsome devil, all bone and muscle—but he had a warm smile and laughing eyes, which in some measure made up for his insolence. Of course he would not approach her father, that would be done by his superiors, which was a pity because she would have liked to meet him again, if only to confirm her first impressions that he was a conceited brute of a man who had no idea how to behave towards a lady.

She wondered what her father would say when she told him of the encounter. He hated change, anything that might interrupt his ordered way of life, and she had heard him rant against the railways so often, she knew he would send the deputation away and threaten to shoot them if they came back on to his land. And he would be angry with her for even speaking to them, so perhaps it would be best to say nothing. He would find out for himself soon enough.

Myles had not returned to his task, but was standing watching her go, admiring the way she rode, her back held straight, the reins held easily in her gloved hands. He realised he had been arrogant and had not explained carefully enough that he and his colleagues were simply trying to find the best route for the line and that the Earl's land, far from being compact, was sprawled all over the place, taking in a farm here, a hamlet there, woodland, heath and pasture, as small parcels had been added over the years. A broad strip stuck out like a tongue between the Gorridge estate and the land on the other side, which his father had bought a few years before to build himself a mansion. The railway, if it took the shortest route, which it was almost bound to do because it was costed per mile, would cross straight over that small tongue before going on to the Gorridge estate. Viscount Gorridge had agreed to sell his section to the railway company and had also assured them that he could guarantee that Luffenham would consent to part with his piece of land. He had intimated that he had some influence over the Earl.

'So that was one of the Earl's daughters,' Joe Masters commented. 'I heard he had three.'

'I wonder if they are all like her.'

Masters laughed. He was in his fifties and had worked for Myles's grandfather and father since he was old enough to work at all, which made him more outspoken than most employees. 'God help the Earl if they are. He has to find husbands for them. And dowries.'

'Are we really on the Earl's land?'

He shrugged. 'Doesn't matter if we are. If he won't agree to sell, then the land will be compulsorily purchased—you've been in the railway business long enough to know that, haven't you?'

'Yes, of course I have, but I hate dissension. It makes for bad feelings all round.'

'You know your trouble, lad,' Joe said, laughing. 'Great lump that you are, you're too soft.'

'I'll show you whether I'm soft or not,' Myles said, putting up his fists and punching the other man lightly on the shoulder. Martin Waterson, the third man of the party, watched in amusement as they began sparring, though neither would have dreamed of hurting the other.

'Pax,' Joe said, holding up his arms in surrender. 'I give in. You're not soft.'

Myles, who was hardly out of breath, dropped his hands. 'Come on, let's get on with the job. I don't fancy a run in with the Earl's men. Not until it becomes necessary, anyway.'

They worked on and by late afternoon had surveyed the land along the valley bottom, which would be the easiest route for the line, and were approaching the village of Luffenham. 'I reckon this is as far as we need go today,' Waterson said. 'I suggest we start again at the other end tomorrow and work our way back to this point. We might find a better route.'

'Right. We'll call it a day,' Myles said, finishing his notes and putting them in his pocket.

After arranging where to meet, they mounted the horses they had been leading and went their separate ways. Masters and Waterson went north where they had lodgings while Myles rode home over the hills on a huge black stallion called Trojan, which his father had bought for him four years before on his twenty-first birthday. 'The size you're getting, you need a big horse,' he had said. 'I'm blowed if I know where you get it from. I'm not much above average in height. As for your mother, she's tiny. Must be a throw-back to some distant ancestor.'

His mother's ancestry was unquestionable. She was the daughter of Viscount Porson, the last of a long line, which had not thrived in the way the Gorridges and Luffenhams had thrived. His lordship had been glad enough to let his daughter marry the son of a mill owner with no pretensions to being a gentleman, but who had become wealthy through business. It was that money, and a generous contribution to Wellington's army in the shape of uniforms, that had led to his being created a baron. Myles could just remember his grandfather, who worked all the hours God made, driven by ambition and a fear that whatever wealth he had created could disappear in a puff of wind and he would be back where he started. It was a trait he had passed on to his son, Myles's father.

'My father worked himself into the ground,' Henry Moorcroft told his own son. 'He was either at the mill or the factory every morning before seven and we didn't see him home again until late evening. His efforts meant I could be educated and learn new ways, but that doesn't mean I could take my ease. I worked, too, and so must you. You can take your pick where you start, but start at the bottom you will.'

Of his father's many interests, Myles could have chosen the woollen mill in Leicestershire where the original fortune had been made, or the engineering works in Peterborough, but he had plumped for building railways, which his father had only then begun to contract for. They were the transport of the future and the whole concept excited him. Starting at the bottom, he had become a navvy and developed muscles, along with a clear understanding of how the men worked, shifting tons of rubble every day with nothing but picks and shovels. He had discovered how they lived, married and looked after their children. Under the tutelage of the contractors employed by his father, he had learned about explosives, cuttings and viaducts, bridges and tunnels, about surveying and costing and keeping within a budget, which was of prime importance if the shareholders were to be paid. He considered himself the complete railway man.

He had been so busy he had had little time for the ladies, but he supposed that sooner or later he would have to begin thinking about marriage. His father, who was still rooted in his working-class past, would not care in the least whom he chose, so long as she was not extravagantly frivolous, but his mother might be more particular that he chose someone of breeding. The Earl's daughter certainly had breeding, but was she frivolous? Judging by the riding habit she was wearing, she was certainly accustomed to extravagance. She was spirited, too, but he could deal with that.

His laughter rang out, startling a flock of starlings who had settled on a tree beside the road. What on earth had made him think of her, the spoilt child of a stick in the mud peer, who would certainly not consider him a suitable husband for his elegant daughter? He would probably never meet her again.

On the other hand, if he had cause to visit the Earl on railway business… He laughed again, raising his face to the sun. You never could tell.

Chapter Two

The Earl of Luffenham arrived home that evening in time to take dinner with his family. He was, Lucy noticed, not in a good mood. He snapped at the servants and criticised Rosemary's gown, saying it was unsuitable for a young lady not yet out. 'What is that shiny stuff?' he asked.

'Taffeta, Papa.'

'What's wrong with muslin?'

'Nothing for day wear, Papa, but it is not the thing for dining.'

'You are getting above yourself, miss, and I wonder at you, madam, for allowing it.' This last was addressed to his wife.

'It is not new, my lord,' she explained. 'It is one of mine I had remade. That deep pink colour suits Rosie and I thought it would recompense her a little for not having all the new clothes Lucy has had this year.'

Slightly mollified, he grunted and nodded at the footman to begin serving. His economies seemed unnecessary and inconsistent to Lucy. He grumbled about money spent on clothes, yet would never have dreamed of managing with fewer servants, particularly those, like the footmen, who were seen by visitors. He insisted on frugality at family meals, having only four courses, but, when entertaining, the food on his table was lavish in the extreme. His horses were the best money could buy, his hospitality at the annual hunt meeting was legendary, but he begrudged the repairs to his farmer-tenants' buildings, maintaining that if they let them go to rack and ruin, why should he have to stump up for their negligence?

They ate in silence for some time until Lucy ventured, 'Did you have a good journey, Papa?'

'It was as abominable as usual.'

'Did you come home by road, then?'

'No, I did not. I came on the railway, but it kept stopping for no reason that I could see.'

'I expect it was because you went from one company's lines to another,' Lucy said. 'You have to be coupled up to their locomotives.'

'What do you know of it?'

'I read it in the newspaper. There was a report about a debate in the Commons about the number of lines being agreed to and Mr Hudson's plans to amalgamate them so that there is no need for constantly changing in the middle of a journey.'

'Not suitable reading for a young lady, Lucinda. And Hudson will come to grief, you mark my words.'

'Why are you so against the railways, Papa? I should have thought they brought enormous benefit.'

He looked sharply at her. 'What is your interest in them, young lady?'

'It is only that I journeyed by train for the first time when we went to London and I found myself wondering about them.

It is a very fast way to travel. Over forty miles an hour, we were told. It felt like flying.'

'So it may be, but the countryside where they go is ruined for ever. They run over good farm land and are so noisy they frighten the cows so they don't produce milk, the sparks from their engines are a danger to anyone living near the line, and they ruin the hunt because the fox can escape on to railway land where horses can't follow. And that is after all the desecration to the countryside the navvies cause when they are building them. They throw up their shanty towns wherever they fancy and spend their free time drinking and quarrelling. Their children run round in rags with no education and no notion of cleanliness. Does that answer your question?'

'Yes, Papa. What would happen if a landowner refused to allow the railway to go over his land?'

'Then they would have to go round it. Now, enough of that. Let us have the rest of our dinner in peace.'

Lucy decided it was definitely not the time to mention seeing the surveyors, and after a few minutes of eating in silence her mother began to talk about their visit to Linwood Park. 'I do not know how big the house party will be,' she said. 'Nor exactly what plans have been made for our entertainment, but we must go prepared.'

'Naturally we must go prepared,' the Earl said. 'There will be riding and excursions, shooting and cards in the evening and undoubtedly at least one ball.'

'I wondered if you might consent to allow Rosemary to accompany us. The invitation was for the whole family....'

'Whole family,' echoed Esme, speaking for the first time. 'May I go?'

'Certainly not!' snapped her father. 'But I will think about allowing Rosemary to go, if she behaves herself.'

'Rosemary always behaves herself,' Lucy put in, winking at her sister. 'And I shall be glad of her company if we are to be with a crowd of strangers.'

'They won't all be strangers,' the Countess said. 'Many of them you will already have met in London.'

Lucy did not see the surveyors again and supposed they had either decided she was right about their trespassing or they had finished what they were doing and gone elsewhere. In a way she was sorry because she could not get thoughts of that tall man out of her head. She could see him in her mind's eye, standing facing her with his feet apart, his hands carefully crumbling soil, his head thrown back and his lively eyes looking up at her. His stance had been almost insolent and she should have been repelled; instead, she found him strikingly attractive. She found herself wondering what it would be like to be held in those powerful arms and, even in the privacy of her room, blushed at the scenario she had created. She must stop thinking about him, because he was nothing but a labourer, a brute of a man used to working with the strength of his broad back, and, though she might be attracted by his physique, he would never fit in to the kind of life she led. He would, for instance, never be at home in a ballroom. On the other hand, Mr Gorridge was to the manner born and knew how to dress and behave among ladies. And Mama and Papa approved of him.

Linwood Park was not above thirty miles from Luffenham Hall and, for a short stretch, their lands abutted, so it was an easy carriage ride to go from one to the other, which was how the Countess and her two daughters travelled, followed by a second coach containing Annette, Sarah to look after the girls and the Earl's valet, together with all the luggage piled in the boot and strapped on the roof. The Earl decided to ride so that he would have his own horse with him. Lucy would have liked that, too, but he had said arriving on horseback would not create the right impression; if she wanted to ride, she would undoubtedly be provided with a mount from the Viscount's stables.

The house stood halfway up a hill above the village, which in times gone by had been known as Gorridgeham, from which the first Viscount had taken his name, but was now simply Gorryham. The house, at the end of a long drive, was surrounded by a deer park, an enormous lake, a large wood in which game birds were reared and several smaller woods and farmsteads. Behind the house the land rose to Gorridge-ham Moor, shortened by the locals to Gorrymoor, a wild, un-cultivated tract of country ideal for riding and hunting.

The house itself was built of stone with a façade at least a hundred feet in length. There was a clock tower at one end and a bell tower at the other. In its centre above the imposing portico with its Greek columns was a huge dome, above which fluttered the Gorridge family flag. The evenly spaced windows on the ground floor reached almost from floor to ceiling, though matching rows on the first and second floors were not quite so deep.

'I was right,' Rosemary said in awe. 'It is a palace. Fancy being mistress of that, Lucy.'

Lucy did not comment. It was not the place that concerned her, but the people. The size and opulence of a house could never make up for arrogant, unkind people. Not that Vis-countess Gorridge had ever been arrogant and unkind on the few occasions when Lucy had met her before going to London. And in London, when they had attended the same events, she had been most affable. She could not speak for the Viscount because she had hardly exchanged half a dozen sentences with him. He had a way of ending all his pronouncements with a barked, 'Eh, what?'

As the carriage drew up, the doors opened and Lady Gorridge came out to welcome them. All the corsetry in the world could not disguise the fact that the Viscountess was fat. She had a round, rather red face, which gave her the appearance of jollity. And her welcome seemed to bear that out.

'My dear Lady Luffenham, how glad I am to see you here at last,' she said, as the Countess left the coach followed by the girls. 'And Lady Lucinda. How do you do?'

Lucy curtsied. 'Very well, my lady. May I present my sister, Rosemary.'

Rosemary curtsied. 'My lady.'

Lady Gorridge acknowledged her and then said, 'Do let us go inside. Tea is about to be served.' As she spoke, the second coach rolled up the drive and disappeared round the side of the house. 'Oh, good, your servants have arrived. They will be directed to your rooms and will begin unpacking while we drink our tea.' She took the Countess's arm to lead her indoors. 'Come, my son and daughter are in the drawing room, waiting to welcome you. Gorridge will come in later. He had some business on the estate to deal with, which he could not leave.'

'I understand,' the Countess said. 'Lord Luffenham is coming on horseback. He will arrive shortly, I expect.'

The hall into which they were conducted was vast. It was big enough for a ballroom, with a huge brick fireplace at one end. A lackey in livery sprang from a chair beside the door as they entered and stood stiffly to attention. The visitors were divested of capes and gloves, which were piled on his outstretched arms, and then Lady Gorridge hurried the little party forward into a second smaller hall lined with doors, one of which was open. 'Here we are. Edward, Dorothea, our guests have arrived.'

Edward, who had been standing by the hearth where the empty grate was concealed by a screen painted with flowers, came forward to take the Countess's hand. 'Welcome, my lady.' He turned to Lucy. 'And you, my dear Lady Lucinda. Welcome, welcome.' Before she could move, he had seized her hand and raised it to his lips. Startled, she withdrew it and put it behind her back. She had not liked the damp pressure of his mouth on her skin.

'Mr Gorridge.' She bowed her head.

'And this is Lady Rosemary.' He looked her up and down, as if sizing her up, and Rosemary blushed to the roots of her hair, bobbing a curtsy as she made a polite reply.

'And this is my daughter, Dorothea,' Lady Gorridge put in. 'I hope you will become great friends. Dorothea, make your curtsy to Lady Luffenham and the Ladies Lucinda and Rosemary.'

Dorothea was about the same age as Rosemary, but, like her mother, on the plump side. She wore her dark hair in two plaits looped around her ears. She was evidently shy, because her response was hardly audible.

By the time all these introductions had been made, the tea tray had been brought in and her ladyship busied herself dispensing tea and sandwiches. 'We have arranged some little amusement and diversions for your stay,' Lady Gorridge told them. 'But not immediately. We thought we would have a quiet evening with a little homemade entertainment and music. Time enough for jollity tomorrow when our other guests arrive, don't you think?'

The Countess murmured her assent. Lucy, sipping tea and nibbling delicate sandwiches, used the opportunity to study

Mr Gorridge. She wanted to see if he was any different in the country from his persona in town. Was he more relaxed, less formal? Was he dressed any differently? Were his eyes any less cold? Had he had time to change his mind about her, even supposing he had made up his mind in the first place? She realised suddenly that he had turned from speaking to the Countess and had caught her looking at him. She quickly turned her head away, but not before she had seen him smile. She could not make up her mind if it was one of amusement or condescension.

She dare not look at him again and turned her attention to the room. It was sumptuously furnished, with a thick Aubusson carpet, several sofas and stuffed chairs, like the one she occupied. There were little tables scattered everywhere on which small ornaments were displayed. The walls were crammed with paintings, from very small ones to large, formal family portraits. She rose, teacup in hand, and wandered over to the window, which gave her a view of a terrace with stone vases and statues lining the steps down to a lawn with flower beds brilliant with colourful summer blooms. It was all too perfect to be true. Beyond that was a park, and she could see the sparkle of water and longed to be outside.

'Shall you like to explore?'

She whipped round to find Edward standing so close behind her he was brushing against her skirt. 'Perhaps later, Mr Gorridge.'

'Oh, yes, later. After dinner, perhaps.'

'It depends whether Mama feels like it. She is often tired after a journey.'

'Ah, the need for a chaperon. We must not forget that, must we? Perhaps Lady Rosemary would like to join us, if

Lady Luffenham doesn't feel up to it. The sun setting over the lake is a particularly beautiful sight.'

She did not commit herself, but he appealed to her mother, who graciously said she would allow Rosemary to chaperon her sister, which was not at all what Lucy wanted. She was reluctant to be alone with him and she did not think Rosie's services would be adequate. Tea over, they were shown upstairs to their rooms to rest before changing for dinner. Lucy had barely sat down and kicked off her shoes, when Rosemary arrived from the adjoining room.

'It is perfect, Lucy, just perfect,' she said, sitting beside her sister on the bed. 'My room is huge and there is a canopied bed and a dressing room that has a bath. Just imagine, a bath all to myself.' She looked about her. 'Yours is the same. Oh, Lucy, I am entranced and full of envy.'

'It's all show.' If Edward Gorridge proposed, she could, one day, be mistress of this magnificent house. She had as yet not explored it and had no idea how many servants there were, but it was plain there were many more than were employed by her father. She could entertain, buy extravagant clothes, ride magnificent horses. But was that what she wanted?

'Don't be silly, even a show needs pots and pots of money. I thought we were wealthy, but this far exceeds anything we have. Our house is poky by comparison.'

Lucy laughed. 'In that case, you don't know the meaning of the word *poky*. Try going into one of the cottages on the estate and you'll see truly poky.'

'Ugh, no, thank you. And I did say by comparison.'

'And I would rather have our comfortable home than this opulence. It frightens me.'

'Why ever do you say that? You can't stay at home for ever.

You have to marry and move on, that's the way things are, and you would soon get used to it. It isn't as if Mr Gorridge is an ogre. He isn't ugly, he's handsome, and his manners are perfect. What more do you want?'

Lucy declined to answer. Instead she said, 'Go and change. We mustn't be late down for dinner.'

Rosemary left her and she sat a little longer, musing on the day so far. If she was going to do as her mother had asked her and try to think of Mr Gorridge as a husband, she was going to have to make an effort. A month before it would have been easier; she had returned from London thinking that perhaps she could learn to love him, but that was before she met a certain giant of a navvy who had warm brown eyes and a ready smile and who had somehow managed to mesmerise her. How else could she explain why she was constantly thinking of him and seeing things through his eyes? What would he make of Linwood Park and its occupants? What did he think about inherited wealth? He would despise it. Had he forgotten her the minute she had disappeared from his view? It was all so silly and so impossible and she was thoroughly vexed with herself.

The maid came in to help her to dress and she forced herself to concentrate on what she was going to wear.

It took an hour, but at the end of it she was ready. She had chosen a simple gown in lime-green silk. It had a boat-shaped neck and small puff sleeves; its only decoration was a band of ruching in a darker shade of green, which ran from each shoulder to the waist in a deep *V* and then crossed to spread in a wide arc down and around the skirt. The ensemble was finished with elbow-length gloves, a fan and a string of pearls her father had bought her for her presentation. Her hair was parted in the middle and drawn to each side, where it was secured with ribbons and allowed to fall into ringlets over her ears. Taking a last look in the mirror, she made her way downstairs. A footman in the hall directed her to the drawing room.

She was, she realised as he opened the door for her to enter, the first lady to arrive and the room contained her father, Viscount Gorridge, Mr Gorridge and Mr Victor Ashbury, Edward's cousin, whom she had met in London. They stopped their conversation to acknowledge her little curtsy, and for a moment there was silence.

'Am I too early?' she asked, wondering whether to retreat.

'No, no,' the Viscount assured her. 'It is refreshing to find a lady who is punctual. Would you care for a cordial or ratafia, perhaps?'

'No, thank you, my lord.' She seated herself on a chair near the window some distance from them. 'Please don't mind me,' she said. 'I shall sit quietly here until the other ladies arrive.'

Edward came and stood by her chair. 'I fear you will be immeasurably bored by the conversation,' he said. 'They are talking about the railway.'

'I do not find that boring.'

'Lucinda has a lively curiosity and interests herself in many things,' her father told the others, though whether he was praising her or excusing her, she could not tell. At least he was smiling and seemed more relaxed. 'And her first journey in a railway carriage has excited her interest.'

'How did you find it?' the Viscount asked. 'Not too noisy or dirty? Eh, what?'

'It was both,' she said. 'But exciting, too. Do you think the railway will be the transport of the future?'

'Oh, undoubtedly,' he said. 'It is exactly what I have been saying to your papa.'

The door opened to admit Lady Gorridge and Dorothea, followed by the Countess and Rosemary, and the conversation was dropped. Lucy was sorry, in a way; she wanted to learn more and it was all because of a certain navvy who had somehow inveigled his way into her head and would not go away. She could not tell anyone about him, could not talk about him, but discussing the burgeoning industry of which he was a part was the next best thing. She wanted to learn everything she could, though when she asked herself why, she could not provide herself with an answer.

She looked up suddenly to find Edward holding out his arm and realised that dinner had been announced and he was offering his escort into the dining room. She stood up and laid her fingers on his sleeve and they followed in line behind Viscount Gorridge with her mother, and Lady Gorridge with her father. Rosemary and Dorothea brought up the rear with Mr Ashbury.

'Only a small, intimate gathering tonight,' Lady Gorridge said as they took their seats and the table. 'Almost, you could say, *en famille.* Tomorrow the rest of the company will arrive.'

Lucy looked at Edward to see if he had reacted to the obvious hint that they would all soon be related, but he was busy signalling to the wine waiter to take round the bottle. She felt as if she were being dragged into a deep pool and, unless she swam as hard as she could against the current, she would be dragged under. But it was definitely not an appropriate time to strike out.

Because it was informal, the dishes were set upon the table for them to pass round and help themselves and before long the conversation, which had begun with talk of the weather and the hope it would remain warm and dry for their stay, returned to the subject the men had begun before the meal.

'You should invest in the new railways, Luffenham,' Lord Gorridge said. 'There promises to be rich pickings for anyone who gets in early. I have already made ten thousand pounds into fifteen.'

'Everyone's gone mad,' the Earl said. 'Railways here, railways there, loop lines, branch lines, connections. It's becoming a mania and, like all manias, it will go out of fashion.'

'Don't agree, my friend. It's here to stay. I've taken shares in the Eastern Counties. Hudson's paying dividends on the promise of profits to come.'

'A fool thing to do,' the Earl maintained. 'The line won't earn a penny until it's opened and in use and he'll find himself in dun territory.'

'His problem, not mine, eh, what? Anyway, I've put my profit to good use by taking shares in the Leicester to Peterborough. It's being built by Henry Moorcroft and he's solid enough. The line is going to cross my land down in the village and that in itself has netted me a few thousand for a tiny strip of land I won't even miss. And I'll get my own station into the bargain. I advise you to do the same.'

'Gorridge, do you have to discuss business at the dinner table?' his wife queried. 'It is not polite. Our guests will become bored. Let us change the subject.'

Lucy was disappointed; the conversation was just becoming interesting. The navvy had told her he was surveying a line from Leicester to Peterborough, so it must be the one Viscount Gorridge was interested in. Would it go ahead? Or would her father's opposition put paid to it? If the line went ahead, she might see the man again, but why did she want to? Striking and handsome as he was, he was no more than a common labourer and far beneath her socially, so why think about him? The trouble was that there was nothing common about him. He was extraordinary—he must be if he could set her pulses racing and her mind in a whirl. And he didn't talk like a labourer.

'Lucinda.' Lady Gorridge interrupted her thoughts. 'I may call you Lucinda, mayn't I?'

'Yes, of course, my lady.'

'Do you sing or play?'

'A little of both, my lady, but neither especially well.'

'Lucy is being modest,' Rosemary put in. 'She is more than competent on the pianoforte and she has a pleasant singing voice.'

'I am no better than you,' her sister said.

'Capital!' their hostess said. 'When the gentlemen join us, we shall entertain each other. Edward has a fine baritone. And perhaps later we will have a hand or two of whist.'

'Mama, I promised to take Lady Lucinda and Rosemary for a walk in the grounds,' Edward told her when the idea was put to the men.

'You can do that tomorrow. It will be too late tonight by the time we have finished dinner. The sun will be going down and it will turn chilly. Don't you think so, Lady Luffenham?'

Lady Luffenham agreed.

When the meal ended the ladies retired to the drawing room and the teacups, leaving the men to their port and cigars and their talk.

'Now,' Lady Gorridge said, setting out the cups. 'We can have a little gossip of our own. Did you enjoy your London Season, Lucinda?'

'Yes, indeed,' Lucy replied. 'But I must admit to being glad to be home. London is all very well for a visit, but I prefer the country.'

'I quite agree, which is why I did not stay in town the whole time. Gorridge wanted to come back for reasons of business—railways again, I am afraid—and I decided to come back, too. No doubt you saw something of Edward after we left.'

'Yes, he was most attentive.'

'What he needs is a good wife, and so I have told him. It is time he set up his own establishment. There is our house in Yorkshire, which is unoccupied except by a skeleton staff, and it needs to be lived in. It will make him an admirable country home.'

Lucy had no idea how she was supposed to respond to that and so she sipped her tea and smiled and said nothing.

'I believe there is good hunting country in that area.' The Countess added her contribution to what Lucy saw as persuasion.

'Oh, yes. Edward loves to hunt. Do you hunt, Lucinda?'

'No, I do not care for it. Rosemary is the huntswoman of the family.'

'Is that so?' Her ladyship turned reluctantly to Rosemary.

'Yes, my lady,' she answered. 'We girls have been encouraged to take part since we have been old enough to leave our ponies behind and ride proper horses.'

'We shall naturally invite you and Viscount Gorridge to bring Mr Gorridge with you to our next one,' the Countess said quickly. The Earl was famous for the hunts he held on the Luffenham estate, which Viscount Gorridge had attended in the past. 'That goes without saying.'

'Thank you. I am sure Edward will enjoy that. Alas, my hunting days are over, but I shall enjoy watching from a distance with Lucinda.'

The gentlemen rejoined them at that point and Lady Gorridge busied herself with dispensing tea for them and then calling on Lucy to sing and play, which she did to warm applause. Then she played a duet with Rosemary, while Edward stood by the piano ready to turn over the music. After that he was persuaded to sing and chose 'Greensleeves,' the old ballad supposedly composed by Henry the Eighth, saying it was in honour of Lucy's beautiful gown. He looked at her the whole time he was singing and she felt her face growing hot. When she tried to look away, he stepped round her so that he was in front of her again and took her hand so that she had no choice but to look at him or appear rude. Dorothea was next and sang to her own accompaniment, then the Countess played for the Earl to sing and they rounded the entertainment off by all singing a round song together.

'Now, what about a hand or two of whist?' Lady Gorridge said.

'Mama, there are nine of us,' Edward said. 'I beg you excuse me. I have something I want to do.'

'Me, too,' said Victor, standing up to follow his cousin.

'Edward, that is very uncivil of you,' his mother complained. 'And if Victor goes, too, we shall be seven.'

'Can't be helped, Mama. Find a game that does not require fours.' He turned to Lucy. 'If you wish, I will give you a tour of the house and grounds tomorrow after breakfast.' And with that he took his leave and Victor scuttled after him.

'Oh, he is too trying,' his mother complained.

'I prefer a game of billiards,' Lord Gorridge put in. 'How about it, Luffenham? I've a good table.'

The Earl jumped at the suggestion, leaving the five ladies to amuse themselves.

Myles and his two companions, having surveyed the proposed line from Leicester back to Gorryham village, arrived there late that evening. Waterson elected to go back to his lodgings, but Myles and Joe Masters decided to spend the night at the Golden Lion before continuing the work next day. They would need to take their calculations and findings back to the office and work on them, but they could see no great difficulty, except the short stretch to avoid the village. They were discussing whether a cutting or a tunnel would best serve when Edward and Victor burst in, talking and laughing.

'Landlord, your best ale,' Edward called out. 'Dining at home and being polite to my mother's guests is thirsty work.'

He leaned against the bar and looked round the company, which had fallen silent at their entrance. Most were villagers: tenant farmers, agricultural labourers, the blacksmith, the harness maker and the cobbler, all known to him, all in some measure dependent on the Viscount for a living. They touched their caps or forelocks to him, but none looked particularly pleased to see him. Then he caught sight of Myles and his friend. 'Whom have we here?' he asked. 'Not the usual peasantry by the look of it.' He picked up the quart pot the landlord had filled and put at his elbow and wandered over to them. 'What business brings you here?'

'Who's asking?' Myles demanded, deciding he didn't like the man. He had seen the look of exasperation on the landlord's face when he had taken his drink and made no effort to pay for it.

'I am. You are not the usual sort of labourers, but certainly not gentlemen, so I guess you're railwaymen. Am I right?'

'You are.'

'Ah, then you must be the advance guard of the Peterborough and Leicester.'

'You could say that.'

'There are some—' and he waved the pot at the company

'—who will not welcome you in their midst. Heathen rabble, some say, not fit to mix with civilised folk. And overpaid into the bargain.'

'If you mean the navvies, sir, they are as hard a working set of men as you'll find anywhere and earn their wages.'

'You being one, I suppose.'

'He's—' Joe began, but stopped when Myles laid a hand on his arm.

'Aye, and proud of it.'

'Is that so? What have you got to be so proud of? That you can outswear, outdrink and outwench any ordinary man?'

Myles laughed. 'If you like. We can also outwork him. How many men do you know who can lift twenty tons of muck a day from the ground into a wagon, with nothing but a shovel?'

'None, and I'll wager you can't, either.'

'Oh, but I can.'

'Would you care to prove it?' He ignored Victor, who was pulling on his sleeve to persuade him away from the confrontation. 'Twenty guineas says you can't.'

'Very well, twenty guineas, but you'll have to wait until we start building this line. I'm not disrupting work or any other works in order to satisfy you.'

The men in the room, who had been listening to the conversation with undisguised curiosity, began to laugh. 'Oh, there's a put-off if you like,' one said. 'He'll be long gone afore he's put to the test. I don' reckon he've got twenty guineas.'

For answer, Myles fetched a purse from his pocket and counted out twenty guineas. 'There's the stake and the landlord can hold it.'

He handed it over to the landlord, who looked to Edward

for his stake, but he just laughed. 'Why would I carry cash about me? I have no need of it. You'll have to accept my word as a man of honour.'

It was a statement that made Myles laugh. 'As you have declined to give me your name, how am I to know that?'

'Edward Gorridge, at your service.'

'The Viscount's heir, I presume.'

'You presume correctly.'

'Very well, when the line reaches this village, you will find me among the men, doing my share of the work.'

'Myles…' Joe protested, but Myles took no notice of him. He held out his hand to Edward who, after a moment's hesitation, took it.

'Landlord,' Edward called. 'Let's have a drink to seal the bargain.'

Drinks were brought and Edward and Victor sat down with Myles and Joe. Myles could see that Gorridge was already a little tipsy and wondered if he would remember the wager by the morning. Or perhaps he did not consider a bet with a navvy one that needed honouring. It did not bother him one way or another; he could make good his boast. His father might not be too pleased when he heard of it, but he was tired of having to defend the navvies' reputation and it might help when it came to recruiting men for the works.

Edward, who had imbibed freely at dinner that evening, was not in a mood to be discreet. 'Had to get out of the house,' he said, by way of a confidence. 'It's full of women, chattering about clothes and balls and picnics. Want me to marry, you know.'

Myles smiled. 'And you are not keen on the idea?'

'Don't see why I should when it's just as easy to have my cake and eat it.' He laughed and quaffed ale. 'You married?'

'No.'

'It isn't as if she has a decent dowry, though I don't need money. No one in these parts would dare refuse me whatever I ask for. I bet I could take that whole barrel of beer off mine host and he would not ask for payment.' He pointed to a giant barrel on its stand beside the bar.

'Why would you want to do that?'

'Because I can.'

'What would you do with it when you got it? Could you carry it off?'

''Course not. I'd send someone to fetch it.'

Myles was aware of the look of consternation on the landlord's face. 'Supposing mine host refused to hand it over?'

'He would not dare. The place belongs to the estate and he can easily be sent off with a flea in his ear.'

'A bit hard on him, don't you think? And it seems a waste of time to me to send someone to fetch it when you could have the pleasure of drinking it tonight.' Myles was beginning to enjoy himself. 'Pick it up and carry it out. If you can, I'll undertake to pay for it.'

'You'll pay for the whole barrel?'

'Yes—unlike you, I do believe in money transactions.'

'What happens if he fails?' Victor asked.

Myles shrugged. 'A gentleman would offer to pay…' He left the rest of his sentence unsaid.

'Being a gentleman, I never welsh on a debt of honour,' Edward said with heavy emphasis.

Myles ignored that and went to the bar counter to speak quietly to the publican, watched by everyone in the room. This was the best entertainment they had had in years and they longed for the Viscount's pup to be taught a lesson. No one could lift that barrel single-handed, not even the giant navvy. Myles returned. 'You can have it if you take it now.'

'Right, lads, give us a hand,' Edward said, addressing a group of labourers. 'Bendish, go and hitch up your cart, we'll put it on that.'

'No, that's not the deal,' Myles said. 'You have to carry it out of the door single-handed.'

'Don't be daft, man, it's not possible.'

'Pity. I was looking forward to sharing it with you.'

'You can and welcome, if you help me get it out to Bendish's cart.'

'So, you will not take my challenge and yet you expect me to take yours.'

'If you're so clever, let's see you carry it.'

Myles laughed and took off his jacket. 'Hold this for me, Joe.'

He walked over to the barrel, flexed his muscles and, bending his knees, heaved it on to his shoulder. A gasp went round the crowd. It was three-quarters full and for a moment he wondered if he had taken on more than he could chew, but he stood for a moment to get the balance right and then walked out of the door, which was hurriedly opened for him by the nearest bystander. He set off up the street, the barrel on his shoulder, followed by everyone in the bar, including the publican. It was incredibly heavy and his knees began to feel wobbly, but just to prove a point, he broke into a trot. Everyone cheered. After a hundred yards he felt he had done enough and carefully set the barrel down on a low wall.

Joe joined him. 'You're mad,' he said, as everyone rushed up, laughing and cheering.

'Yes, but I might have made a few friends and that will stand me in good stead when the works reach here,' he murmured, for Joe's ears only.

'Is that why you did it, to make friends?'

'Not altogether.' He had taken a dislike to Edward Gorridge for his arrogance. 'Well, lads,' he said to the men as Edward came puffing up, trailing in everyone's wake. 'I think we should take this back where it belongs and drink to the health of the navvies, don't you?'

This was greeted by a resounding cheer and the barrel was rolled down the hill back to the inn and manhandled back on its stand.

Two hours later, the men, in various stages of inebriation, returned to their homes, until only Myles, Joe, Edward and Victor were left. Victor had tried his best to persuade Edward to leave but he would not go. The whole barrel had been bought and, as it still had some ale left in it, he was of a mind to try to drink the navvy under the table. Joe decided to go up to bed and advised Myles to do likewise.

'I can't leave him like that,' Myles said, pointing at the comatose Gorridge. 'How did he get here?'

'In his gig,' the publican said. 'It's in the backyard.'

'He's in no fit state to drive it.' Myles had taken a few more than he was wont to do, but he was still reasonably in control of his faculties.

'No, and neither is his friend.'

'Nothing for it, I'll have to see he gets safely home.'

'Why?' Joe demanded. 'It's not your fault he can't hold his ale.'

'Nevertheless, I feel responsible. You go to bed.' He bent down and threw the drunken man over his shoulder and marched out with him, followed by Victor, who was just able to stand, though he rolled all over the place when he tried to walk and giggled like a girl.

One of the inn's servants lead the gig out of the yard and

Myles deposited Edward on the seat, helped Victor in and squeezed in beside them. Both men began to sing a bawdy song as they trotted down the street and took the turn on to the lane leading to Linwood Park.

Lady Gorridge was leading the ladies out of the drawing room towards the stairs, when they heard the sound of a carriage arriving and loud singing. They looked at each other in surprise that anyone should arrive so late at night, and Lady Gorridge looked embarrassed. They had not reached the foot of the stairs when whoever was on the outside beat a loud tattoo with the door knocker. The duty footman opened the door and a man marched in with the Gorridge heir slung over his shoulder like a sack of coal.

'Where shall I put him?' he demanded of the footman, and then, catching sight of five ladies standing in the hall with expressions of horror on their faces, checked himself. 'I beg your pardon, ladies. The gentleman is a little under the weather. I think the other one can make it under his own steam.' As he spoke Victor staggered into the hall.

'So I see.' Lady Gorridge moved forward, her face a mask of barely controlled fury. 'Follow me.' And to the ladies, 'Please excuse me. If you need anything, I am sure Dorothea will be able to help you.' She started up the stairs with Myles and his burden behind her. Victor, looking sheepish, bowed to the ladies and almost fell over in the process and then followed the little cavalcade, leaving the rest of the ladies looking from one to the other.

'I think I had better inform Papa,' Dorothea said and disappeared in the direction of the billiard room.

'I think, girls, we had better go to our rooms,' their mother suggested. 'And tomorrow we will behave as if nothing has happened and not mention it. It is only youthful high spirits, but Lady Gorridge was clearly embarrassed and the sooner it is forgotten the better.'

'I wonder who that man is,' Rosemary murmured. 'He did not look like the sort of person Mr Gorridge would associate with.'

Lucy did not answer, but she had recognised the navvy and, though she had tried to hide behind her mother, she was quite sure he had recognised her. It was only a glance, an exchange of messages. From him a kind of 'Well, well, so we meet again,' which was accompanied by a slight twitching of his lips that looked as if he might break into a broad smile if she gave the slightest encouragement. Her message was simple: 'Do not, I beg you, betray the fact that we have met before.' He must have understood, for he had quickly turned away and followed Lady Gorridge.

'No, but it is nothing to do with us and we must forget all about it,' the Countess said, preceding her daughters up the stairs to their rooms. She kissed them both goodnight outside her own room and disappeared inside. Rosemary and Lucy moved on and were standing outside Rosemary's door saying goodnight, when Myles came out of Edward's room and made for the head of the stairs. To do so, he had to pass the girls.

'Good evening, ladies,' he said, maintaining his navvy persona. 'Fine evening, don't you think?'

'You may think so,' Lucy said. She was unaccountably angry with him, as if he had somehow affronted her. That Mr Gorridge was drunk was clear and it was his fault. She had never seen Mr Gorridge even slightly inebriated the whole time they were in London and attending balls and parties, so he must have been plied with drink by the navvy. Everyone

knew they were hardened drinkers and hardly ever sober. She
ignored the fact that the man had been perfectly sober and
polite when she had met him before and did not appear to be
more than a little tipsy even now. And how had the two men
met? She wished they had not, though she could not have said
why she wished it, unless it was her own strange, mixed-up
emotions that wanted them kept apart. She did not want to
find herself comparing them, mentally listing the faults of
each against their virtues. It was a futile exercise, anyway.

Myles compounded his unpopularity by smiling broadly.
'It is indeed a fine evening when a man is privileged to meet
two such charming young ladies.'

Rosemary giggled and Lucy pushed her into her room,
hoping he had not noticed, but she knew he had. 'Goodnight,
sir,' she said and turned on her heel to leave him.

He reached out and caught her arm, making her turn back
to him. 'I am sorry,' he said contritely. 'I had no idea you were
here and I would not have subjected you or any of the other
ladies to the spectacle we must have presented when we came
in.'

She looked down at his hand on her arm. It was a large
hand, brown and tough from the work he did, but surprisingly
neatly manicured. It was not gripping her tightly; in fact, there
was a gentleness about him that decried his size. She knew
she should stand on her dignity, and demand to be unhanded,
but found herself tongue-tied. He was so close to her, close
enough for his legs to be brushing against her skirt. And for
a second, discomforting time, she found herself wondering
what it would be like to be held in his arms. Unable to look
at him, she turned away and he released her.

'Goodnight, sir,' she said and disappeared into her room,
shutting the door firmly behind her.

He went downstairs and met Viscount Gorridge and the Earl of Luffenham in the hall, apparently on their way to find out what was happening. 'Good evening, gentlemen,' he said cheerfully, as the footman opened the front door for him.

'Who are you?' Lord Gorridge demanded.

'Myles Moorcroft, my lord. Your wife will explain my business here. You will find her with your son.' And before he could be detained further, he hurried from the house.

He wished he had never become involved with Gorridge. He certainly would not have done so if he had known the Earl of Luffenham's daughter was staying at Linwood Park.... She had been disgusted with him and who could blame her? Carefully nurtured, she could know nothing of drunkenness and the japes working men got up to to amuse themselves. And he had made matters worse by maintaining his pretence of being a navvy and teasing her. His apology had been too little and too late. And how to redeem himself he did not know.

But, oh, the pleasure of besting that young pup was not to be denied. The villagers would have sore heads in the morning, but he did not doubt they had enjoyed their evening and, when the navvies came to work in the vicinity, they would remember it with pleasure and there would be no trouble between the two communities, as there so often was when the railway builders arrived in a district. That would not be for some time because the survey had yet to be completed and approved, the legal side to be concluded with any landowners along the way, sub-contractors employed to do the work and a labour force assembled. When all that was done, he would make a point of inspecting the work at regular intervals and then he might meet the young lady again.

Seeing her tonight, he realised she was even more beautiful than he remembered. Her hair was as lustrous, her eyes as lively, her figure as perfect and that green dress, simple as it was, had been just right, setting off creamy shoulders and a long neck. She had been angry, though. He smiled as he let himself in through the back door of the Golden Lion; he would meet her again, he was convinced of it, and perhaps in more favourable circumstances. And he would do his best to win her round. It was a question of pride, though. If anyone had suggested he was falling in love, he would have hotly denied it.

Chapter Three

Edward did not appear for breakfast. Nor did Victor. Lady Gorridge, who felt some explanation was called for, told the Countess, in Lucy's hearing, that her son had been taken ill while conducting some business with the railway engineer, a Mr Masters, who was staying at the inn in the village, and Mr Masters had asked one of his men to drive him home. She was sure that he was not to know that dear Edward would be so brutally manhandled. Of course they had been obliged to thank the man, but had made their disapproval clear.

'I felt sure it was something of the sort,' murmured the Countess, lying just as nobly as Lady Gorridge. 'It can hardly have helped his recovery to be carried in that way.' She frowned at Lucy, who was doing her best not to laugh. 'I hope he is better this morning.'

'Yes, indeed. I asked his valet, who assures me he will make a full recovery by luncheon. I am sorry that you will be deprived of his company this morning, Lucinda. No doubt he will make it up to you this afternoon.'

'Oh, please do not worry about me, Lady Gorridge,' she

said. 'Rosemary and I can amuse ourselves, I am sure.' They were in the breakfast room, a small, sunny room looking out on to the park, which was dotted with fine specimen trees and grazing deer. In the distance she could see the sparkle of water. 'Perhaps we will take a stroll in the grounds.'

'Oh, yes, go wherever you please. You will find the path through the park to the lake a particularly pleasant one when the weather is hot. I would ask Dorothea to accompany you, but she has a music lesson this morning and her teacher is a little temperamental. He will not accept excuses.'

Thus it was that Lucy and Rosie found themselves dressed in pale muslin with a parasol apiece, wandering across the short grass of the park. The conversation naturally turned to the events of the previous evening.

'Do you think Mr Gorridge was drunk, Lucy?' Rosie asked her.

'His mother said he was taken ill.'

'She would have to make excuses for him, wouldn't she? I am sure he was drunk.'

'If he was, I expect it was because that navvy plied him with drink and he is not used to it. It is well known that navvies are great drinkers.'

'How do you know he was a navvy?'

Lucy was caught out for a moment, but recovered quickly. 'Lady Gorridge said the man worked for the railway engineer, so I guessed he was.'

'He was magnificent, wasn't he? I never met such a strong man, and the way he had Mr Gorridge slung over his shoulder, it was so funny, I wanted to laugh.'

'It is as well you didn't. It would have affronted Lady Gorridge.'

'And he was so bold, wasn't he? Later, I mean, when we met him in the corridor. He did not seem at all overawed.'

'Overawed! I am sure he doesn't know the meaning of the word. I expect that is the disrespectful way he speaks to all the women of his acquaintance and thinks nothing of it. He probably thought he was being gallant.'

'He was handsome though, don't you think?'

'I am sure I don't think of him at all,' Lucy lied. 'He is nothing but a common labourer.'

'So he may be, but not many labourers are that good to look at. He was clean for a start and I liked the way his hair waved and the gleam in his eye, as if he found the whole world amusing.'

'Rosie! How could you?'

'Oh, go on, Lucy, don't be so stuffy. I am sure you noticed it, too. You turned scarlet when he spoke to us in the corridor.'

'If I did, it was with mortification.'

'Is that why you pushed me into my room, or was it because you wanted him all to yourself?'

'Rosie, I am losing all patience with you. I wish I had not told Papa I wanted you to come and keep me company, if that is all you can talk about.'

'Whatever has got into you, Lucy? I haven't done anything wrong. Talking about the man is not a sin. I am not about to fall into his arms and run away with him.'

'Now you are being silly.'

'Yes, of course I am. I would never jeopardise my future in that foolish way. I mean to make a good marriage, and that means at least eighty thousand a year, a house in town, a country estate and a hunting lodge in good hunting country. That doesn't mean I can't admire specimens like that navvy. If he really was a navvy. I have my doubts about that.'

Lucy was beginning to wonder about that herself, but decided not to encourage her sister by admitting it. 'You have high aspirations, Rosie.'

'Why not? I want my husband to be at least Mr Gorridge's equal. Maybe there will be someone among the guests coming this afternoon who will fit the bill.'

'You are still only seventeen. There is plenty of time to enjoy being single first.'

'And I mean to, don't worry.' They had arrived at the shore of the lake and stood looking across the water. It was so wide they could barely see the bank on the other side. It was edged by reeds and bulrushes and a flock of water birds bobbed up and down, too far away to identify accurately. 'It's big,' she murmured. 'I wonder how far the Viscount's land stretches.'

'I don't know.'

'Just think, you will be mistress of it.'

'Only if I marry Mr Gorridge, and then only on the demise of the Viscount.'

'Well, you are going to marry him, aren't you?'

'I don't know. He hasn't asked me yet and perhaps he won't.'

'Of course he will. That's what this stay is all about, isn't it? For you and he to come to an understanding.'

'But I am not sure I do understand. I do not know why Papa and Mama are so keen on him. If a man can leave his house guests to go and get drunk…'

'Oh, you are not going to hold that against him, surely? All men get drunk sometimes. Why, I have known Papa to get a little tipsy on occasion and Mama thinks nothing of it. Perhaps he was a little nervous of the future. It must take courage to propose, especially if the poor man has no encouragement from his intended.'

Lucy laughed. 'You are probably right. Let us turn back. It must be nearly time for luncheon.'

They turned and made their way back to the house, which was just as imposing from the side as it was from the front. It was perfect; there wasn't a window that did not gleam, not a step that did not dazzle with its whiteness, not a blade of grass out of place nor a weed in the flower beds. It needed an army to keep it like that.

When they arrived they discovered more guests had arrived and luncheon would be taken in the large dining room at the front of the house. Lucy and Rosie went up to their rooms to tidy themselves.

The atmosphere of an intimate family gathering disappeared during lunch. The company consisted of Sir Edwin Benwistle and his wife and daughter, Ursula, distant relatives of Lady Gorridge; Mr and Mrs Ashbury, Victor's parents, who evidently knew nothing of the previous evening's escapade, for Mrs Ashbury continually commented on the fact that her son did not look 'quite the thing,' to which he replied irritably that he was perfectly well. Others of the party were friends of Viscount Gorridge who were there for the fishing and shooting and who had brought wives and daughters, so that the party numbered twenty.

'The lake is well stocked,' his lordship told them as they enjoyed a sumptuous luncheon. 'I propose a little competition to see who can bag the greatest weight. A magnum of champagne for the winner.'

'Supposing the winner is a lady,' Rosemary asked.

'A lady?' he queried in surprise.

'Why not, my lord? I shouldn't think the fish are particular whose bait they take.'

'Well, I suppose a lady could take part.' He beamed at her in a condescending manner. 'A separate prize for the winning lady, then. A new bonnet, eh, what?'

'Silly idea,' Edward murmured to Lucy, who was seated beside him.

'What, that a lady can fish or that she should win a new hat?'

'Neither—the idea of fishing as a pastime.' He was feeling decidedly under the weather, but to have absented himself from luncheon would have been unforgivable in his father's eyes and he was already in trouble as it was, having to beg the price of a barrel of ale because a gambling debt was a debt of honour and he had spent his monthly allowance. But he'd be blowed if he'd let that navvy have the last laugh. He didn't remember being brought home, but Victor had furnished the details and said his mother had put it about that he had been taken ill and Mr Masters had asked the navvy to drive him home in the gig. But, damn it, the fellow did not have to carry him into the house.

'You do not care for it?'

'No, I would rather go for a ride. What about it, my lady, shall you leave them to their fishing and allow me to show you the countryside on horseback?'

'If Mama agrees, I would like that.'

'Lady Luffenham, will you allow me to take Lady Lucinda for a ride this afternoon?' he asked.

Lady Luffenham looked at her husband, who gave a small nod. 'Very well, but take someone with you.'

'Victor will come, won't you, Cousin?'

'I meant a lady,' the Countess put in quickly. 'For appearance's sake. Perhaps Rosemary.'

'Oh, Mama,' she protested. 'I want to go fishing.'

'Then you have been nominated, Dotty,' Edward told his

sister before Lady Luffenham could insist. 'We shall be four. That should satisfy the proprieties.'

As soon as the meal was finished, everyone dispersed. The fishermen and women went to select their rods and bait and to be shown their stations round the lake, others who preferred to stroll set off down the drive and the elderly went up to their rooms to take an afternoon nap. The four riders went to the stables, where Edward made a great fuss about choosing a mount for Lucy.

'Cinder is a good lady's mount,' he said, pointing to a horse with a mottled grey coat. 'Will he do?'

'Yes, thank you,' she said, realising that calling him a lady's mount probably meant he was docile to the point of sluggishness. She was a good rider and would have preferred an animal with a little spirit, but decided not to make an issue of it.

Dorothea had her own horse, which was only slightly more lively, and the two men had big bays. Once they were all saddled and mounted, the four riders set off at a gentle trot across the park. 'We'll go up on to Gorrymoor,' Edward said. 'It has some spectacular views.'

He led the way, skirting the village and trotting through the wood that lay behind it. The path was narrow and there was little opportunity for conversation, which Lucy was glad of. She was studying Edward's back and was obliged to admit he sat a horse very well. It reminded her that she had promised herself to concentrate on his good points, so, while they walked their horses through the leafy shade, she began to list them. There was, of course, his obvious wealth and prospects. He was handsome in his own way, had a slim figure and was well turned out. The cost of clothes would not be an issue with him. He was educated, but how well she had no idea; his manners were polite and he did not appear to be governed by temper. Perhaps she had been unkind to call him a cold fish, because any show of passion would not have endeared him to her.

And then she came to a stop. She had no idea of his likes and dislikes, whether he would be a loving and affectionate father to his children, what his plans were concerning the life he meant to lead. Surely not one of indolence, which appeared to be the case at the moment. No doubt Lord Gorridge was grooming him to take over the estate and that was no mean task. Could she learn to love him? Was love something that could be learned? According to her mother, it was. But her mother belonged to another generation, when young ladies were expected to obey without question, to marry from a very narrow selection of gentlemen. Society was changing and changing fast and the old ideas were dying, but not quickly enough to help her.

They emerged from the trees, trotted up a narrow lane past a single cottage with a few chickens pecking in the yard and a dog on a chain, which barked ferociously as they passed the gate. Then they were on the moor and Edward urged his horse to a canter, followed by Victor, then Dorothea. Lucy kicked hard, hoping to find Cinder had a little life in him. He obeyed after a time and she realised his sluggishness was habit; he had never been given his head before. Once urged into a canter, he went well and she soon caught the others as they reached the highest point and stopped.

'There!' Edward said, waving his crop about him. 'All that is Gorridge land—the farms, the village of Gorryham and goodness knows how many smaller hamlets and farms. There, on the far side of the lake, is Luffenham land. See the river— it's the same one that flows past Luffenham Hall.'

'What are those white posts?' Lucy asked, having noticed a row of them following the line of the river.

'That's the line of the proposed railway.'

'I see. It looks as though they are going to cross my father's estate after all.'

'So they are. There is Gorridge land, then a strip of Luffenham and then Moorcroft's grounds. After that there are several small holdings before it reaches Peterborough and joins up with the proposed line to Grantham.'

'But I do not think Papa will agree to it. He is against the railway going over his property.'

'Oh, he will change his mind. My father will persuade him that it makes sense. We need the railways to carry freight as well as passengers and having to avoid the Earl's strip will cause no end of problems and put the cost up.'

'You sound as if you know a great deal about it.' Now they had touched on the subject of railways, she began to ponder the navvy again, just when she thought she had put him out of her mind. Would it remind Mr Gorridge of him, too?

It was Victor who laughed and said, 'We had a lesson in railway building last evening, didn't we, Teddy?'

He looked daggers at his cousin. 'From Mr Masters, the engineer, yes. I met him to discuss progress.'

'Is that what it was?' Dorothea put in. 'I thought it was to enjoy a convivial evening with the hoi polloi. I cannot think why you like to frequent that common alehouse. It is full of peasants.'

'Why should I not go there?' he demanded. 'It belongs to our father and the men I see there owe him their living and they know their place. And they know mine, too.'

Lucy wasn't sure what to make of that statement. 'But the railway engineer wasn't one of those,' she said.

'No, of course not, but he's working in the area and so decided to stay there.'

'What about the man who brought you home last night?' Dorothea posed the question Lucy did not like to ask.

'His assistant, I think, some sort of jumped-up navvy. I cannot be sure, for we were not formally introduced and then I was taken unwell.'

'Are you fully recovered?' Lucy asked him.

'Yes. It is a weakness I have that occurs now and again, but nothing to concern yourself with, my dear. I am, as my physician will confirm, hale and hearty.'

'Goodness, I wasn't questioning the state of your health, Mr Gorridge, simply making a polite enquiry. I suggest we change the subject.'

'I could not agree more. Shall we ride on?'

They walked their horses in silence for a moment, not at all sure what subject would be acceptable, then Edward suddenly said, 'My horse is getting lazy. I'm going to give him a gallop.' And with that he set off across the moor, followed by a determined Victor.

'You must forgive my brother, Lady Lucinda,' Dorothea said as they followed at a more sedate pace. 'He knows he ought to be thinking of marriage and he has said how much he favours you, but he is perhaps a little anxious as to your reply and that makes him behave in a silly fashion. He has always been the same, ever since childhood. I suppose it is a kicking over the traces, a way of showing he is not to be coerced and will make up his own mind, even when it is what he wanted in the first place.'

'I hope he does not think he is being coerced into marrying me. If I thought that, I should never entertain the idea.'

'But it would be such a good match. You would be good

for him, I think. Mama thinks so, and of course Papa and the Earl have so much in common, both from ancient families with adjoining estates.'

'I cannot see how having adjoining estates matters. I am not an heiress—I have a brother, you know, so no advantage would come to Mr Gorridge through that.'

'Yes, I know. I heard your mama talking to mine about him. She is devoted to him, isn't she?'

'Of course she is, but she has no favourites and loves us all.'

'How fortunate you are. I think I should like to have you for a sister-in-law.'

'Thank you.' She did not want to continue with the conversation. Even if Edward was not being coerced, she felt as if she was, and, like Edward, she wanted to rebel. How could two people who had been pushed into a marriage expect it to be happy? She pointed at the men, who had stopped and dismounted a little way ahead. 'Shall we join the gentlemen?' She spurred her horse and this time he responded a little more enthusiastically.

Edward and Victor were standing on the highest point of the hill deep in conversation, but stopped when the ladies rode up. Lucy noticed they were standing with their backs to a large boulder, which was a shelter from the wind that blew across the moor, and were facing a second valley. Here, too, were white stakes, but they stopped short on the opposite slope. 'More of the railway surveyors' work?' she queried.

'Yes. They are down there, can you see?' Edward said.

Her heart jumped into her mouth when she saw where he was pointing. The tall navvy and his two companions were pacing the ground, quite oblivious to the people who watched them from the opposite hill. 'So I see.' She tried to sound indifferent.

'I want a word with that fellow,' Edward said.

'I must go back,' Dorothea said. 'My horse is tiring and I promised Mama I would visit Nanny this afternoon.' To Lucy, she explained, 'Nanny is our old nurse and lives in a little cottage in the village and Mama likes to keep an eye on her to see she wants for nothing.'

'Would you like me to come with you?'

'No, you enjoy the rest of your ride. Victor will keep me company, won't you, Victor?' The young man was addressed with heavy emphasis. He looked surprised for a moment, but a meaningful look from Dorothea stopped him protesting and he chuckled and remounted. 'Delighted, my dear.'

Before Lucy could say a word, they had ridden off and she was left with Edward.

'Not very subtle, are they?' he commented. 'But no matter, we will continue our ride. You will not mind if I stop and speak to those railway people, will you? You need not speak to them yourself, or even approach if you think it will be distasteful. I shan't be above a minute or two.' He did not sound like a man with marriage on his mind, though he undoubtedly realised why Dorothea had inveigled Victor away.

Lucy smiled. 'I shall not mind in the least, Mr Gorridge. With you to protect me, what have I to fear?'

He looked sharply at her, but decided to take her words at face value and began the downward descent to where the men worked.

Myles heard the horses and looked up as they approached. 'Hey up,' he said to Joe. 'Here's our friend of last night.'

'I said we hadn't seen the last of him,' Masters said. 'And he's got the Earl of Luffenham's daughter with him.'

'So he has,' Myles said, as if he had only just seen the

man's companion, though she was the one he had noticed first.

'Good afternoon, gentlemen,' Edward greeted them and dismounted.

'Good afternoon. My lady.' Myles spoke guardedly.

'You know Lady Lucinda?' Edward queried.

Myles saw Lucy shaking her head behind her escort. 'No, sir, I have not had the honour of being presented.'

'Nor will you have,' Edward said. 'Lucy, my dear, take no notice of him. Wait a little way off. My business will not take long.'

Lucy had no intention of being dismissed in that fashion and she resented Mr Gorridge's condescending attitude towards her. She dismounted and stood beside her horse. He started to nibble the grass, while both she and Myles waited to see what would happen next. He was looking at Edward, but he was all too aware of Lucy. She was wearing the same elegant habit she had worn before; it clung to her breasts and waist before flowing out around her feet. Her face was slightly flushed and her eyes were alight. With amusement? Mischief? He could not tell and wished the others could be made to disappear so that he could be alone with her. He might be able to explain many things he wanted her to know, but there was no chance of that, so he prepared to listen to whatever it was Gorridge had to say.

'I believe I owe you the price of a barrel of ale,' Edward said. 'It has been left in cash with the publican at the Golden Lion. Let it not be said Edward Gorridge does not honour his debts.'

'It is of no account. A barrel of ale was a small price to pay for an evening's entertainment.'

'No doubt.' Edward's voice was clipped. 'But a debt is a debt. On the other hand, there was no call to extend it beyond the hostelry and humiliate me when I was too ill to protest.'

'Ill?' Myles smiled, knowing exactly what he meant. 'I would have done the same for any man.'

'No doubt you would, having no pretension to the manners of a gentleman.'

'I say,' Joe protested. 'That was uncalled for.'

'Hush, Joe,' Myles said. 'Mr Gorridge is right and I should apologise.'

It was more than Edward had expected. 'Apology accepted. But that doesn't mean the other matter is forgotten.'

'Other matter?'

'To shift twenty tons of rubble in a day.'

'When the line goes through.'

'When do you think that will be?'

'As soon as the surveying is done and the rest of the finance raised. I believe Viscount Gorridge is one of the principals, so I do not envisage any problems. Except, of course, the Earl is holding back.'

'He will come round. He and my father were discussing it only yesterday. I am sure, when the advantages are pointed out to him, he will let you have his piece of land. He might even be persuaded to invest some of his own money and you will need to look no further for your finance.'

'That would certainly hurry things up.'

'What are the advantages?' Lucy asked, determined not to be left out of the discussion, though what she could contribute she did not know. It was simply that she did not like being ignored and she wanted the navvy to notice her.

'Why, with our own railway station we can hop on a train any time we like, go wherever we like,' Edward answered. 'Once the line from London to York is completed, I can reach our house in Yorkshire inside a day.'

'And there is the question of freight,' Myles added. 'Farm

produce can reach the markets of London in hours. We can send milk that would otherwise turn sour before it arrived, and chickens and fish from the rivers, all farm fresh. Heavy goods like coal and fertiliser, even livestock can go by rail. Soon there will be railways all over the country. Every town and village will have a station. It will provide work for men for years.'

'Yes, well, you had better not try poaching our labourers,' Edward said.

Myles laughed. 'They would be useless. It takes a year to turn a farm labourer into a navvy. They don't have the muscle.'

Edward also laughed. 'For shifting twenty tons of rubble a day.'

'Exactly.'

'Well, we shall see if it can be done when the time comes. I bid you good day, sir. Come, Lucy, time to go home.'

He flung himself on his horse, leaving Lucy, who was already annoyed with him for being so familiar with her, to look about for somewhere to mount. The navvy, seeing her dilemma, came to Cinder's side and bent to offer his clasped hands. She put her foot in them and he lifted her easily into the saddle. When she had settled her skirt about her, he picked up the reins and put them into her hands and somehow managed to put his own hand over hers and leave it there for a fraction of a second. Even through her gloves she was aware of the slight pressure and, startled, looked into his upturned face. 'Take care, my lady,' he murmured. 'Until we meet again.'

Thoroughly confused, she managed to thank him and rode after Mr Gorridge. The effrontery of the man! Until we meet again, indeed! He was a bad as Mr Gorridge, who had deliberately tried to give the impression that he owned her. They had made no commitment to each other; it had never been discussed between them. Surely he was not taking it for granted? Or was his behaviour something to do with the navvy? Why did she suddenly feel as if the two men were in competition and she was the prize? She didn't even know the navvy's name, where he came from or anything about him. All she did know was that he disturbed her and that she seemed destined to keep meeting him.

'He's a strange one.' Joe, like Myles, watched until they had gone from sight. 'Didn't seem to bear a grudge for last night at all.'

'He couldn't with the lady present, could he? I'll wager he won't forget it.'

'Then watch your back.'

'He was very familiar with her. You don't suppose they are to marry, do you?'

Joe shrugged. 'How should I know? What does it matter?' He looked closely at Myles. 'You aren't thinking of setting your cap at her, are you?'

'It might be fun.'

'It might be dangerous, especially if you want the Earl's co-operation over the line.'

'I thrive on a challenge.'

'You won't get anywhere with her by playing the navvy. I don't know why you do it.'

'Yes, you do. I feel more comfortable talking to the men dressed as they are, and they are more comfortable with me. Besides, I would look an idiot, using a shovel in drawing-room clothes.'

'And you don't have to do that, either.'

'No, which is why the men respect me. I don't ask them to do anything I can't do myself.'

'Like shifting twenty tons of crock. You'll look an even bigger idiot if you fail that test.'

Myles laughed. 'Oh, ye of little faith.'

Joe shrugged. 'Let's get back to work. I would like to finish this section and go home tonight, even if you don't.'

'Oh, I'm going home. I don't fancy another evening in Gorridge's company.' He smiled to himself. Her name was Lucy and he had Gorridge to thank for that piece of information. He savoured the name, repeating it in his head. Lucy. It suited her. And, dangerous or not, he meant to pursue her. He couldn't let her marry that man who would make her thoroughly miserable, when she was meant to laugh and to be happy. 'Lucy, my sweet,' he murmured to himself. 'We shall meet again and then we'll see what we shall see.'

'Did you enjoy your ride?' the Countess asked her daughter. Lucy had gone up to her room to change and had met her mother on the landing.

'Yes, thank you, Mama. I was just coming up to change for dinner. I imagine it will be formal tonight.' She opened her door and her mother followed her in and sat on a *chaise-longue* at the foot of the bed.

'Yes. Wear your dark-blue watered taffeta. It is very becoming and shows off your figure.'

'Yes, Mama.' She kicked off her riding boots and began taking off her habit. 'I couldn't make up my mind between that and the cerise silk.'

'There is no need to hurry. Sit down, child, and talk to me for a moment. Tell me what happened this afternoon.'

'Happened, Mama?' She sat next to her mother in her chemise and petticoats and pulled the pins from her hair, making it tumble about her shoulders. 'Nothing happened. We rode up on to Gorrymoor and looked at the view. It is splendid. You can see for miles and miles. Right across the lake to the edge of the Luffenham domain.'

'Dorothea and Mr Ashbury came home some time ago.'

'Yes, she said she had to do an errand for Lady Gorridge and Mr Ashbury went with her. I am sorry, I did not know she was going to do that. There was nothing I could do about it.'

'But why should you want to do anything about it? I expect Dorothea was being tactful.'

Lucy laughed. 'She was more clumsy than tactful, Mama.'

'Whichever it was, did Mr Gorridge use the opportunity to propose?'

'No, Mama.'

'Why ever not?'

'I imagine because he did not want to.'

'But I have been assured that he does. You must have said or done something to put him off.'

'I did not. Or if I did it was unintentional.'

'What did you talk about?'

'We were riding. We did not talk much at all. He was more interested in the railway line. You could see the stakes marking the line all the way to Luffenham land.' She omitted to mention the encounter with the navvy, though there was no reason why she should.

'Oh, you make me lose all patience. Everything has been contrived to make it easy for you both and you still hold fire. It is too bad of you.'

'Mama, why is it so important? If he does not want to marry me, I am not going to throw myself at his feet and beg him to propose. Quite apart from the humiliation, it would only end in misery for both of us.'

'But he does want to marry you. He has told Lord Gorridge so and he has said so to Papa. It is only shyness holding him back. I suggest you try a little harder.'

'Why, Mama? Why is it so important?' Shy was one of the things she decided Edward Gorridge was not.

'Your papa has said it is. It is something to do with the families being united and the settlements. Don't ask me what they are. I do not involve myself in financial matters.'

'Perhaps you should. I feel as though I am being sold to the highest bidder.'

'Lucinda! Do not let me hear you say anything like that again. It is a shocking thing to say about your papa, who has loved you and looked after you and wants only the very best for you. And Mr Edward Gorridge can and will provide it. You will never get a better offer. It is the duty of every young lady with any claim to rank and position to marry and marry well—that's how great families keep the lines pure and increase their wealth. But I shouldn't need to tell you that, should I?'

'No, Mama, but Mr Edward Gorridge is not the only bachelor in the world.' Even as she spoke Lucy was presented with a mind picture of the navvy, big and powerful, his hand on hers, promising they would meet again. Was he a bachelor? She shook herself. She must not, she really must not, keep thinking of that man. He was certainly not a good reason for refusing Mr Gorridge.

'Lucy, you are shivering,' her mother said, noticing the shudder. 'You must not catch a chill. Wrap yourself in your robe until your hot water is brought. I'll go and ask them to hurry it up.' She stood up. 'And, Lucy, please make an effort tonight.'

Make an effort, Lucy thought, as her mother left her, make an effort to do what? Like Mr Gorridge? She did like him. At least, she didn't dislike him. Encourage him into making a proposal? How could she do that if he had made up his mind he would not? His behaviour towards her that afternoon had been proprietorial, as if he had already done so and she had accepted. Were they just going to drift into it, with no romance at all? She put on a dressing gown, sat on the bed with knees clasped to her chest and contemplated a future with Edward Gorridge. She could not deny the material advantages, they were plain to see—but what of the rest, mutual affection, interests in common, the passion her mother had so vehemently denied as if it were a sin? Was it a sin?

Her hot water arrived along with her maid and the next hour was spent getting ready for the evening.

The evening was a convivial one, the food sumptuous and the conversation varied. The fishing had been good and Rosemary had won herself a new hat; the gardens were superb and the gardeners to be congratulated; in someone's opinion, French chefs were infinitely superior to British cooks, which statement was attested by the splendour of the Viscount's table. Music was discussed and literature; *The Three Musketeers,* so someone said, was a good read if you took the story with a pinch of salt, and someone else preferred home-grown stories and recommended Dickens's work.

It was inevitable that some of the guests should remark on the line of stakes they had seen and that led inevitably to a discussion about railways. The company was evenly divided when it came to embracing the changes the railways were bringing and deploring the desecration of the countryside and the invasion of the men who came to build them.

'Uncouth, foul-mouthed savages,' one red-faced, whiskery gentleman said. 'They throw up their evil huts just wherever the fancy takes them, their children run around in rags with no schooling and no notion of cleanliness, and the least said about their morals the better, but if I were you, Gorridge, I should tell your people to lock up their women.'

'They aren't all bad,' another said. 'I know Morton Peto and his lines are well managed and so are Henry Moorcroft's. If he is building this section, then I doubt you'll have trouble.'

'Trouble,' a third put in. 'If you want to know about trouble, I suggest you go and inspect the Woodhead tunnel. Nothing but trouble there.' The building of a tunnel through the Pennines to link east to west had already been going on for years. There were some who said it would never be finished.

'The more I hear, the more I am inclined not to allow the line anywhere near my land,' the Earl said.

'That would be a pity,' Lord Gorridge told him. 'It would mean taking our line round the far side of the lake. You would lose the advantage of being close to a line.'

'It seems to me the disadvantages outweigh the advantages.'

'It is always the same,' Lady Gorridge complained. 'Whenever Gorridge has a few friends about him, the conversation inevitably turns to railways. I don't know what he finds so fascinating about them. They are nasty, dirty, smoky things.'

'My dear,' he said patiently, 'we cannot hold back progress, it is inevitable. I find the whole concept exciting, but, as you are so right to point out, I should not bore the ladies with it, so I will say no more. What had you planned for our evening's entertainment?'

'I thought we might play charades,' she said. 'If everyone agrees. Or we might have some music. Dorothea has been practising a new piece by Chopin and I know of others in the company who are talented.' She beamed round at one or two of the young ladies. 'Or cards. We could set up the tables for whist.'

Charades was decided upon and, while the ladies repaired to the drawing room and the tea cups and the men continued their discussion about railways, Lady Gorridge sent two footmen up to the attic to bring down a box of costumes and props. When the gentlemen joined them, everyone was paired off to decide what they would enact. Inevitably Lucy found herself with Edward.

After some deliberation, they chose *The Pickwick Papers,* for which the props were easy. A candle was called for and Lucy made great play of pulling at its wick, while Edward fetched a bundle of newspapers from the library, which the gentlemen had discarded earlier in the day. Someone said, 'Burning the candle at both ends,' but everyone decried that as having nothing to do with newspapers. They went through it again. 'Hiding one's light under a bushel' was another suggestion, but it was Rosie, watching Lucy plucking at the wick of the candle, who finally guessed it. Others took their turn. *Hamlet* was soon guessed, as was 'A bird in the hand is worth two in the bush,' but Victor and Dorothea's *Persuasion* foxed them all.

After that some of the older members of the company retired while the younger ones asked Dorothea to play for dancing. Lucy found herself dancing a waltz with Edward. He danced well and she allowed the music do its work, but because he did not talk, she found herself wondering and dreaming. She began to imagine that it was not Mr Gorridge who held her, but the navvy whose name she did not know, but whose presence in her heart and mind could not be denied. Could he dance? If Edward were to propose now, would the very fact that she seemed obsessed by another man make her refuse him? Even if the other man was a not-so-common labourer who should not be in her thoughts at all? How could she banish him? Did she even want to? But she must. This nonsense had gone on long enough. If Edward proposed, she might as well say yes and be done with it; holding out for no good reason could only bring heartache to everyone concerned.

Except he didn't. The dance ended, the evening ended, they said goodnight and parted, and he didn't say a word, except, 'Goodnight. Pleasant dreams. Tomorrow is another day.' What was she supposed to make of that?

Chapter Four

The next day and those after that followed a predictable course: the men went shooting and fishing, the ladies occupied themselves in more genteel pursuits, like sketching, strolling about the grounds and gossiping. Edward was frequently in Lucy's company, but she waited in vain for a proposal. She did not know whether to be affronted or relieved. Perhaps he was waiting for their last evening when there was to be a grand ball, to which anyone who was anyone in the area had been invited. Preparations had been going on in the background for most of the week and a huge tent was being erected on the lawn. It was an annual event to celebrate the bringing in of the harvest. The labourers had their party in the barn of the home farm, but this was for the family to show their appreciation to the middlemen: farmers, factors, the doctor and the parson—not, in Lady Gorridge's view, the sort to be invited into the ballroom of the house. Lucy had heard that the railway engineer had been invited, but nothing was said about his assistant. He was probably expected to sup with the labourers.

The ladies spent the afternoon resting in order to be at their best for the event. Lucy, too agitated to stay in her room, set off alone for a walk. Her feet took her, without any forethought, through the village and on to the bridge which spanned the river. She stood leaning over the parapet, looking down into the water.

'It goes all the way to the sea.'

She whipped round to find the navvy behind her. 'You are still here?'

'As you see, my lady.' He came and stood beside her, so that they were both looking down into the water. 'The river is low at the moment, but I am told that in winter it can flow very fast.'

'Your railway line must cross it?'

'Yes, but farther downstream, I think. We have to continue along the side of the hill until we have cleared the village, then we must build a bridge to carry the line over and continue it on the other side.'

'Towards my father's land.'

'Yes, though we may do it in reverse and start from the Peterborough end, in which case we shall come to Luffenham first.'

'And if you cannot get my father's agreement, what will you do? He is very determined against it.'

'Then we shall have to make it worth his while.' He didn't want to talk about his job, but she seemed interested and it was better than nothing if it kept her by him a little longer. 'Locomotives cannot work efficiently uphill, especially with a full load, nor can they go round corners, so we have to make the ground as straight and level as possible and that means surveying the route carefully, but even so we often have to make cuttings through hills and fill in valleys; when that is not possible, we build viaducts and tunnels. Avoiding Luffen-ham would mean taking a different route, cutting right through a hill and going round the other side of the lake, which would put the cost up considerably.'

'I doubt that will carry any weight with my father. When it is a matter of principle, I do not think you will shift him.' It was said with a smile that knocked him for six. She was beautiful in repose, but when she smiled, she came to life and set his pulses racing.

'It will not be down to me, but the directors of the company, to persuade him.'

'Of whom Viscount Gorridge is one.'

'Yes, indeed he is.'

'He hasn't had much success so far. They talk about the railways a great deal and the company is divided on the ne-cessity for them, and even those who agree they are the way forward do not like the prospect of the trouble they cause in the construction.'

He laughed. 'You mean the men who build them, don't you? A few years ago naughty children were frightened into good behaviour with the threat that Boney would get them. Now it's the navvy who is set up as the villain.'

'Perhaps with good cause.'

'What reason have you to say that? Have you met and talked to any navvies?'

'No, of course not. Except you, of course, and I don't know why I am talking to you now.'

'Don't you?' he queried with a smile.

She felt herself colour, but refused to meet his eye. 'I suppose it is because I am interested in the work you do.'

'It is a strange interest for a lady. I should have expected you to be concerned with fashion and entertainment and finding a husband.' When she did not answer immediately, he added, 'Unless, of course, you have already found him and I am to felicitate you.'

'That would be a little premature. And why should a lady not be interested in something that is set to become part of everyday life?'

'No reason at all.' So, she wasn't engaged to Gorridge, that was something to be thankful for, but she had said premature, not out of the question. He hoped nothing would come of it, not only because he had realised that if any woman was made for him, this one was, but also because he had taken a dislike to Gorridge and was convinced the man would not make her happy. 'Anything else I can tell you, please do not hesitate to ask.'

'There is one thing. Why did Mr Gorridge owe you the price of a barrel of ale? Did he wager he could drink more of it than you could?'

'No, though that would have been as foolish a wager as the one he did embark upon.'

'Do tell.' Her eyes were alight with mischief. 'I promise I won't divulge that you have told me.'

He was tempted to tell her of Gorridge's boast that he could take the ale without paying for it, but decided that would not be the honourable thing to do. 'We were talking about strength and he bet me I could not carry the barrel the length of the village street. The loser to pay for it.'

'And you did.' She laughed. 'But he said he owed the moncy to you.'

'Only because mine host would not let us make use of the barrel without paying for it, considering I might drop it and break it open and he would be the loser, so I bought it first.'

'But you did not break it and so the ale had to be broached, is that what happened?'

'Yes. I apologise for the way I brought the gentleman home. If I had known you were there…'

'It is not to me you need apologise, but poor Lady Gorridge, who was mortified.'

'Oh, I know that. She took pains to tell me exactly what she thought of me. I think perhaps that is why Joe Masters has an invitation to the ball tonight and I do not, which is a great pity—I would have enjoyed taking a turn about the floor with you.'

She decided not to rise to the bait of commenting on his impertinence in even thinking she would consent to dance with him. It was what he wanted, if only to argue with her about it. 'Mr Masters is a gentleman.'

'Oh, he is, one of the best. I have known him since I was in petticoats.'

She choked on a laugh. 'You, in petticoats! That I find hard to imagine.'

'My mother has a picture of me at eighteen months old and there is no doubt of the garment. One day, I will show it to you.'

'You are presuming we shall meet again.'

'Oh, we will, when the railway comes through.'

'Then you will be with your own kind, using pick and shovel. Tell me, is it true you can shift twenty tons of soil a day?'

'Soil, stones, mud, tree roots, solid rock, everything that gets in the way of our progress. We call it crock.'

'Crock, then. Is it true?'

'Yes.'

'And you have another wager on it?'

'Yes. When a man's word is challenged, he must respond.'

'I cannot envisage what twenty tons looks like.'

'You have seen a freight wagon?'

'Yes, of course. There were some hooked on behind our

carriages when we came back from London. I think they were filled with coal.'

'They hold forty tons. Two good navvies can fill one in a day. You see, they not only dig the crock out, they lift each shovel full over their heads into the wagon.'

'Then I begin to think Mr Gorridge's wager is safe.'

'We shall see.'

She would like to witness that, but she doubted if she would be allowed anywhere near the workings. Hadn't one of the Viscount's guests advised her father to lock up his womenfolk? Papa would not take that literally, of course, but she knew her movements would be severely restricted if the railway builders ever came within a furlong of Luffenham Hall. Yet, looking at the man who stood beside her, so obviously at ease, but so courteous, she found it hard to believe the dreadful tales that were told of the depravity of the navvies. In different clothes, with a little more polish, he could pass for a gentleman. Oh, if only he was!

'A penny for them,' he suggested.

'What?' His voice, coming so suddenly out of the silence, startled her. 'I'm sorry, I was miles away.'

'So I saw. What were you thinking of?'

'Nothing. Nothing at all.'

'It was enough to make you sigh. I have not made you sad, have I?'

'No, not at all.'

'I should not like to think I had.' His voice was soft; the grittiness of the navvy was gone and the eyes, which had been so full of amusement, much of it at her expense, had become serious. 'I would rather make you happy.'

'I am happy.' He was probing too deeply and she was beginning to feel afraid, not of him, but of her own feelings.

They were stirring something inside her that she had never felt before and she did not know how to still them.

'Then I am glad of it.' He laid his hand gently over hers as it rested on the stone parapet of the bridge and she jumped as if she had been burned. 'I beg your pardon, my lady, I did not mean to startle you. It was a simple gesture of empathy and presumptuous of me.'

What answer could she give to that? Was this how navvies went about choosing their conquests? But, empathy? What a strange word for a navvy to use. But she could not help feeling it was the right one. There was something between them, something intangible, something like a thread, a very strong thread, that drew them together, no matter what their differences might be. It bridged the gulf of wealth and class and thoroughly confused her. She should not have feelings for this man at all. 'I must go,' she said sharply and walked away so fast she almost broke into a run.

It did not take many strides for him to catch up with her. 'Slow down, my lady, there is no need to run from me. I mean you no harm. In fact, I'll fell any man who does. You have my promise on that.'

'You are very conceited if you think I am running from you.' She slowed a little to prove her point. 'And I beg you not to think of felling anyone. I abhor violence. Now, please do not pursue me any further. I have no wish for your company.'

He stopped walking and stood in the middle of the road, laughing. He had not done with her yet. *'Au revoir,'* he called. 'Enjoy your ball.'

By the time she had been up to her room, stripped off her day clothes, soaked in a bath, dressed in the cerise gown and the maid had done her hair, she had calmed herself. She was back in the world she knew, a world of fine clothes, good food, impeccable manners and the grand occasion. Dressed in her finery, she was once again Lady Lucinda Vernley, daughter of the Earl of Luffenham. The young woman who had dreamed of being held in rough-clad arms was gone. And she must stay gone.

She went downstairs to join the house guests for dinner and afterwards they strolled out to the marquee to greet the guests coming from far and wide. Lucy, her hand on Edward's arm, was introduced to some of the newcomers before the musicians struck up and the dancing began. Edward whirled her off into a country dance, whose steps she did not know, so he spent the whole time murmuring instructions. Later she danced with a succession of young gentlemen, all of whom paid her pretty compliments. She smiled and answered their flattery with a light rejoinder and the evening passed pleasantly until supper was announced. This was held in a smaller tent and Edward offered her his arm to escort her across the grass.

'We have this shindy every year,' he told her. 'The locals expect it and it keeps them sweet, but Mama finds it more wearying every year. Dotty does what she can, but she does not have the presence of Mama.' He paused. 'I think they like you.'

'Do they? I have hardly exchanged half a dozen words with any of them.'

'You will get to know them better.'

She waited, expecting him to enlarge upon that and end with a proposal, but he suddenly changed the subject. 'Just look at Victor with a lady on each arm. They will be disappointed if they expect anything from him. He has been singled out for Dotty since they were both in the schoolroom.'

'Is you sister happy about that?'

'Never asked her. Why should she not be?'

'I thought perhaps she might prefer to choose her own husband.'

He laughed. 'So she shall and she will choose Victor.'

'Is that how it works in your family?'

'It's how it works in every great family—surely you knew that?'

'No, I did not. I am sure I shall not choose whomever I'm told to. Goodness, that sort of thing went out at the turn of the century.'

'Ah, a rebel,' he said, smiling. 'I like that.'

'You do?'

'Yes, I like a challenge.'

So he saw her as a challenge, did he? She laughed suddenly. 'So do I.'

'Then we are at one and we shall enjoy keeping them guessing, shan't we?' He led her to a table and pulled out a seat for her. It was after he had left to fetch food from the buffet for her that she realised she was sitting opposite Mr Masters.

'Good evening, my lady,' he said. 'It is a splendid occasion, is it not?'

'Yes. You are alone tonight?'

'Yes, my wife has only recently been confined with our third child or she might have accompanied me. She would have enjoyed meeting you, I think.'

'Perhaps another time.'

'Yes. This reminds me of the spread put on by Lord Moorcroft for the navvies whenever a section of line is finished. Fine man, Lord Moorcroft.'

'I'm sure he is.'

'The Earl would have no trouble with the men on his works.'

'Then you should tell him that. I have no influence or even interest in the subject.'

'No, of course not. Silly of me to mention it. I only meant to reassure you there would be nothing to fear from them.'

'You are the second person to tell me that today, and if you have come as his emissary, I beg you to save yourself the trouble.' It was snapped at him, which just went to show how unnerved she was. Thank goodness they were going home tomorrow and the whole subject could be dropped, because she was very sure her father would not allow the railway anywhere near his land.

Edward returned with two plates of food, one of which he placed before her. It held chicken and ham and a cold salad. 'I hope I have chosen something you like.'

'Yes, thank you.'

He sat down beside her and they began to eat, but before long Edward and the engineer began talking about the railways again and, losing all patience with them, she excused herself and left the tent. No one saw fit to follow her.

It had been very warm under the canvas, and the cool air drifting across her face, was welcome. Leaving the lights, the hum of conversation and the occasional burst of laughter behind her, she strolled unhurriedly down between the trees to the lake. A long finger of crimson light from the dying sun reflected in the water. It was breathtaking and she stood admiring it until the sun sank below the horizon and she found herself in darkness. But it wasn't completely dark. The moon came up behind her and threw part in light, part in shadow where the tall reeds grew. The boathouse was another shadow and her own slim shape another. She stepped forward to the edge and watched her other self dancing on the rippling water. It was magical and she laughed aloud.

It was then she heard a slight splash and became aware of a man in a rowing boat pulling towards her, but she was so mesmerised that she felt no fear. A few more deft strokes with the oars and he had drawn up by the bank beside her. The boat rocked as he stood up, but, bracing his sturdy legs slightly apart, he was easily able to control it. She knew who he was, of course, had known almost from the beginning and the strange thing was that she wasn't at all surprised.

He held out his hand. 'Can I tempt you to a boat trip, my lady? The view is even better from on the water.'

'How did you know I would be here?'

'I didn't. I simply hoped you would be.'

The hand was still outstretched. She could reach out and take it and seal her own fate, or she could turn and run and her fate would still be sealed—in another way. The choice was hers. She took the hand.

He drew her into the boat, made sure she was sitting comfortably and took off his coat to drape over her bare shoulders. 'It is cooler on the water, my lady.' Then he sat down opposite her and picked up the oars.

It was like a dream. It could not be real. Surely she had not been so lost to all sense as to get in a boat with a man she hardly knew and not even a gentleman. She would wake up in her bed any minute. But the rough coat was real, the creak of the oars in the rowlocks, the ripple of the water, the hoot of an owl, the croaking of a frog among the reeds and the silver moon, lighting their way, were all real. And the man in his shirtsleeves, pulling them along with the strength of an ox was no figment of her imagination. She could see the whites of his eyes and the gleam of his teeth. They were strong and white—did all navvies have good teeth? Did they all have clean fingernails? Did their coats smell of whatever soap they used to wash themselves?

'Where are you taking me?'

'To a mystical land of make-believe, where there are no boundaries and no rules, where a man and a woman may say what is in their hearts without any of it being misconstrued, where truth is more important than form, where no one is rich and no one is poor, where the sun warms everyone and the moon and stars are for lovers.'

'No jealousy, no envy, no hate,' she added, caught up by his mood. 'Is there such a place?'

'It is to be found in the heart,' he said. 'In everyone's heart who takes the trouble to seek it. Yours and mine.'

He stopped rowing and allowed the boat to drift. Her silky gown was spread across the little craft like a froth of pink sugar. Her upper body, shrouded in his coat, was dark, making her head seem disembodied. Her face was in shadow, but he could see her eyes and they were shining in a kind of understanding of what he was saying. 'Look into your heart, Lucy, and tell me what you see.'

'I don't know,' she murmured. 'I am afraid.'

'Of me?'

'No, not of you, of what might happen.'

'Nothing will happen that you do not want to happen. That's what it means.'

'I think,' she said slowly, 'that I should like you to take me back now.'

'Your wish is my command.' It was said cheerfully; the soft mood had gone and he was once again the navvy. She watched him pick up the oars and begin to pull. She could see the muscles through the sleeves of his shirt as they did their work.

She did not have the courage to follow him to that mythical land and half of her regretted it. The other half suddenly began to wonder if she had been missed and what she would say to explain her absence if she had. Real life had thrust its way into the dream.

He pulled into the bank at the spot they had left—how long before? Was it minutes or was it hours? He tied the mooring rope to a stake and jumped out, then turned to offer her his hand, steadying the little craft with his foot. She jumped out in a flurry of silky skirts and he grabbed her other hand to prevent her falling. The next moment she was in his arms and her face was lifted to his. He bent and kissed her lips, gently, reverently, like the kiss of summer rain on parched earth. She lost herself in the sensuous delight of it, made no pretence of a struggle. It seemed so right.

He lifted his head at last. 'I must go before I disgrace myself.'

'I believe you already have.'

'Then so have you.'

'If I have, it is not polite to point it out to me.'

He laughed and hugged her to him. 'As we are so past all redemption, we might as well make it worth our while.' And he kissed her again.

It was a little while before she wriggled away from him. 'I don't even know your name.'

'It's Myles.'

'Then, Mr Myles, I suggest you get back in that boat and row yourself away from here before someone comes looking for me.'

She had taken his Christian name for his surname and he did not correct her. 'I'll walk you back.'

'You will not!' It was said with a degree of panic that made him realise she was not completely lost to her position. It might be the little bit of mystery surrounding him that intrigued her, or the danger of allowing herself to be kissed by a navvy, notorious for their licentious ways, but she was not yet ready to acknowledge that she felt anything more. He smiled.

'Then I will not. But we will meet again.'

'I think not. We return home tomorrow.'

'Makes no difference. We shall meet again. It is written in the stars, in the very air we breathe. Remember that if you are tempted to marry someone else.'

'Whom I marry is no concern of yours.'

'Oh, but it is, most decidedly it is.'

'Nonsense. I have foolishly allowed you to take liberties tonight. I cannot think why, but it does not mean anything....'

'No? Do you think a brutal navvy has no finer feelings? That he cannot be hurt by rejection?'

'I begin to wonder if you are a navvy.'

'Oh, I am that,' he said. 'I've got muscles to prove it. And bruises, too.' He lifted her hand, slowly and deliberately removed her glove and put his lips to the back of her hand, then turned it over and kissed the palm. She shivered as his lips explored her flesh and her whole body seemed to turn liquid with desire. Terrified of her own reaction, she snatched her hand away and fled.

He stood and watched her and then went slowly back to the boat, where he sat patiently waiting for Joe, whom he had rowed over from the other side of the lake earlier that evening. It was much shorter and quicker than going by road and he had hoped he might watch the jollity from a distance and perhaps catch a glimpse of Lucy, tormenting himself with the thought that she was dancing with Gorridge. And then she had appeared like a wraith, pale and achingly beautiful. The opportunity to have her to himself for a while had been too good to miss. It was all very well to talk nonsense to her, saying whatever came into his head, watching her slow smile, but then he hadn't won her over completely, not as a navvy. Why had he continued with that pretence?

But it wasn't a pretence. He *was* a navvy. And a gentleman. And the two sides of his nature did not sit easily together. His mother deplored the navvy, his father laughed and said it had been the making of him. But when it came to dealing with young ladies like Lucinda Vernley, his two sides warred with each other. Having started out the navvy, it was becoming increasingly difficult to show her the other side of him. He could dance just as well as Edward Gorridge, could dress as finely. Easy compliments that meant nothing could just as easily trip from his tongue and yet he chose the other way, even when she had given him the opportunity to explain.

He could see the lights about the gardens between the trees, could hear the music, and a stray dog barking. Was she in Gorridge's arms? Was he even now proposing marriage? Would she accept?

The music stopped; several carriages made their way from the stables behind the house to the gravel at the front. He could hear, rather than see, the horses. Voices calling goodnight, the clop of hooves and the rumble of wheels told him that the guests were departing. A few minutes later Joe appeared. 'You waited, then?'

'I said I would.'

Joe climbed into the boat and picked up one of the oars. Together they set off across the moonlit water.

'A good evening?' Myles asked.

'The usual thing. The gentry and the hoi polloi in the same

space, but not connecting. You didn't have to wait about. I could have gone to the Golden Lion for the night.'

'Oh, my evening was not entirely wasted.'

Joe laughed. 'Did a bit of poaching, did you?'

'Yes.'

Joe decided not to comment on the lack of evidence of success. He had seen the lady disappear and had a feeling that rabbits did not figure in his friend's evening at all. He just hoped he wasn't storing trouble up for himself.

The Earl was furious with Lucy. He blamed her that they had returned home without a proposal or even the hint of one. She had been too cool towards Mr Gorridge, she had said something to upset him. 'You have too sharp a tongue, Lucinda,' he said when they were once more at home. 'No doubt you found fault or more likely proffered an opinion on something ladies should have no opinion on.'

'I was not aware I had done so, Papa. In fact, I was careful not to do so. And Mr Gorridge was perfectly at ease with me. He simply did not see fit to commit himself, that is all.'

'I felt sure he had proposed last evening,' her mother said. 'You both disappeared and I thought you had gone off to be private somewhere.'

She had not known that Mr Gorridge had taken himself off almost immediately after she had, until she met him as she was returning to the house. He seemed a little put out at first, until he realised she had not been looking for him and had only come out for a breath of fresh air. Then he had tucked her hand into his arm and they had rejoined the company together. 'We simply went for a walk round the garden to cool down. It was terribly hot in the tent.'

'Whatever is the matter with the man?' the Earl demanded

in exasperation. 'There have been opportunities in plenty and he has not seen fit to take them up.'

'I think, Papa, that he enjoys keeping everyone on tenterhooks. He as good as told me so.'

'Well, all is not lost then. He is coming with his parents for a week's shooting next month and no doubt he'll come up to scratch then.'

Lucy wanted very much to tell him she had made up her mind to reject the proposal, but decided not to anger him again after managing to pacify him. Time enough for that when Mr Gorridge did manage to find the courage or inclination to propose and she could find a reason that would satisfy him. The real one was all because of the navvy. Oh, she knew marriage to him was out of the question, not only because of what he was; everyone knew that the navvies were hardly ever married to the women who shared their lives. And what a life! She could not even begin to contemplate that. It was more to do with the way he looked at her, searching her face as if he could not get enough of her, the way he spoke to her, his concern for her and the strange sensations he aroused in her. Edward Gorridge had never done that, never attempted to do so and, having met the navvy, she was more than ever convinced that Edward Gorridge was a cold fish. She must look elsewhere for her partner in life.

Her father let the matter rest, much to her relief, and her life returned to its normal pattern. She went riding, paid visits with her mother to friends in the neighbourhood and to the poor people in the village. Life had been hard for the agricultural community for years; harvest after harvest had been bad and many of them were hungry. The Countess did what she could by taking them little presents of food and clothing for which she was loved. Lucy, taking her cue from her mother, interested herself in their welfare. She played tennis and croquet with her sisters and brother, wrote letters to distant friends, sewed and sketched.

She was in the morning parlour three weeks after her return home, working on a sketch of the bridge at Gorryham, which she had started from memory, when a footman came to tell her that two gentlemen visitors had arrived and asked to see her father.

'I told them the Earl was not at home,' he said. 'But they say they will wait. Her ladyship is also out, so what am I to do?'

'Who are they?' she asked.

'One of them says he is Lord Moorcroft. I cannot bundle a nobleman out of the door, can I? Not that I would want to, considering the man with him is built like a navvy.'

Lucy's heart began to beat in her throat. Could it be? If it was, what was he doing with Lord Moorcroft? She had never met his lordship, but she had heard of him. He owned a neighbouring estate and she had heard his name mentioned more than once in connection with railway building. It was undoubtedly why they were here. Was it any part of her duty to intervene? In the absence of her mother, it was. She was the eldest daughter and should stand in for her. 'Where are they?' she asked.

'In the waiting room. I did not know where else to put them. If Lady Luffenham had been at home, I would have shown them into the drawing room.'

'I will go and speak to them.' She rose and made her way to the small sitting room beside the front door where uninvited visitors waited to see if they would be granted an interview, people like farmers, business people, his lordship's steward, those not considered drawing-room visitors. The door to the room was ajar and she could see the navvy as she approached. He had his back to the door and was studying a portrait of her grandfather, which hung above the fireplace. Her step faltered, but then she took her courage in her hands and entered.

'Good morning, gentlemen. My father is not at home, nor, I am afraid, is my mother. I am Lady Lucinda.'

Myles whirled round and stood looking at her, his head turned slightly sideways as if he could see her better that way. She was dressed in pale blue muslin dotted with white spots. Her hair was simply arranged in ringlets tied back with matching ribbon. His memory had not been at fault: she was beautiful and he loved her. He bowed formally. 'My lady.'

He was, she noticed, dressed in a grey frockcoat and narrow trousers whose exquisite tailoring could do little to hide his physique. His scarf had given place to a pristine silk cravat. His unruly hair had been smoothed down and he carried a top hat. The change in his appearance startled her so much that, for a moment, she forgot her role.

A slight cough from the other gentleman brought her to her senses and she turned to face him. He was a portly man of middle years with a red face and gingery whiskers, dressed in a brown tailcoat suit and a buff-coloured waistcoat. 'Lord Moorcroft, I believe.'

'Yes, my lady and this is…' He turned to his son.

'I have already had the pleasure of meeting Lady Lucinda,' Myles put in quickly. 'When we were surveying, her ladyship came upon us. Accused us of trespass, as I recall.'

'Then, my lady, you will know the reason for our visit.'

'I can guess,' she said, guessing also that the navvy had gone to a lot of trouble and expense to make a good impression for his visit to the great house. She should at least acknowledge that and treat him accordingly. Knowing what her mother would have done in the circumstances, she turned to the footman, who still hovered in the hall behind her. 'Watkins, take the gentlemen's hats, then go to the kitchen and ask for refreshments to be sent to the drawing room.' Having deposited the hats on a side table in the hall, he disappeared on his errand and she turned back to the visitors. 'Gentlemen, please come with me.'

She led the way across the hall to the main drawing room. 'Please sit down.' She indicated one of the sofas set at right angles to the hearth and seated herself on the other, controlling the shaking of her limbs with an effort. 'I am sorry you were kept waiting in the vestibule, but as both my father and mother are out, the footman was at a loss to know what to do. I am afraid you will have to make do with me.'

'That is certainly no hardship,' Myles said.

'How long will his lordship be?' Henry asked.

'I believe he is on the estate,' she said. 'But as to how long he will be, I have no idea. Is the matter urgent?'

'We should, perhaps, have sent notice of our coming,' he said, 'but as we need to conclude our business with the Earl before we can proceed with our plans, we decided to take a chance of catching him at home.'

From that she gathered that they had tried contacting her father and he had been making himself unavailable or refusing to answer letters. 'Mr Myles is aware of my father's stance on railways being built on Luffenham land,' she said.

Henry looked at Myles with an eyebrow cocked. 'Mr Myles?' he murmured.

'Yes,' Myles said quickly, a mischievous gleam in his eye. 'Her ladyship was kind enough to enquire my name when we met.'

She did not want to be reminded of that. 'Perhaps the Earl will be here by the time you have had your refreshment,' she said, as the footman returned with the tea tray and set it down by her elbow. To Watkins she said, 'I will see to it. See if you can find Lady Rosemary and ask her to join us.' If her father came home and found her all alone, dispensing tea to two men, one of whom was certainly not a gentleman, she would be in trouble.

She was gratified to note that Mr Myles's manners were impeccable, as he sipped tea and made small talk. Coming from him it seemed absurd. His lordship seemed to be enjoying a private joke, for he smiled a lot, no doubt at his young friend's expense. Of the two, he seemed the more rough and ready, which surprised her. Perhaps that was why her parents had never visited Goodthorpe Manor, nor invited the Moorcrofts to Luffenham Hall. But he intrigued her almost as much as the navvy did.

The footman returned to say he could not find Lady Rosemary and supposed she had gone with the Countess; he had hardly left them when they heard voices and her father entered the room. Both Henry and Myles stood up.

'Lord Moorcroft. I understand from my footman that you wish to see me?'

'Yes, my lord. This is—' He indicated Myles.

'I know who the young man is. I see my daughter has seen fit to entertain you.'

'Indeed, yes.'

'Mama was out,' Lucy put in. 'I stood in her stead. The gentlemen said their business was urgent.'

'Then we had better get on with it. Come to the library, gentlemen, where we can discuss matters more freely.' And with that he left the room. Lord Moorcroft followed him.

Myles looked at Lucy, a broad smile on his face, but he did not speak. She watched him go after the two older men and then sat down again and let out her breath in a long sigh. There was no shaking him off. Wherever she went, he was there. He must have hoped he would see her today and had dressed himself up for the occasion, but it made no difference to her view of him. He was a navvy dressed in the clothes of a gentleman and she would rather he did not pretend to be something he was not. It did not impress her.

'Lucy, who have you been entertaining?' Her mother had entered the room and noticed the used tea cups. She was still wearing her outdoor coat and hat.

'Two gentlemen who came to see Papa. They are in the library with him now.'

'Then send for someone to take these things away and bring a fresh pot while I go and take off my hat. I am parched. Old Mrs Whitby offered me tea, but her cups are so stained and chipped I could not bring myself to accept. Besides, the poor dear can hardly afford to keep giving me tea.' She disappeared without questioning Lucy any further.

She had returned and was enjoying her tea and listening to Lucy's carefully edited account of what had happened when they heard the visitors leaving and the Earl joined them. The Countess looked up. 'Have they gone? I am surprised you did not see fit to present his lordship to me.'

'It was business, Maryanne, and Lord Moorcroft, for all his title, is not a gentleman.' He turned to Lucy. 'And I am surprised at you, miss, entertaining them as if they were royalty.'

'I only did as I thought Mama would have done,' she protested.

'You knew that young man was the one who had the temerity to bring Edward Gorridge home on his back.'

'I did not recognise him, Papa.'

'No, perhaps not,' he conceded. 'He was dressed up like a popinjay and I suppose it did no harm to let Moorcroft see how civilised people behave.'

'Is he not civilised?' his wife queried.

'He is a businessman. He works for his living. Not that he's done too badly out of it, but he's not the sort we should be entertaining. His father was the foreman of a cloth mill before he had the luck to marry the mill owner's daughter. He's come up in the world, but it doesn't make him a gentleman. He can't forget his roots, speaks in the common idiom when he forgets himself and is determined to bring his son up the same way. I hope when Johnny grows up he will conduct himself according to his station in life and not go slumming with his inferiors.'

'Did you conclude your business with him? I assume he came about the railway.'

'Yes, he did. I can see why he is successful at what he does. He had facts and figures at his fingertips, quoted stocks and shares and compensation and tried blinding me with science. He's probably right; the railways are here to stay and it would be commercial suicide to have an estate that could not be reached by rail. Agriculture is in the doldrums, has been for some time, and, if I cut Luffenham off from the advantages of sending produce to the best markets by rail, I am condemning my farmer tenants to penury. And if they are poor, how will they pay their rent?' He was evidently repeating Lord Moorcroft's words. 'He asked me how much coal we used in a year, and though I could not tell him precisely, I knew it must be several tons a month, especially in winter, what with fires and boilers and heating the glasshouses. And that doesn't take account of what the tenants use. He told me the cost would drop by at least a third if it were brought to us by rail.'

'It sounds as if you have been convinced,' the Countess said.

He was reluctant to give up his stance. 'Not at all. You know I hate doing anything that might diminish the estate, but we are only talking about a small strip of land on the far side. And Moorcroft said the navvies would be gone in a matter of weeks and he would guarantee their discipline. Or rather the young fellow did. It may be why Moorcroft brought him. I have said I will take other advice and let him know, but that was only to get rid of him.'

Lucy excused herself and returned to her sketch of the bridge. Would her father give in? If he did, it meant the navvies would be coming and she might see Mr Myles again. The prospect was both exciting and frightening. Would she see him in his shirt-sleeves, loading twenty tons of soil into a wagon? Would he laugh and take Mr Gorridge's money? Edward Gorridge would not like it. She looked down at the pad on which she had been sketching and realised, with a sense of shock, that she had put Mr Myles on the bridge, leaning over the parapet, and he was easily recognisable. She tore the page out, folded it carefully and put it in her skirt pocket, just as Rosemary dashed into the room. 'Is it true that tall navvy has been here?'

'Yes. Who told you that?'

'Miss Bannister. She saw him arrive and she heard Papa talking to Mama about Lord Moorcroft. He's not Lord Moorcroft, is he?'

'No, of course not. He's a navvy, but Lord Moorcroft brought him. They came to persuade Papa to part with some land for the railway.'

'Oh, railways, is that all? I'm sick and tried of hearing about them.'

'Then let us talk of something else. I thought I might take Johnny for a ride this afternoon. He missed us while we were away and he's longing to show off his prowess. Shall you come?'

The upheaval was over, the danger passed and Lucy was back to being what she had always been, the Earl of Luffenham's daughter.

'Mr Myles,' Lord Moorcroft chortled as they left Luffenham Hall behind and were driving along lanes lined with hawthorn and elder hedges back to Goodthorpe Manor. 'Mr Myles! What have you been up to, my boy?'

'Nothing. It was a simple misunderstanding on her ladyship's part.'

'Which you did nothing to correct. Ashamed of the name of Moorcroft, are you?'

'No, Father, not at all.'

'She's a handsome wench.'

'Yes, she is, but I do not think she would appreciate you calling her a wench.'

Henry was still laughing. 'Had some conversation with her, did you?'

'When?' Myles was thinking of Lucy, remembering her in his arms, soft and compliant. She had not cared who he was then.

'When you met her. You said she accused you of trespassing.'

'So she did. I met her again later. At Gorridge's place. She was a guest there. Took me for a navvy.'

'It was easy enough to prove her wrong, wasn't it?'

'Not after what happened. I am afraid I tangled with young Gorridge.'

'Tell me about it.'

Myles had never had any trouble in confiding in his father

and they often enjoyed a joke together, which was what they did now over the tale of the barrel of ale. Henry's laugh was a loud rumble that started in his belly and shook the coach in which they were travelling.

'It's not that funny,' Myles said.

'Not if you've fallen for the lady,' Henry said, wiping his eyes with an enormous handkerchief. 'You haven't exactly begun on the right note.'

'Perhaps not. But when she asked my name and I said Myles, she assumed it was my surname and I decided not to correct her. If she can like me as a navvy, then she likes me because I am me, and not because of who I might one day become.'

'Well, that's a daft reason if ever I heard one. Navvy or my son, makes no difference, you haven't a hope of marrying her.'

'Why not?'

'You are too bourgeois, my lad. Your grandfather was a mill owner, a working man, and the fact that he was granted a peerage by George the Third for making soldiers' uniforms won't cut any ice with the Earl. As far as he is concerned, the old King was soft in the head and ennobled anyone who took his fancy.'

'Is that true?'

Henry shrugged. 'Who knows?'

'But it was a long time ago and you have proved your worth since then. And Mama's people did not look down their noses at you.'

'No, they were on their uppers with an estate going steadily downhill, so they gave in. We should have defied them and married anyway. We both knew there would never be anyone else for either of us.'

'It could happen again.'

Henry laughed. 'You have to win over the lady first. And the Earl. Mind you, if what I've heard is true, he's land rich but cash poor, which is why he might be persuaded, given the right incentive.'

'You have offered him a lot of money for his little piece of land. More than it's worth.'

'There is that, of course, but I was thinking of Gorridge. He's got an interest, too, don't forget, and if he thinks you are poaching his preserves, he might cut the rug from under us and advise the Earl to hold out for more. He might, if you put young Gorridge's nose out of joint, withdraw his own backing.'

'Are you saying I should stand back and let that drunken, selfish lout marry Lucy?'

'No. I wouldn't expect you to comply if I did. But hold hard, will you, until everything is signed and sealed? I could make up the shortfall myself, but it would mean some retrenchment in other areas and I would rather not. And we need the Earl's bit of land. To go all the way round it means digging a huge cutting through the hill.' He laughed again. 'You will get plenty of practice shifting crock if that happens.'

Myles knew that it could make the whole line unviable if they had to spend more than they had bargained for, but it was not the line Myles was thinking about, but Lucy. His father seemed to read his thoughts, for he suddenly said, 'Be patient, Myles, and remember you are as good as a Vernley any day, and certainly better than young Gorridge, because you are not a parasite on the land.'

Myles fell silent, thinking of Lucy, contrasting the way

she had fallen into his arms beside the lake, the sheer
pleasure of kissing her, knowing he was giving her pleasure,
too, with the stiff way she had dispensed tea in her father's
drawing room. Which was the Lucinda Vernley she felt most
comfortable with?

Chapter Five

Lucy was at sixes and sevens. She could not settle to anything. Whatever she did, wherever she went, something served to remind her of the navvy. It might only be a spade left lying about by a gardener or the sound of the river on its way down to the sea, or a kestrel flying high above the moors, or even a white post stuck in the ground. He was everywhere; he was nowhere. It was no good hiding the truth from herself; she had fallen in love, and it was hopeless and she was miserable. All sorts of fancies filled her head. She thought of elopement, but she had no idea if he would contemplate such a thing; of living together unwed, as so many navvies were reputed to do, but the idea of that appalled her. It was the height of wickedness and she had always been God-fearing. If they did that, they would pay for their sin in hell. On this earth their love for each other would be eroded by the guilt and poverty until they ended up hating each other and by then she would be beyond redemption, a fallen woman no longer recognised even by her own family.

She dreamed of him finding long-buried treasure while excavating crock, or doing her father a great good turn for which he was prepared not only to sanction a marriage but to make sure they wanted for nothing. It was all too silly for words. Life was not like that. And besides, he had never said he wanted to marry her, or even be with her. All he had ever said was, 'We will meet again,' which could mean something and nothing.

She was angry with herself for her obsession and tried her best to interest herself in all the things she normally used to fill her time—needlework, sketching, riding, visiting—but they all seemed so pointless. She wished she could go away, somewhere where there were no reminders, where she had never encountered him and no one knew anything about him. She might then realise he was not important to her happiness at all. And then the opportunity arrived in the shape of an invitation one day in early October.

Georgina had been her friend since they were at a young ladies' seminar together and they had always corresponded and met regularly. Georgina had married Sir Gerald Brotherton earlier in the year and had come back from her wedding tour to settle in Peterborough. 'Come and visit me,' she had written. 'Stay a week or two. I have so much to tell you and I want to hear all about your Season in town.'

She had asked her mother if she might go and, after consulting the Earl, the Countess agreed and the arrangements were soon made. She would be sent in the family coach with Sarah to attend her and the coach would come back empty, so that the Countess could have the use of it. It would be sent to fetch her at the end of her stay in time for the arrival of the Gorridges.

A week later found her alighting from the carriage outside a substantial villa in the middle of Peterborough, within walking distance of the cathedral and the shops. The door was flung wide and Georgina ran down the steps to embrace her. 'Oh, you are finally here. So much has happened since we last met. It seems years ago.'

'It was at your wedding, Georgie, only six months ago.' Lucy was kissed on each cheek and taken by the arm and dragged indoors while a manservant helped Sarah unload the luggage. The coachman was going to stay a night at a nearby inn before returning to Luffenham. It crossed Lucy's mind that when the railway was built, there would be no need for a coach to travel from her home to Peterborough, but thinking of railways was a risky thing to do considering it inevitably led to thoughts of Mr Myles. She had promised herself she would not think of him at all and quickly turned to more immediate matters. She was here for a change of scenery and to enjoy a visit with an old friend, and that she meant to do.

Georgina was rosy cheeked and a little plumper than Lucy remembered, but she was just as bubbly, full of questions, hardly waiting for the answers before moving on to the next, and enthusiastic about everything. Gerry, who practised as a lawyer in the town, would be back for dinner, she told Lucy, and in the meantime they would catch up on the gossip. She led the way into the drawing room where tea was laid out. 'We'll have tea while your maid is unpacking and then I will show you to your room. We don't keep a large staff and we don't stand on ceremony, so you must make yourself at home.'

'Marriage seems to suit you,' Lucy said when she was able to get a word in.

'Oh, it does, it does, I can thoroughly recommend it. With the right man, of course. Nothing could be worse than being tied to the wrong man, but luckily for me Gerry is a pet and we love each other dearly.'

'You are very fortunate.'

'Indeed, I am, but that is not to say you cannot be equally happy. Tell me about your coming-out. Did you meet the man of your dreams?'

'Not exactly.'

'Not exactly. What sort of answer is that?'

Lucy laughed. 'I mean, no. I met someone my parents seem very keen on…'

'But you are not?'

'I like him well enough.'

'Well enough is not good enough, Lucy. It has to be much stronger than that. It has to be love, passionate love, nothing less.'

'Then perhaps I will never meet him. I am told passion is something a lady never feels.'

'Rubbish! If that were so, then I cannot be a lady.' This, coming from the daughter of a marquis, was clearly not true.

'Tell me, what is it? How do you recognise it? How do you know if the other person feels it, too?'

'You know. It is a meeting of souls and minds and bodies, all three welded into one huge emotion that takes over your whole being. You can hardly think of anything else but when you last saw him, what you did, what you said, the feel of his hand in yours, how you trembled when he kissed you, what you will do until you see him again, and you know life without him is unthinkable.'

Lucy recognised the symptoms. 'Even if he is entirely unsuitable?'

Georgie gave her a startled look. 'So, you do know what I'm talking about?'

'Perhaps.'

'Is he very unsuitable?'

'Out of the question.'

'Oh, dear, you are in a pickle, aren't you?'

'Yes, I suppose I am.'

'Do your parents know?'

'Good heavens, they would throw up their hands in horror. I hoped coming away for a few days might cure me.'

'It might, but if it does, then it wasn't love in the first place.' She laughed lightly. 'But I shall do my best to divert you.'

'Thank you.'

'Shopping is one remedy and meeting new people another. I attend a reading group, which is great fun and not at all serious. You'll come, won't you?' She did not wait for an answer before continuing. 'We will take a picnic into the country on Wednesday and, on Saturday week, Lady Croxon is giving a ball in honour of Harriet's engagement to the Honourable Leonard Sumpter. You remember Harriet, don't you?'

'Yes, of course I do.' Harriet Croxon was another of their school friends, though Lucy had not kept in touch with her.

'I told her you would be staying with me and she has extended the invitation to include you. You have brought a ballgown, I hope.'

'Yes. Mama said to bring one in case.'

And so they chatted. They talked all through tea, all through a tour of the house and when Lucy was shown her room, and Sarah sent to fetch hot water for her to wash and change for dinner. They hardly drew breath through dinner itself, much to the tolerant amusement of Sir Gerald. He did not sit alone after the meal, but came with them into the drawing room where they talked some more, until they suddenly ran out of breath and subjects to discuss. In all that time, Lucy's dilemma was never mentioned.

'There's going to be a public meeting at the Assembly

Rooms tomorrow evening,' Sir Gerald said, finding that at last they had stopped and he could contribute more to the conversation than the occasional affirmative or negative. 'It should be interesting. I've a mind to go, if you can spare me.'

'What is it about?' his wife asked him.

'This new railway from Leicester. Lucy will know about that, considering the proposed line goes over her father's land.'

There was no escape and Lucy resigned herself to this new topic. 'My father is not inclined to agree to it. He thinks the disruption to our way of life will be too great. Surely that is not why they need a meeting?'

'No, I don't think so. There are already proposals to include Peterborough on the proposed Northern Direct and to join it to East Anglian and the Midland via Blisworth, and some people think enough is enough, so the meeting is to persuade them otherwise. And raise more finance.'

'Are you interested?' Lucy asked.

'As a lawyer, I must be. I am sometimes asked by my clients what I think of such and such a proposal. I should like to hear what these railway people have to say for themselves.'

'So would I,' Lucy said suddenly. 'Would it be possible for me to attend?'

He looked startled for a moment, then smiled. 'Of course. It is open to all. What about you, Georgie?'

'If Lucy wants to go, then of course I will come with you. I only hope we shall not be bored to death.'

They took their seats early, which was just as well because the hall soon became packed. It was a mixed audience. There were working men and women, many businessmen and a few railway employees, anxious to hear about new jobs. There were farmers, doctors, engineers and a scattering of gentry sitting near the front, murmuring among themselves. The subject, Lucy realised, was of universal interest. Most people were interested in the practicalities, the costs, the engineering, the advantages, the returns they might expect should they decide to invest, how strong the opposition was. Some wanted to be reassured the navvies would be disciplined and held to account for any damage they did. The damage they could do, and had done, was legendary. Lucy was perhaps the only one interested in the navvies as flesh-and-blood people who could, as Mr Myles had pointed out to her, feel pain and rejection. Here she was, thinking about him again and it was her own fault for asking to come. Did she enjoy giving herself grief?

The murmur of conversation ceased as a gentleman came on to the stage. 'That's our mayor,' Georgie whispered to Lucy.

He began by welcoming everyone and then proceeded to introduce the gentlemen who were going to speak to them and answer their questions. The first to take his place on the row of chairs behind him was Lord Moorcroft. And then Mr Joseph Masters, who was followed, to Lucy's consternation, by Myles, who was introduced as Mr Myles Moorcroft. It was definitely her navvy, her Mr Myles, but this one was a gentleman. He dressed like a gentleman, carried himself like a gentleman and, when he was asked to speak, his voice was cultured, his accents refined. She realised she had taken his given name for his surname and she felt herself blush to the roots of her hair. He was Lord Moorcroft's son! That was why he had come to Luffenham with his lordship and why her father had been so scathing about the way he had been brought up. Oh, what a fool she had been and how he must have laughed at her.

She was so busy with her confused thoughts and emotions,

she did not hear any of the proceedings. It was not until questions were invited from the floor that she felt able to pay attention. The audience hurled questions at the speakers, particularly Myles, but he fielded them well, being patient and knowledgeable, answering frankly, sometimes seriously, sometimes with humour, which had his listeners laughing. 'It is the conveyance of the future,' he told one questioner. 'Unless a man wishing to do business lives or works near a railway line, he will be left behind. He will be reliant on road transport for everything. His goods cannot be sold except in his own locality. He will pay twice as much for his coal to be delivered. And when he travels by road he will find it increasingly difficult to find post houses.'

'Yes, yes, we understand all that,' his questioner put in. 'But do we need so many lines, all vying with each other for business? Why can't they get together and agree about who goes where? At the moment, we have to stop and get out to cross to other lines every time we come to a town or a junction. It is as bad as changing horses. Worse, in some instances, because there are gaps and passengers have to walk or find other means of transport from one line to the next. The government should step in.'

'I agree,' Myles said. 'And one day it will happen. The lines will amalgamate and they will work to a common timetable with a standard fare…'

'Much hope of that when London time is not the same as York time,' someone called out and everyone laughed.

'That, too, will have to be addressed,' Myles said. 'But it is not the business of this meeting to decide on government policy, but to explain about the Leicester to Peterborough line, which will be an important connection between this city and the west, linking the east with the Midlands Railway. It is an important section for everyone and will repay investment in the years to come.'

'Ah, it's our money he wants,' someone cried out amid laughter.

'It is not my function to ask for your money,' Myles said. 'My fellow directors will tell you about that. I am here to talk about the works.'

'The navvies, you mean. Is it true you were once a navvy yourself?'

'I pride myself on being able to undertake any work I ask my men to do,' he said.

'Your men! Heathen rabble, you mean. I don't want them anywhere near my home.'

There were cries of 'Here! Here!'

Myles smiled and held up his hand for silence. 'The men under my command are not rabble. They are hardworking and skilled men and they are certainly not heathens. Many of them are devout.'

'They are made to work on Sundays, so how can they be devout?'

'There is no work on Moorcroft projects on Sundays.' This was a rule his father had insisted on right from the beginning. The men needed a break from unending toil, he had said; they worked the better for it the other six days of the week.

'Better if they did,' someone else shouted. 'Less time to go drinking.'

Myles smiled at the speaker. 'Do you not enjoy a glass of beer occasionally, sir?'

''Course I do. But I don't go mad with it.'

'Neither do my men.'

'Can you guarantee that?'

That was a tricky one and Myles knew his answer would

determine whether he won them over or not, but he also knew that if he lied he would be called to account later if any of his men imbibed too freely and caused trouble. 'The navvies are the same as any other working man,' he said. 'Their work is hard, much harder than most, and frequently dangerous. They are paid well for it and occasionally they like to celebrate. Trouble often comes because there are so many of them crowded together, cut off from basic amenities like dry shelter, clean water and wholesome provisions. What I can guarantee is that on Moorcroft works, these things are provided. Also, the men are paid every two weeks and the temptation to drink their wages away is much reduced.'

Mr Masters intervened to tell them that Mr Myles Moorcroft was beloved and respected by his men and they would follow him anywhere. Anyone living along the Leicester to Peterborough line would have nothing to fear from the navvies.

There were a few more questions put to Lord Moorcroft about stocks and shares and expected returns and the mayor closed the meeting. The audience applauded politely and began to file out. Lucy rose, but could not move until the others in the row had gone. It was then that Myles saw her and his eyebrows rose in surprise, then a broad smile lit his features. This was the last place he had expected to see her, and the drab assembly rooms seemed suddenly light and cheerful. He excused himself from his companions on the platform and made his way down the aisle, arriving at the end of her row just as she did.

'Lady Lucinda, what a surprise to see you here. Is Lord Luffenham with you?'

'No, Mr Moorcroft.' She addressed him clearly and correctly, making him smile. 'I am with my friend, Lady Brotherton, and Sir Gerald Brotherton.' She turned to her companions. 'May I present Mr Myles Moorcroft?'

Georgina bowed her head and Sir Gerald shook his hand. 'Very interesting meeting,' Sir Gerald said. 'But it has left me curious to learn more. Perhaps we could meet?'

'Delighted,' Myles said, casting a glance in Lucy's direction. She was looking enchanting in a pale green dress with a narrow pointed bodice that emphasised a neat waist. Her forest-green hat sat on her curls and framed a face that was looking decidedly flushed. It was hardly surprising, since she had caught him out for what he really was.

'I did not know you knew Mr Moorcroft, Lucy,' Georgie said. 'You did not say so when you said you would like to come to the meeting.'

Lucy's colour deepened. 'I did not know Mr Moorcroft was to be one of the speakers.'

Georgina looked from one to the other and read the signs accurately. 'Mr Moorcroft, you must come and take tea with us while Lucy is with us,' she said, delving into her reticule for a calling card to give him. 'Then Gerry can ask all his questions and you can tell us all about working on the railways. I am sure it is a fascinating story. You will accept, won't you, sir?'

'Nothing would please me more,' he said. And he certainly looked pleased. Lucy had a feeling he was laughing at her and she squirmed inwardly and wished she could put a curb on her friend's tongue.

'Tomorrow afternoon at four o'clock,' Georgina said, and then gave a trill of a laugh. 'Peterborough time.'

'I shall be there.' He bowed and left them and Georgina took Lucy's arm and they left the hall in the wake of Sir Gerald.

'He's the one, isn't he?' They had had supper and said goodnight, but Georgina had come to Lucy's room to quiz her.

Sarah had come and gone after helping Lucy undress. Now she was sitting at the dressing-table mirror in her nightgown, brushing her hair, and her friend was seated on the bed, watching her. 'He's the one you said was unsuitable.'

'Who?'

'Mr Moorcroft.'

'What makes you say that?'

'It was as plain as day to me. You could hardly look at him and your face was scarlet.'

'It was warm in that room.'

Georgie laughed. 'Oh, Lucy, don't try deceiving me. I know you too well. But why is he unsuitable? He seemed perfectly civilised to me, though to be honest I found his size overwhelming.'

'He is a navvy.'

'Don't be silly, he is Lord Moorcroft's son.'

'I know, but Lord Moorcroft is only a second-generation peer and Papa despises him. He hates having to do business with him.'

'How did you meet him? Go on, tell me everything. I can't help you if I don't know the whole.'

'Help me? How can you help me?'

'I do not know unless you tell me all about it. Has he declared himself?'

'Goodness, no. He laughs at me.'

'I didn't see him laughing at you. He was perhaps sharing a joke with you. That's what it looked like to me.'

'The joke is on me. I made a mistake. He told me his name was Myles and I thought it was his surname and he really was a navvy. He says he is and he's proud of it.'

'He is certainly built like one. When did you discover who he really is?'

'Tonight.'

'Oh, no wonder you were hot and bothered.'

'I wish you had not asked him to tea. I must excuse myself.'

'You will do no such thing. Lucy, you have an ideal opportunity to get to know him better without your papa being any the wiser. Surely you are not going to turn that down?'

'I can't see what good it will do.'

'Neither do I at the moment, but no doubt something will occur to me. I am not going to stand by and watch you throw yourself away on someone you do not care for simply because your papa has picked him out for you, when with a little contrivance you can have the man you really want.'

'But he doesn't want me. At least, I do not think so. Not as a wife.'

'How do you know? Has he told you so?'

'No, of course not. He would not be so ungentlemanly.'

'Oh, so you do believe he is a gentleman.'

'Georgie, you are confusing me. I do wish you would go to bed. I am tired.' She put down her brush and left the dressing table.

Georgie got up and kissed her. 'I am a brute, aren't I? But I want you to be as happy as I am. Go to sleep now and have pleasant dreams and in the morning you will be more optimistic.' And with that she picked up the lamp she had brought with her and left the room, closing the door softly behind her. Lucy, left with the light of a flickering candle, got into bed and pinched it out. Pleasant dreams. Yes, she would concentrate on pleasant thoughts. Myles, no longer *Mr* Myles, rowing her into the middle of the lake and talking nonsense to her, taking her in his arms and kissing her. The memory of that made her squirm farther down the bed. She had thought she was being kissed by a navvy and that should have repulsed her, but she must have known, deep inside her, he was no ordinary navvy. She ought certainly to have realised it when he came with Lord Moorcroft to the house. But it made no difference; her father had made it perfectly clear what he thought of Lord Moorcroft and his son.

Myles, trying not to betray his eagerness, arrived at exactly four o'clock and was shown into the drawing room, to find the two ladies apparently engrossed in a discussion about the relative merits of flowers and feathers for decorating a bonnet. They rose and Georgie made him welcome.

'Do sit down, Mr Moorcroft. I'll go and tell Gerald you are here. I don't suppose he heard the doorbell. His study is at the back of the house and he becomes engrossed in his work and hears nothing.' And she was gone.

'Mr Moorcroft,' Lucy said, after several seconds' silence, during which they simply stood and looked at each other.

'I liked it better when you called me Mr Myles.'

She wished he had not reminded her of that. 'You knew I had misunderstood and yet you did nothing to correct me. That was unkind of you.'

'I am sorry. I would not for the world be unkind to you. I liked to hear you use the name and it meant you took me for what I am, an ordinary man who works for his living, and perhaps liked me the better for it....'

'There is nothing ordinary about you, Mr Moorcroft. You like to deceive and tease and play tricks. You assured me you were a navvy.'

'So I am.'

'But you are also the son of a peer and presumably his heir.'

'That, too. I am a man divided. Sometimes it is not very comfortable.'

'What do you mean?'

'To men like your father I am a contemptible upstart, pretending to be a gentleman and making a poor hand of it. To the navvies, I am one of the privileged rich who likes to think he is one of them.'

'Which would you rather be?'

'Neither. I would rather people accept me for what I am. I hoped that you would.'

'How could I, when I did not know the truth? How long would you have kept it from me, if I had not been in your audience last night?'

'Ah, there you have me. I don't know. It would have depended on how close we became, how often we met.'

She felt herself colouring. 'Close, Mr Moorcroft?'

He smiled. 'I live in hope.'

'I am not sure I understand you.'

'Oh, my lady, you cannot be so naive. I wish to know you better. I wish you to know me for the man I am, perhaps to grow to like me a little.'

'Stop! Stop this instant.' She put her hands over her ears. 'You know that isn't possible.'

He stepped forward and took her hands in his, pushing them away from her face. 'Not possible? Why not? Am I so dislikeable?'

'Yes. No. Oh, you are confusing me.' He still held her hands, but his grip was gentle. She knew she had only to pull away and he would release her, but she did not even try. He was supporting her, for one thing; for another, it meant she was held close to him, the warmth of his body warmed her and gave her a kind of comfort. But it was a false comfort, because soon he would let her go and she would have to stand alone. 'I don't know what you are asking of me. I do not understand.'

He wanted to tell her what was in his mind, that he wanted to make her his wife, but he remembered his father's request and bit off the words. 'You are the only young lady I have met who could help me to reconcile my two halves. You do not look down your nose at me because I am a navvy.'

'I never thought you were one. You are too clean, too well spoken.'

'And how do you know how clean navvies are? How do you know that some of them might not be educated?'

'I don't.'

'There you are, then. I am a navvy and therefore far beneath you. I acknowledge it. But I am also a stubborn man and not easily discouraged.'

She did pull herself away then and stepped back, breathing erratically. 'You are talking nonsense, Mr Moorcroft, and I do not want to hear any more of it.'

He understood that she was afraid, afraid of her own feelings, and he might talk all day and she would not admit to them. He had been an idiot to expect anything different. She had been brought up to know her place in society; it had been bred into her over generations and she would never defy her father. He could only admire her for it, but his frustration made him irritable. 'But mark my words, there will come a time when the working man will come into his own,' he said, repeating something his grandfather had told him when he was a small boy. 'Those that endeavour to work with their brains and hands to make their fortunes will become the country's elite, not the aristocracy. Birth will matter less than achievement. It is already happening. Men like Isambard

Kingdom Brunel, Morton Peto and Thomas Brassey are already paving the way. Sooner or later, the Earl of Luffenham, and those like him, will have to come to terms with that.'

'Mr Moorcroft, I beg of you not to speak of my father in that way.'

'I beg your pardon, my lady.' It was said with stiff formality.

'I am surprised at you when your own father is a peer of the realm.'

'He will tell you, were you to ask, that his late father had earned the title and it is in deference to his father he continues to use it.'

'I understand your mother is a lady born and bred.'

'So she is, so she would be, even if her father had not been a Viscount. I adore her and you will when you meet her.' He smiled suddenly. 'I did tell you that I was not always comfortable with myself.'

'Then you have my sympathy.'

'That is a step in the right direction. Only a little one, to be sure.'

The humour was back in his eyes and she found herself smiling. He grinned back at her and picked up her hand, lifting the back of it to his lips. 'Shall we be friends?'

She nodded. Oh, how she longed to give way, to tell him what he wanted to hear, but she was too afraid.

The door opened a crack and Georgie put her head round it before coming into the room. Myles dropped Lucy's hand and went to stand looking out of the window to recover his equilibrium. Lucy, now that his large frame had distanced itself from her, felt the seat of a sofa behind her knees and sat down suddenly. She felt drained. The whole episode had been so unreal, the stuff of novels, and her head was spinning.

'Gerry is just coming,' Georgina said, looking from one to the other. 'Wherever has Thomas got to with the tea things?' She picked up a bell from a side table and rang it vigorously. When the servant appeared, she said, 'Thomas, you may serve tea now. Sir Gerald is just coming.'

The spinning slowed; Lucy found that she was back in the real world, listening to the conversation, hearing Georgie ask if Myles liked milk and sugar, offering him cake, and his polite replies. When Sir Gerald came into the room, she heard the men greet each other and talk about the weather and then go on to speak of the railway. It was all so normal, she began to think she must have imagined that she and Myles had been alone together and had that strange conversation. Her heart was singing with the sheer joy of it, but even as she felt she would burst with happiness, her head spoiled it all, bringing her back to earth. Nothing could come of it unless her father softened and she could not see that happening. Marrying the son of Lord Moorcroft was only marginally better than marrying a common navvy in his eyes. She could not marry against her father's wishes; he would disown her if she did, cut her off from her mother, her sisters and Johnny—and that would break her heart. She had been brought up on the Bible's teaching, 'honour thy father and thy mother,' and it would take more courage than she possessed to go against it. Besides, Myles had not asked her to marry him and it was well known that half the women who lived with the navvies were not married to them. Did his strange philosophy embrace that, too? Did he think she would be like the other women and live in a hut with him without benefit of clergy? He had sadly misjudged her character if he did. Had she misjudged his?

'I am often asked by my clients for advice about investments,' Gerald was saying. 'Everyone seems to be buying into railways these days. People seem to be making fortunes doing nothing at all. Is it really the bonanza it is made out to be? Shall I advise for or against?'

'I should advise caution,' Myles said, trying to concentrate on the question he had been asked and not on Lucy. She looked pale and troubled and he blamed himself for starting to talk about his feelings for her when he could not ask her to marry him. Not yet. Quite apart from the caution his father had advised, she was not ready to stand up to her father. 'Pick your company carefully. Many of the proposed lines now receiving Parliamentary assent are wildly optimistic and will never be finished and some may run out of money before they even start. Money has to be found for setting up the company, legal expenses and getting a bill through Parliament, then there is engineering, surveying and paying compensation to landowners, not to mention buying rails, rolling stock and all the necessary equipment. Many thousands, sometimes the whole of the debenture, are gone before a spade full of earth has been turned. You need to be sure the company can deliver what it says it can, that the main contractor is reliable and that, at the end of the day, the line will be used and return a profit.'

'You make me feel I should advise against it.'

'No, I am not saying that—you cannot halt progress and the day will come when railways are taken for granted—but it is wise to go into facts and figures and the character of the proposers carefully before laying out capital.'

'What about your own enterprise?'

'That is sound. The line is vital to connect east and west and will be well used when the whole system is in place. The costs have been carefully calculated and we use our own team of navvies as far as possible. It is easier to control them than if it is left to sub-contractors to hire them.'

Lucy was listening now. She felt what he was saying was important to her personally, that in a way he was speaking directly to her. 'What happens if a landowner refuses to allow you to cross his land?' she asked.

'We try to come to a reasonable settlement, my lady,' he said, turning towards her and paying her the compliment of treating her question seriously. 'If we cannot, then we go to law to make a compulsory purchase.'

'I see. Then you may expect a battle with my father, the Earl. He is adamant.'

They both knew what that would mean. Luffenham and Moorcroft at daggers drawn and their offspring caught in the middle of it. The future, as far as Lucy was concerned, looked bleak indeed.

'Oh, I think we shall reach an accommodation,' he said, and she knew he was not speaking entirely about railways. How could he be so confident? Because he did not know her father as she did, she answered herself. Papa was of the old school, who wanted to keep everything exactly as it was, his domains, his way of life, his hold over his family, his tenants and workers, exactly as they had been in his father's time and his father's before him. He would fight tooth and nail not only to keep every acre of land he owned, but to dictate whom his daughter should marry. Well, perhaps he would not force her to marry someone she did not like, but certainly he would forbid her to marry someone of whom he disapproved.

Deep in her sorrowful musings, she did not at first realise that the tea hour had come to an end and Myles was taking his leave. She was startled when he moved over to her and bowed. 'Lady Lucinda, your obedient.' The formality seemed to bring home to her that he had accepted her refusal to discuss the feelings they felt for each other; though she knew that was sensible, she was none the less cast down about it.

She forced a smile to her lips, though she could not make the rest of her face follow suit. 'Goodbye, Mr Moorcroft.' Oh, how final that sounded. She might see him again, but she could not foresee a time when they would be able to talk to each other as they had done that afternoon.

After he had gone, Sir Gerald returned to his study and Georgina subjected Lucy to a grilling, which she tried to withstand, but in the end she fled to her room in floods of tears. Georgie followed her. 'Oh, Lucy, I am so sorry. I thought I was being helpful, leaving you alone together. I did not dream he would behave badly....'

'He didn't behave badly. Nothing happened, nothing, do you hear? Please don't mention it again.'

Georgie looked contrite. She put her arm about Lucy's shoulders. 'Don't upset yourself, Lucy dearest. If you do not want to talk about it, then of course we will not. But when you do feel like confiding in me, I will listen.'

The subjects of Myles Moorcroft, railways and marriage were carefully avoided for the rest of Lucy's stay. They picnicked, went to the reading group, visited some of Georgina's friends, toured the cathedral, shopped for presents for Rosemary, Esme and Johnny, and gossiped about their schooldays. By the time her visit was coming to its end, Lucy prided herself on bringing her emotions under some semblance of control. They laughed a lot, too; if Georgina noticed Lucy's laughter was a trifle hollow, she did not comment. What Lucy was unprepared to find, when they arrived at Lady Croxon's for Harriet's engagement ball on her last night, was that Myles was among the guests.

She saw him first, talking to a group of men. She could hardly miss him, because of his height. He was in impeccable evening dress, his normally long hair carefully groomed. She noted his easy stance, the way laughter was never far from his mobile face, the face of a man at ease with himself, which was very different from the picture of himself he had painted to her. She almost stumbled, but Georgie had a hand on her elbow and steadied her. 'You do not have to speak to him,' she murmured. 'Just nod your head as you pass him.'

She tried, oh, how she tried, to be cool and mature. She walked the length of the room beside her friend, her chin in the air and her pink-feathered fan working furiously. Coming abreast of where he stood, she paused and bowed. If he had only bowed in return and not spoken, she could have carried on. Instead he excused himself from the group and walked towards her, not hurriedly, but as if he had all the time in the world, and she stood mesmerised like a rabbit facing a loaded gun.

'Lady Brotherton, Lady Lucinda, good evening,' he said. She was, he noted, wearing the dress she had worn at the Gorridge ball, a delicate pink froth of silk and lace. It did not seem to have come to any harm from being in a rowing boat. She still looked wonderful and desirable. 'Good evening, Sir Gerald. This is a pleasant surprise.'

'Surprise, sir?' Lucy queried, piqued. 'I fancy it was more of a surprise to us than to you. How did you manage it?'

'Lucy!' Georgie exclaimed, shocked by the tartness in her friend's voice.

Myles smiled. Lucy Vernley was rattled and that was a good sign. Or so he thought. 'My lady, I have known the prospective groom since childhood,' he explained, refusing to rise to her bait. 'Our fathers are lifelong friends.'

'What a small world it is!' exclaimed Georgie brightly. 'Miss Croxon is an old schoolfriend of ours, isn't she, Lucy?'

Lucy nodded silently.

The music had struck up for a waltz and Myles turned to Lucy and held out his hand. 'May I have the pleasure of dancing with you, Lady Lucinda?'

She had meant to refuse, she really had; she would not put herself through the torment of being close to him again, but somehow she found herself on the dance floor with him. For a big man he was very light on his feet and they danced in silence for a complete circuit of the floor. And then he spoke. 'I truly did not know you would be here tonight,' he said. 'But now you are, it has made my evening happier than I could have hoped for.'

'Mr Moorcroft, I hope you are not going to resume the conversation we had the last time we met, because as far as I am concerned there is nothing more to say.'

'I was merely paying a compliment to the lady I am dancing with,' he said. 'If you do not care for compliments, you must be unique among women.' He laughed softly. 'But then you are unique. There is not another Lady Lucinda Vernley in the whole world, certainly not for me. And you must acknowledge there is not another Myles Moorcroft, either.'

'I do not doubt it,' she said. 'Who else could dress the gentleman and fill a lady's head with nonsense one day and fill a wagon with twenty tons of crock on another? You see, I do remember what you call it.'

He laughed. 'Oh, my dear, can you not unbend just a little and smile? Everyone will think we are quarrelling.'

'Why should anyone be interested in us?'

'Because, my dear, I am who I am and you are who you are.'

'Yes, and I beg you to remember that,' she snapped. But she smiled. She went on smiling all through the evening. She smiled at the other young men who came and claimed a dance; she smiled at their hostess and complimented her on a splendid occasion; she smiled when she congratulated Harriet. She smiled when she chatted to Georgina; she was still smiling when Myles came and asked for another dance. She smiled all through it, though they hardly spoke. Only once did she falter and that was at the end of the evening when he came to take his leave as everyone was making their way out to their carriages. He bowed and lifted her hand to his lips, looking into her eyes as he did so. '*Au revoir,* my dear,' he murmured. 'We shall meet again, you and I. Put a little of your pin money on me when Gorridge comes to challenge me.'

She did not know whether he was talking about that wager or something else entirely and it puzzled her all the way back to the Brothertons' residence.

The next morning, after a sleepless night, the family carriage came to fetch her and she went home. Her visit had been a respite, but it had done nothing to settle her unease. The problem she had left behind was still there, made more poignant because of her meetings with Myles and the things he had said. She had called it nonsense, but it was sweet nonsense and made her realise that she could never contemplate marrying anyone else. She could not make herself fall out of love with Myles Moorcroft and into love with Edward Gorridge, however much her father might wish it.

Chapter Six

She had been home several hours, had given her siblings their presents and answered their questions about what she had done while she was away, then changed for dinner and was on her way to the drawing room when she encountered her father, who had evidently only just come indoors at the end of his day's business on the estate.

'Into the library with you,' he said when she tried to greet him. 'I want to speak to you.' His tone was brusque and she followed him into the room with some trepidation, and stood waiting for him to speak.

'Lucinda, I am displeased with you. I hear you have been talking to that navvy.'

She knew perfectly well whom he meant, but pretended she did not. 'Navvy, Papa?'

'Moorcroft. You were seen at a public meeting, conversing with him.'

'Georgina and her husband were interested in what the railway directors had to say and, as it is a subject that interests me, I agreed to accompany them. I did not know Lord Moorcroft would be one of the speakers.'

'I am not talking about Moorcroft, but his son. He does not even pretend to be a gentleman.'

'He behaved like one.'

'Oh, I do not doubt he can put on airs and graces if he needs to, but he has no breeding. And you should not encourage him.'

'I was no more than polite,' she said hotly. 'He spoke to Sir Gerald and Georgina and answered their questions about the railway while I listened. I can see no harm in that.'

'Why on earth you should want to go to such a meeting is beyond me. It is not the sort of gathering a young lady of your rank should attend and I am surprised at Sir Gerald taking you to it. If Edward Gorridge had not told me he had seen you there, I do not suppose you would have seen fit to tell me.'

She had not seen Edward in the audience, but then she had had eyes for no one but Myles. 'I did not think it was of any great importance.'

'Not important! What my daughter gets up to not important! You will go to no more such meetings and if you should encounter that upstart again you will not speak to him, is that clear?'

'Yes, Papa.'

'Now go to your mother. I will join you directly.'

She made her escape, thankful that he did not seem to know anything about the Croxon ball. She would have been even more firmly scolded if he had known she had danced with Myles. Luckily he believed his displeasure was punishment enough and life at Luffenham Hall went on as it always had.

The railway was coming after all. Lucy learned this one afternoon two weeks later after her father had met Lord Moorcroft and Viscount Gorridge and their respective lawyers in Peterborough. She was passing the library on her way out for a ride when she heard his voice. 'I decided to let it go ahead,' he said, apparently in answer to a question from her mother. 'They made me an offer for that land I could not refuse. It will help to pay for the repairs to Home Farm. Sayers has been on at me for some time about them and there's other things that need doing too. I made certain provisos, of course. It is to take the shortest line across the Luffenham land and stay on the other side of the river. I have also stipulated a station and coal yard where the rail crosses the road just outside the village. And the navvies are to be forbidden to enter the village.'

'Lord Moorcroft agreed to that, did he?'

'Yes. After Gorridge had had his say. He is all for it and was prepared to add his own inducement.'

'Inducement? You mean if Lucy marries Edward?'

'It wasn't said in so many words, but I understood he meant something of the sort.'

'I am reluctant to push Lucy into it if she doesn't want him.'

'Why shouldn't she? It's an ideal match. It's up to you to make her see it.'

'What about Edward? He did not seem in any hurry to propose when we were over there.'

'Oh, you know what young men are, they like to pick their moment. I have no doubt he will come up to scratch when they come here.'

Lucy hurried away before they came out and found her eavesdropping. She did not want to marry Edward Gorridge. How could she, when she did not have an atom of feeling for him? She would have to make it clear that she would not entertain marriage to him. But supposing doing that meant putting her father in a difficult situation with Viscount Gorridge over the railway? He would be furious.

She hurried to the stables and took Midge out. In a furious mood, she rode hard until she found herself at the top of the rise from which she had first seen the men surveying. Here she drew rein and slipped from the saddle, standing beside the horse's head and contemplating the view. There was no one there. It was green and peaceful. The river wound its placid way to the sea; a small stand of deciduous trees were showing their autumn colours, red, gold and brown; the sheep, beginning to grow their winter coats, dotted the opposite hill with flecks of white. The only evidence that a line was to be built was the row of white stakes hammered into the ground at intervals along the side of the hill on the other side of the river.

How long before the railway builders arrived? How long before Myles was there, directing the men, shovelling crock alongside them, so near and yet as far from her as ever? The shape of the countryside would be changed. For a time at least it would be scarred, but she had seen on other lines how soon the grass returned once the men and all the paraphernalia they brought with them had gone, leaving behind only the gleaming rails. When that happened Myles would be gone, too. Where was he? Did he ever think of her? Angrily she brushed the back of her hand over her face to stem the tears, and climbed back into the saddle. She must endure and hope that something, anything, would turn up to solve problems that seemed insoluble.

The Gorridge carriage, containing the Viscount, his wife and daughter, rolled up the drive one day at the end of October. Edward rode over on horseback. They arrived on the same day as the vanguard of the navvies, which gave everyone a talking point at dinner that evening and saved Lucy having to force a conversation with Edward, who was seated beside her.

'We saw them as we came along the road,' Lord Gorridge said. 'They were bringing in dozens of wagons loaded with their stuff. There was a couple of dozen of them, but no doubt the rest will be arriving in the next few days.'

'Yes, I expect so,' the Earl said. 'I've been watching their progress as they came nearer. The line has reached the cross-roads on the edge of the estate and they have been bringing up their equipment as far as that by rail. They have made a dreadful mess on the lane, breaking down hedges and dropping litter. I had to go down and speak to them about it. Moorcroft's son was there and promised me they would clear it up once they had everything on site, so I shall go down tomorrow and see that they have.'

Myles was there! Lucy's heart gave an erratic jump before settling back to something approaching a normal beat. It only needed someone to mention his name to set her off dreaming and wishing, making her lose sight of her surroundings. The dining room faded, the long table with its gleaming cutlery and sparkling glass, the colourful gowns of the ladies, her own pale blue organza with its cream bertha, faded and she was back in that rowing boat, peacefully dabbling her hands in the water, watching his strong arms wielding the oars and listening to him talk nonsense and loving it. Would she see him again? Dare she?

'He's there, is he?' Edward was saying. 'I have some un-finished business with him.'

'Oh, Edward, I beg of you not to provoke him,' his mother put in. 'He is such a big man and no doubt he has a temper, too.'

'Oh, I do not intend to fight him, Mama,' Edward said. 'We have an outstanding wager, which he promised to fulfil when the line came through. He has bet me he can lift twenty tons of earth into a wagon in one working day and I mean to stand over him while he does it. He'll be given no opportunity to arrange for help.'

Lucy wanted to protest that Myles would never cheat, but held her peace. She would learn more by simply listening.

'Does he really work alongside the navvies?' Lady Gorridge asked.

'He says he does, but I have yet to see it.'

'Are you speaking of that man who came here with Lord Moorcroft?' the Countess wanted to know. 'I thought he was his lordship's son.'

'So he is,' her husband answered her. 'I told you the family were not acceptable in polite circles, didn't I? Now you know why.' He looked hard at Lucy, reminding her that he had forbidden her to speak to Myles again.

'Oh, dear, shall we be expected to entertain him again?'

'Certainly not!' He turned to Lady Gorridge. 'You need have no fear, my lady, neither he nor his men will be allowed anywhere near the house. You will be perfectly safe, so long as you do not venture out of the grounds without an escort. I had hoped they might not reach here before your visit, but they have apparently made good time. Now they are here, the sooner they get on with their work and leave, the better.'

Anyone would think Myles Moorcroft was a monster, Lucy thought, and was tempted to defend him, but the look her father had given her had spoken volumes, so she bit her tongue and they continued their conversation, unaware that she was seething inside.

'I had heard they live in the ground in burrows, like rabbits,' Dorothea said.

Edward laughed. 'Breed like them, too, you know.'

'Edward!' His mother was shocked. 'That is hardly a subject for the dinner table. There are young ladies present.'

The Countess rose. 'Ladies, I think we will leave the men to talk,' she said. 'I am sure we can find a more edifying subject for our conversation in the drawing room.' She left the room, followed by Lady Gorridge, Dorothea, Rosemary and Lucy, who went reluctantly. If she could not see Myles and talk to him, she wanted to hear about him, even if what was being said was not complimentary. She minded very much about that on his behalf and she was glad he could not hear it.

Did the navvies really live in holes in the ground? she asked herself, as her mother dispensed tea and began talking about an intricate piece of embroidery she was engaged upon. Surely they did not bring wives and children to the works to live like that? But they would need their wives to cook and clean and darn their clothes, wouldn't they? She meant to find out and, if conditions were as bad as that, she would defy her father and confront Myles to do something about it. She had no idea how she could do that, nor if he would take any notice if she did. But it would be an excuse to see him, to see if he changed his character as well as his clothes when he worked among his men. Would he be rough and coarse and lacking in manners?

'Lucy, whatever are you daydreaming about?' her mother asked. 'You haven't heard a word I said.'

'Sorry, Mama. I was wondering if I would be allowed to go riding. Midge will get fat and lazy if I cannot ride her.'

'I am sure Edward will be pleased to escort you,' Lady Gorridge put in. 'You do not need to go near the works, do you?'

'No, there are other places,' she said, resigning herself to riding with Edward.

The men joined them and it appeared the subject of the railway had been exhausted because it was not mentioned again and the evening was spent making music and reciting poetry. Edward proclaimed a speech from Shakespeare as if he were in a huge theatre, making Lucy want to laugh. She controlled herself with an effort to sing a duet with Rosemary and then someone suggested dancing. To do that they went into the hall where the marble floor lent itself to dancing better than the carpet of the drawing room.

Lucy wanted to play for the others, but that suggestion was vetoed and it was Rosemary who sat down at the piano. Inevitably Lucy found herself dancing a waltz with Edward. She tried imagining it was Myles, but that did not work because Myles was so big and broad, and though Edward was by no means short, he was slimly built and paradoxically nothing like as light on his feet.

'Mama has told me you would like to go riding tomorrow,' he said.

'Yes, Midge needs exercise.'

'Then I shall be happy to accompany you. You can show me round the estate. Is it really as extensive as Linwood?'

'I really do not know its dimensions. I have a rough idea of its boundaries and that most of it has been in the family hundreds of years. Papa is very proud of that.'

'And it will all go to your brother one day?'

She wondered why he asked. 'Of course.'

'Linwood will be mine. But you knew that, didn't you?'

'I hadn't given it a thought.'

He laughed. 'I don't believe you. I am sure your mama and papa have been at pains to tell you so.'

'Yes, but that doesn't mean I spend my time thinking about it.'

'Then you should.'

'Why?' Asking that was a mistake—she knew it as soon as the word was out.

'You have been brought up in luxury, nothing smaller that Luffenham would contain you, so it behoves you to look for a husband who can provide its equivalent and that without the enticement of a dowry.'

'I am sure I have not considered marriage in such mercenary terms. I must love the man I marry.'

He threw back his head and laughed, making everyone in the room look towards them and smile indulgently. 'Oh, Lucy, you are such a romantic. But it won't do, you know, it won't do at all. You would soon tire of a penniless lover.'

'He might not be penniless.'

'He soon would be, if you tried marrying against Lord Luffenham's wishes. He is a powerful man, your father. And you wouldn't even have a dowry to subsist on.'

'Papa would never withhold that.'

'Did you not know?' he queried lightly. 'There is no dowry. Your papa cannot afford one.'

She gaped at him, unable to believe what she was hearing. He was laughing again and that made her stiffen her spine and refuse to rise to his bait. 'Then I should be sure the man whom I married, married me for love and not for money,' she snapped.

'Oh, I agree that money isn't everything,' he said, still laughing. 'There is land and breeding and consequence. The Earl of Luffenham could be as poor as a church mouse, but he would still be the Earl of Luffenham and his daughters would still be the daughters of an earl.'

'Yes, but a poor man, whether he was an earl or not, could

not afford the upkeep of somewhere like Luffenham Hall, so there is no point in making comments like that.'

'No point at all,' he said, whirling her round as Rosemary brought the music to an end. He offered her his arm to return her to her seat beside her mother, who was smiling happily to see Lucy apparently on good terms with Edward. She had no idea what the two had been talking about and Lucy did not enlighten her.

Lucy herself was puzzled by what Edward had said. He seemed to be hinting that her father was in financial difficulties, but she did not see how that could be. They lived at the same standard they always had. They ate well when alone and extravagantly when there were guests. She had no idea how much their clothes cost because all the bills were sent to her father and, though he might occasionally grumble, he never refused to pay them. The horses, the carriages, the guns were the best money could buy. The Luffenham cellar and the Earl's hospitality were renowned throughout the county and beyond. On the other hand, that snatch of conversation between her parents she had overheard made her wonder if things were not as comfortable as appeared on the surface. And her father's solution seemed to be to marry her off for a consideration! She wondered what it was. Just how much was she worth in monetary terms? Oh, how angry that made her.

She would have liked to have ridden alone the following morning, but could see no way of bringing that about, especially as Edward was already at the breakfast table when she went downstairs. He was dressed, as she was, ready to go riding. They bade each other good morning and made desultory comments about the weather while they ate their breakfast and then went out to the stables where their horses were being readied.

A few minutes later they were riding across the park towards the belt of trees that screened Luffenham Hall from the north-east wind. Beyond that they came to open country-side, most of it farmland, but it was criss-crossed with bridle-ways that led up to grazing land on the higher slopes. 'You can see most of the Luffenham estate from here,' she said as they reached the highest ground. 'These pastures, the farms, the village, all belong to it, except the church and the Glebe Farm. A cousin of my father's has the living.'

'Is he a member of the hunting, shooting and fishing fra-ternity or one of the hellfire-and-brimstone brigade?'

'Neither to excess. He takes the middle ground.'

He looked about him. 'I expected to see the railway works.'

'That's on the other side of the village, not visible from here.'

'I should like to go there.'

'Why?'

'You know why. I have business with Moorcroft.'

'I am not sure I should encourage that by taking you there.' The prospect of seeing Myles again would have been a de-lightful one if she had not been accompanied by Edward. Myles would jump to quite the wrong conclusion.

He laughed. 'Oh, Lucy, you goose, your encouragement or lack of it would make no difference. The wager has been made and will not be unmade, at least, not by me. All I wish to do is settle the details. I will find my own way if you do not choose to come.'

Normally she gave little thought to her title, but she hated his familiarity; it was as if they were already be-trothed and, considering he had not even asked her and given her the opportunity to refuse him, it annoyed her.

'Then the best way is back through the village.' She set off in that direction.

It was a small village with the usual buildings and businesses. There was a mill, a blacksmith, a cobbler, a shop that sold everything from candles and twine to flour and tea and several cottages grouped around a village green. On the only crossroads stood the Plough, which had once been a thriving coaching inn and had accommodation for several horses, but was far less busy than it used to be. She pointed out the church, Glebe Farm and Home Farm, which she noted looked neglected. The paint was peeling from the windows and the outbuildings looked decidedly tumbledown. No wonder her father had said his tenant had been asking him about repairs. The railway company money was going to pay for those, but where did she come into it? She did not want to conjecture.

Edward followed as she rode through the village and past the gates of Luffenham Hall. After a while they came to a bridle path going up beside the wall of the estate and they turned on to that, following the wall until the track divided. 'That way leads round to the other side of the house,' she said, pointing to the left. 'We go this way. It's quicker than taking the road.' She turned right and rode up the hill; once at the top, they could look down on the valley where the navvies worked.

They were already, only a day after their arrival, making inroads in the opposite hill, digging out a cutting. There were hundreds of them, working in a kind of frenzied unison. A temporary line had been laid from the crossing on the lane to where they worked so that empty wagons drawn by horses could be brought up and filled with soil, which was taken away to be dumped elsewhere. There were huts dotted about, too, with smoking stove-pipe chimneys. Washing lines had been strung up and children played in the dirt. She could not believe all this had happened in the space of twenty-four hours.

She saw him before Edward did. He was so tall, his curly head stood out above the others, but even without that, she would have known him. She was so attuned to him and his presence, her eyes were drawn almost involuntarily to where he was. Standing in the doorway of one of the huts, he was dressed in a working man's moleskin trousers, an open-necked shirt with the sleeves rolled up and a gaudy red-and-green striped waistcoat, the traditional garb of the navvy.

'There he is,' Edward said, spotting him. 'He doesn't seem to be doing his share of digging.'

'Someone has to oversee what they are doing.'

'Let's go down and challenge him.' He dug in his spurs and set off down the hill at a gallop. Lucy hesitated, knowing she would be disobeying her father, but she needed to know what was going to happen; if Edward was with her, she did not suppose Papa would grumble about it. She followed, but, having more consideration for her horse, cantered down at a less bruising pace.

She heard Edward call out, 'Moorcroft, good day to you' as he pulled up in front of Myles and slipped from the saddle.

'Gorridge.' Myles had not known the man was at Luffen-ham and had not expected to come across him again until he was on Gorridge land. He looked up and saw Lucy riding over the bridge and his eyes lit up at the sight of her. Hastily he rolled down his sleeves and did up the top button of his shirt. 'My lady.' Ignoring Edward, his eyes were on her, searching her face, trying to read something in her expression that would tell him how she was and if anything had changed.

'Mr Moorcroft.' She did not dismount. 'You have made a start, I see. I did not realise it would take so many men.'

'The more we have, my lady, the quicker we work and the quicker we work the sooner we shall be off Lord Luffenham's land and the sooner the railway will be in operation. Six weeks, perhaps two months, and we shall be gone.' He wanted to say more, to speak privately to her, but that was impossible with Gorridge watching and his own men looking on with open curiosity.

'Then what about that wager we had?' Edward said. 'Not backing out, are you?'

'Not at all.'

'Then all I want to know is when you are going to prove your boast.'

'Any day you like. I shall be here until we move on to Gorridge land and we shall be several weeks there, so you may take your pick.'

'Tell me,' Edward said, 'how long is a working day?'

'It depends on what needs doing and the state of the contract, but for the sake of this wager, shall we say seven until seven?'

'Very well.' He turned to Lucy. 'Lucy, my dear, what entertainments have been arranged for us this week?'

Again that use of her given name, and she saw Myles's eyebrows raised quizzically. 'I believe Papa has arranged some shooting on two of the days, and if the weather remains mild we are all going to make an excursion to the abbey ruins on Tuesday. It is sheltered among the old walls and there are some magnificent views. And on Friday there is to be a formal dinner for some of Mama and Papa's friends in the neighbourhood.'

'Then shall we say Thursday?' Edward suggested.

'As you wish.'

'I shall be here at seven on Thursday morning to see you begin and there will be someone watching you all day, so do not think of recruiting help. Perhaps we should have a referee. I've a mind to ask the parson. Lucy tells me he always takes the middle ground.'

'That is acceptable to me,' Myles said. 'But filling a wagon requires two men. I need a mate.' He laughed suddenly. 'Want to have a go yourself?'

'Certainly not! *I* do not pretend to be a labouring man. Find your own man.' It was said with scorn.

'Very well. The navvies themselves will judge whether the wagon is full.'

'And the parson will say how much of it is down to you.' Edward held out his hand, which Myles shook. 'Until Thursday.' He heaved himself into the saddle. 'Come, Lucy, my dear.'

She looked at Myles, but his face betrayed nothing of what he was thinking. 'Good day, my lady,' he said, touching his forelock in the manner of a peasant while giving her a lopsided smile. 'Until we meet again.'

She did not answer, but rode after Edward, more confused than ever. Myles seemed to have forgotten he was a gentleman and had reverted to being the navvy, sleeping in a hut like all the other men, rolling up his shirtsleeves and digging alongside them, getting hot and dirty. Of the two sides of his nature he had spoken of, he seemed to prefer the common labourer. Did he think she would also prefer it? Was he making a statement with those rough clothes? 'This is me. Take me as you find me.' Or was he not trying to tell her anything at all and she was simply reading more into his words and actions than he intended?

He watched her ride after Gorridge and ached to call her back, to take her into his arms and tell her that he loved her. But was it too late? Was she already engaged to that popinjay?

He must see her and find out. He turned to see Joe Masters laughing beside him. 'What is amusing you, my friend?'

'The scrapes you manage to get yourself into, lad. When did you last do a whole twelve-hour shift?'

'I don't know, not so long ago.'

'A couple of years at least. If you are not careful, you will have to own yourself bested by that…' He nodded in the direction of the disappearing horseman.

'Not I. I have the rest of the week to get back into shape, beginning now. Fetch me a shovel.' He could dig and lift, dig and lift, and at the same time decide how he could see Lucy and talk to her. The railway contract had been signed; his father's strictures about holding back no longer applied, or they would not in a few weeks' time. He must convince her that he loved her, wanted to marry her and could amply provide for her; if she loved him, as he hoped she did, she would face up to her father and refuse Edward Gorridge, who was not the man for her.

He had begun work late, but by the time the men stopped for the night he was aching in every muscle. If he was to carry on the following day, he could not take the long ride home. He stayed in the hut of the man he had asked to be his digging mate. Pat O'Malley had been a navvy ever since he came over from Ireland as a young man twenty years before, first on the canals, but lately on railways. He was not particularly tall but he had a wiry strength and could easily match Myles spade for spade, as most of the really good navvies could. He had brought his wife and family with him and his first task before lifting a single turf had been to build a hut for them.

Unlike many employers Lord Moorcroft provided wood for the navvies to make themselves homes and that was brought in the wagons along with all the other paraphernalia of railway building. His men did not need to live in holes in the ground. The huts were not large, but were divided into a living room and bedroom, where several bunk beds were erected so that bachelors could lodge and be looked after by the woman of one of them. Myles shared their meal and tumbled into a bunk bed and was asleep within seconds. But before that happened, he knew he would defy the Earl's ban and seek Lucy out.

Edward made no secret of what was to happen on Thursday; though the Earl might disapprove, he could not voice that to a guest and a guest, moreover, whom he hoped would marry his daughter. 'The hill above the works makes a fine viewing platform,' Edward said at dinner that evening. 'Shall we all go and watch? I'll have a little wager with anyone that he is done for by mid-day.'

'I'll take that.' The Viscount laughed, having heard the tale of the barrel of ale. 'A guinea says he will last until tea time.'

The Earl did not want to appear a bad sportsman by refusing to take part. 'It is all very well to dress as a working man and strut about the works, but that doesn't mean he can work like a labourer,' he said. 'So my guinea says he won't last beyond ten o'clock.'

'Really, gentlemen,' the Countess put in, 'what a thing to gamble on. And I am sure I do not wish to witness a man labouring in such a vulgar fashion. If Lord Moorcroft has any affection for his son, he will forbid it.'

Lucy listened to it all in horror. Myles was going to be made a spectacle, a figure of fun, and her heart ached for him. She wished she could warn him. Dare she do so? But he was a man and, she guessed, a stubborn one—he would not back out simply because she asked him to. Could he do it? Could he

win his wager? If he did, how would Mr Gorridge react? A
wager was a wager and he would have to pay up and smile
while he did it, but Myles would have made an enemy.

Party games and charades were arranged for the evening,
but she could not concentrate and begged to be excused, saying
she had a headache. Her mother looked sideways at her, but did
not try to stop her leaving the room. Glad to escape, she went
to her bedroom and flung herself on the bed. Sarah arrived soon
afterwards with a tisane and stayed to help her into bed.

She slept badly and woke early. Unable to stay in bed, she
dressed in a warm wool gown, threw a shawl over her shoulders and went out. The dew was on the grass and moisture-
laden cobwebs decorated the trees. The sun, still low in the sky,
was a huge orange ball. She walked down the drive and on to
the lane towards the village. A milkmaid was driving a herd of
cows in to be milked. A ploughman was already at work on
one of the fields. A cock crowed in the yard of the Home Farm
and a dog barked somewhere behind one of the cottages. The
landlord of the Plough was sweeping out his yard.

She bade him good morning and passed on, aware that he
was looking after her, no doubt wondering why she was out
so early. She turned towards a cottage and knocked on the
door. It was opened by an old lady whose lined face broke into
a smile at the sight of her. 'Lady Lucinda, you are up betimes.'

'I was restless and remembered I should have visited you
yesterday to see if you were better.' Mrs Staines was grandmother to her maid, Sarah, and so crippled with rheumatism
she could not leave her cottage. The last time Lucy had visited
with her mother the old lady had been laid low with a hacking
cough. They had brought her medicine and fruit and Lucy had
promised to go to see her again soon.

'Come on in and sit ye down,' she said. 'I didn't expect you. I know you've got important visitors up at the big house. A young gentleman, so I am told.' And her old eyes twinkled mischievously.

Lucy entered the cottage which, though tiny and poorly furnished, was clean as a new pin. The Countess allowed Sarah to go home one day a week to clean and dust and do a little cooking for her. 'Sarah told you.'

'Yes. Was that why you were restless?'

'Partly.'

'Undecided, are you?'

'It hasn't come to that yet.'

'My advice is to be sure, my lady, be very, very sure.' She spoke with emphasis while searching Lucy's face and then went on. 'What do you think of them there navvies what are buildin' the railway over yon hill? I never thought to see the day his lordship would allow it.'

'They are ordinary working men, Mrs Staines, and will soon be gone. And the railway will benefit everyone.'

'The women in the village are frightened to death and the men are up in arms.'

'Who told you this?'

'Joshua. He said there was a meeting last night and they were going to do something about it.' Joshua was her grandson and Sarah's brother. He lived with his wife in a tied cottage on Glebe Farm.

'What are the women frightened of?'

'Of having their fences and winders broke and being set upon by a drunken rabble, of having the livestock and their food stolen and their children carried off.'

'I do not think you need worry, Mrs Staines. My father has forbidden them to come into the village.'

She laughed. 'Do you think that will stop them? Two of 'em were in the Plough last night and drunk as lords. Sorry, my lady, shouldn't have said that. But they made a great racket with their singing, and this morning two of Mrs Green's chickens are missing.'

She thought that her father ought to know that his ban had been disobeyed, but that would get Myles into trouble and she did not want that. Disputes between her father and the man she loved must be avoided. 'What are the villagers going to do?'

'They are getting everyone together, from hereabouts and other places along where the line is going, and they are going to march to the works to let them know we ain't puttin' up with their lawless ways in Luffenham and, if they come into the village again, they can expect to be met with trouble. And they want the two who stole the chickens.'

'They mustn't do that, Mrs Staines. It will inflame tempers and blood will be spilled. And it will anger my father.'

'I told Josh that, but he would not listen. He says someone has to stand up to them. He's a hothead, always has been. I'm afeared for him.'

'When is this going to happen?'

'This morning when they get everyone together.'

Lucy sprang to her feet. 'I must be going, Mrs Staines. Things to do.' She almost ran from the cottage and sprinted back to the Hall, but, instead of going indoors, went to the stables and had Midge saddled. She did not even stop to change into her habit. As soon as the saddle was on the mare she was up and riding away, leaving the stable boy scratching his head and wondering if he ought to report her strange behaviour.

Poor Midge was winded by the time she arrived at the navvy camp. Lucy flung herself off her and stood looking about for the tall figure of Myles, ignoring the stares of the men already working. One of them threw down his shovel and walked over to her. 'You ain't no business here, miss.'

'I need to speak to Mr Moorcroft urgently. Is he here?'

'I'll fetch him.'

He disappeared into one of the huts and a moment later Myles ducked his head under the lintel and emerged in shirt-sleeves, which served to confirm that he lived among the men. He strode over to her. 'Lucy, what has happened?'

She hardly registered his use of her name, but would not have minded if she had. He had been Myles in her mind for a long time now. 'Nothing yet, but the villagers are up in arms about two of your men going into the village and getting drunk last night. They are coming here.'

'They'll get bloody noses if they do.' The man who spoke was a small, wiry fellow wearing a very battered top hat and a red-and-white spotted neckerchief. He turned to the men nearest him. 'What say you, mates?'

They murmured agreement and some were already shouldering their shovels to meet the threat.

'No,' Myles said. 'I'll deal with it. I want no conflict. I gave my word none of you would cause trouble. If any have, they can collect the pay owing to them and be off.'

'We won't strike the first blow, but if the village men come looking for trouble, they'll get it. We've a right to defend ourselves.'

'But they are no match for you,' Lucy said. 'They're farm-hands, most of them, and many have had little enough work this past year.'

'They should have thought of that.'

'If any man leaves the works in the next two hours, he needn't bother coming back,' Myles told them. 'And he'll forfeit the wages he's earned.' To Lucy he said, 'Wait here while I saddle Trojan.'

She stood by Midge's head and looked about her. The men were looking belligerent, but she was determined not to show fear. Myles would look after her if any of them took a step towards her. But none did. She smiled. 'I am amazed at how much you have done since you arrived,' she said, in friendly fashion. 'It must be very hard work.'

'Oh, it is that and it don't 'elp to be accused of makin' trouble.'

'No, I can see that.'

A group of barefoot children surrounded her and one reached out and touched her skirt, fingering the material. She squatted down to be on their level. 'Hallo,' she said, smiling at them. They were very dirty and ill clad, but none looked hungry. In that respect they were better off than the village children, many of whom relied on hand-outs from Luffenham Hall. 'What are your names?'

They giggled and continued to stare at her, but one boy, braver than the rest, answered her. 'I'm Adam O'Malley, miss. And this is me sister, Matty.'

'What are you going to do with yourselves today?'

'Fetch water for Ma. From the river.'

'Then we are goin' to school,' added Matty, touching the back of Lucy's hand and stroking it. Lucy was overcome with tenderness towards them. She took the little one's hand in hers. 'School. Where do you go for that?'

'There!' She pointed at one of the huts. 'I'm learnin' me letters.'

Myles returned, leading his big horse, and Lucy straightened up and said goodbye to the children.

'Off with you,' he said to the children, and to the men, 'Get on with your work. I'll be back and then I shall want to know who it was went into Luffenham last night.' He bent to lift Lucy into her saddle, jumped on his own mount and led the way across the bridge and up the opposite hill.

'They have a school on the site,' she said when they were able to ride side by side.

He smiled. 'One of the women has a smattering of education and the company pays her to teach the children. It keeps them out of mischief. They are not welcome in the village schools.'

She did not answer because she could see a crowd of men, some villagers, some she had never seen before, coming up the rise towards them. They were lead by Joshua Staines. Myles reined in and they stopped to face him. Joshua was looking mulish and he glared at Lucy. 'Tell me your grievance,' Myles began reasonably.

They all started shouting together and he held up his hand. 'Speak one at a time or I cannot answer you. Who is your spokesman?'

Someone prodded Joshua in the back and he was forced to take a step forward. 'We don't want the navvies in Luffenham,' he said. 'They frighten the women and children.'

'Why?'

'They are a godless rabble and would as soon rape a woman as look at her. Two of them came into the village last night and got drunk in the Plough and then ran up and down the street shouting. My missus was mortal afraid. They stole a couple of chickens, too.'

It was not unheard of for the navvies to be blamed for any wrongdoing anywhere near a works whether they were guilty or not. Myles decided not to argue the point. 'What is your name?'

'My name don' matter.'

'It's Joshua Staines,' Lucy said.

'An' you've no business siding with 'em, my lady. What would his lordship say?'

'He would say I did right,' she said, not really believing it. 'I am only concerned with keeping the peace and seeing justice is done.'

'An' what about 'im?' The young man nodded at Myles.

'I, too, wish for peace,' he said. 'My men are not heathens, nor a rabble. They do not rape women or abduct children. The two you spoke of will be paid off. They are only two among three hundred—the other two hundred and ninety-eight have obeyed my instructions not to enter the village. It goes hard on them. After a day's work, they like to sit and enjoy a beer and a chat, just as you do, but in order to keep the peace they obey. Go back home, let them get on with their work. The owner of the chickens will be compensated.'

Joshua looked at Lucy. 'Is he telling the truth?'

'Yes, I am sure of it.'

One or two mumbled dissent, but when Myles dug in his pocket and found a couple of sovereigns that he handed to Josh for the chickens, which was several times their value, they turned and went back the way they had come. Lucy heaved a huge sigh of relief. Myles looked at her and saw for the first time that she looked drained. 'My poor darling,' he said, dismounting and holding out his arms to her. She slid from the saddle and into them. After a poor night's sleep and all the excitement she was exhausted. She wanted only to be held in the warmth of his arms and made no effort to break away. 'Thanks to you, no harm's been done. But you are shaking. Surely you were not frightened?'

She heard his gentle endearment and looked up into his face. His expression was one of deep concern. 'Not when you had the situation under control. You have a way with people, don't you?'

'I try.'

'Will you really turn off those two men?'

'I have no choice. I warned them what would happen if they went against me and I keep my word. The last thing I want is the wrath of your father on my head.'

She smiled. 'If he could see us now, I do not think there is any doubt of it. I dread to think what he would do.' Mentioning her father reminded her how long she had been absent. She pulled away from him. 'I must go home. I shall be missed.'

'What will you tell them?'

'I do not know. I went to visit Mrs Staines. She is Joshua's grandmother and it was she who told me what the men planned to do.'

He smiled. 'Visiting on horseback dressed like that? Do you think he will believe you?'

'Oh, dear. I shall have to sneak Midge back in her stall and swear the stable boy to secrecy.'

He reached for her hand. 'Lucy, I must know. Have you accepted Edward Gorridge?'

'He hasn't asked me yet.'

'But you expect him to?'

'I think so. His parents and mine both wish it.'

'But do you wish it?'

'I don't know. It is a big step to take and for everyone's sake I must consider it seriously....'

He took her shoulders in his hands and shook her gently. 'Lucy, while it is true that marriage is a big step, it is not for everyone's sake you should consider it, but for your own. It is your future, your happiness. Do not let yourself be persuaded against your will.'

'It is all very well for you to say that. You are a man and may do as you please.'

'Do you love him?'

'I do not think so, but perhaps I might learn to love him.' She was only repeating the arguments her mother had used, not because she believed them, but because she did not know how to answer him. It was a fruitless conversation; she and Myles could have no future and she was afraid to let him think they might.

'You don't believe that, do you?' In his anxiety he gripped her more tightly than he intended.

'You are hurting me.'

He let his hands fall. 'I am sorry, my lady. I did not mean to. Saving you from hurt is my sole mission. Please forgive me.'

'I do. But I really must go.' She turned back to Midge and put her foot into the stirrup. He took her other foot and lifted her easily into the saddle. 'Take care,' he said, as she hitched up her skirt a little, revealing trim ankles and a pair of ordinary shoes.

'You take care. You know Mr Gorridge is laying bets on how long you will last on Thursday. He is making a joke about it. I wish you did not have to do it.'

'You have no need to worry. I would not have accepted his wager if I did not think I could do it.'

'He will be angry if he loses.'

He laughed. 'Oh, he will lose, have no fear, and I hope not only the wager.'

Midge was restive, anxious to be away again. Lucy settled her before speaking again. 'What do you mean?'

'I will tell you another time. We have to talk, but not now. I do not want you to be in trouble for coming here. Later I will find you. But, Lucy, my love, do not accept Gorridge until we have spoken together.'

'Goodbye,' she said, digging her heel into the mare's side and galloping away so that he would not see her tears. It was all so hopeless.

Chapter Seven

Somehow Lucy got through the rest of the day. It was made easier for her because the men had gone shooting game and she did not have to make conversation with Edward. The ladies strolled about the grounds and gossiped until it was time for afternoon tea. It was when they dispersed to rest before dressing for dinner that the Countess came to her room.

'Lucy, where did you go this morning? You were absent at breakfast and when I sent up to ask after you, I was told you had risen early and gone out. I know you have been used to coming and going as you please, but with those navvies in the area it is not wise.'

'Mama, they are simple working men and I think it is unfair of everyone to brand them as monsters.'

'Well, where did you go?'

'To see Mrs Staines.'

'On horseback, Lucy? In a morning gown?'

'Oh, someone told you. Does Papa know?'

'No, he does not, but I am not at all sure I shouldn't tell him.'

'Oh, please don't. He will be angry and it was nothing,

except… Oh, Mama, I had to do it and Papa would never understand.'

'Then you had better tell me and see if I can.'

Lucy told her how she had visited Mrs Staines and what Mrs Staines had told her and that she felt something must be done to stop trouble, so she had ridden to find Mr Moorcroft, who had spoken to the village men and they had gone away peaceably.

'Lucy, I am appalled. You should have come home and alerted your father, not taken it upon yourself to ride out to the works. He forbade you to speak to Mr Moorcroft, didn't he?'

'Yes, but this was an emergency. Please, Mama, it turned out all right in the end, so please, please do not tell Papa.'

'With guests in the house it would be difficult for him to punish you, so I will not tell him. He is in a good humour and enjoying the Viscount's visit. Let us keep it that way.'

'Thank you, Mama.'

'But it is not to happen again. You will not speak to that man again, is that clear?'

'Yes, Mama.'

'Now I will send Sarah in to dress you for dinner and you will behave in a manner befitting your rank, and that means not taking part in the men's conversation or asking questions about things that do not concern you. And you will try to encourage Mr Gorridge to pay his addresses.'

'Yes, Mama.'

She held her tears in check until the door had closed and then she flung herself on the bed, burying her face in the pillow, and wept.

The whole party, including Esme and Johnny, set off the following morning to walk to the abbey ruins, which dominated the skyline. The weather was good for so late in the year, but the wind was a little chill and everyone was warmly clad. They wandered about the broken walls and climbed the remains of a circular stone staircase to admire the view. They were some way from the railway works and could not see them, but they could hear the distant clamour of a multitude of men working: the ring of spades on stone, the rumble of wagon wheels, shouts and laughter, and once the dull thud of an explosion.

'Goodness, what was that?' Lady Gorridge asked.

'It's only the navvies, Mama,' Edward said. 'They are blasting rock.'

'I had no idea we would be able to hear them from here,' the Countess said.

'What are navvies?' Johnny asked.

'They are workmen, properly called navigators because they once dug out canals, but now they are building a railway,' Lucy explained to him. 'One day we shall have trains coming to Luffenham station and you will be able to see them steaming along.'

'May I go and see what they are doing now?'

'No, certainly not,' his mother said. 'They are rough men and not at all nice to talk to. You must not go anywhere near them.'

'Mama,' Lucy protested. 'You will make him afraid of them.'

'So he should be.'

'I could take the little fellow to watch on Thursday, if you agree, my lady,' Edward said. 'He'll come to no harm watching from the top of the hill and he will see his very own railway taking shape.'

'Oh, Mama, may I?' Johnny begged. 'I'll be good, I promise.'

The Countess found it difficult to deny her young son anything. 'You must ask your papa.'

The result of this was that Johnny asked his father, who suddenly said he would take him himself if Miss Bannister said he had been good, and that led to Esme wanting to go and before long everyone, ladies included except the Countess, had agreed they might enjoy a ride to the top of the hill from where they could view the men at work in safety. Lucy was appalled, knowing that Edward had manipulated the company to witness Myles labouring like a common workman, and perhaps his downfall. Myles had seemed confident of success when she spoke to him, but that would only confirm, in her father's eyes, that he was not a gentleman. And perhaps he was not. Perhaps it was only because he was so different from every other man she had met that she felt so drawn towards him. If he behaved like every other gentleman of her acquaintance—like Edward, for instance—would she think him quite ordinary? Oh, she wished she were not so confused! She had been forbidden to speak to him again and, being a dutiful daughter, she must obey.

Convinced her demeanour would give her away, she did not want to go with everyone else, but Edward was being particularly insistent and for the sake of peace she gave in. She would ride up to the vantage point, but that did not mean she had to watch. She would take her sketch book and draw wild flowers.

The days were shortening now and it was barely light when they set out, with Johnny proudly riding his little pony between Lucy and Edward and everyone else following on behind, including the Reverend Mr Cedric Luffenham, who was flattered to be asked to referee and determined, so he told the Earl, that he would take the opportunity to minister to the workmen.

They could hear the clatter of work on the site before they

topped the rise, and the sight that met them when they could finally look down into the valley astonished them. A huge swathe of the opposite hillside had been cut open and the men were busy levelling it. More huts had been built, more wagons brought in and more horses being worked by boys, among them, Lucy noticed, Adam O'Malley. An empty truck stood at the head of the cutting and beside it was the tall figure of Myles in shirtsleeves, leaning on a shovel. He must have heard the neighing of one of their horses, because he looked up. She could not see his expression, but her heart went out to him. Navvy or not, she could not help her feelings for him.

'He's turned up at any rate,' Edward said, and started off down the hill with the parson. The Earl and Viscount Gorridge decided they, too, would ride down and inspect the works. Lucy took Johnny's bridle when it looked as though he meant to follow. 'We must stay here,' she said.

He was full of questions: Why were the men digging such a big hole? How many of them were there? What were the children doing? Did they have lessons? When would the first train come? She endeavoured to answer them all, but in spite of her determination not to look, she could not take her eyes from the drama being enacted in the valley. She saw Edward speak to Myles and shake his hand, then the reverend also shook his hand and Myles dug his first spade of crock. He worked in rhythm with the man on the other side of the wagon: dig, lift, empty, dig, lift, empty; unstopping, unstoppable. Lucy was fascinated. She forgot about wild flowers and began sketching the scene.

Lady Gorridge soon became bored and suggested they might as well leave the men to it, but Johnny set up such a wail of protest. Lucy volunteered to stay with him until his father returned to take charge of him.

'Can't we go down there?' he asked when they were the only two left on the hill.

'No, we will only get in the way.'

At noon the workers stopped when Mrs O'Malley brought them food and a tankard of ale apiece. Myles, quaffing his, looked up and saw Lucy, still there, still watching him. He likened her to a guardian angel. It gave him fresh impetus; as soon as he had finished his frugal meal, he set to again with renewed vigour. He knew what he was doing would not help his cause with the Earl, or even Lucy herself, but he could no more have refused the challenge than taken wing. When it was all over, he would be the gentleman again. He would dress as befitted the son of a nobleman, he would cultivate the friendship of those who mattered and hope that word would reach the Earl that he was someone to be reckoned with, someone worthy of his daughter. But would Lucy wait that long?

The Earl and Viscount watched him for a few minutes and then turned to rejoin Lucy and Johnny and they rode home, leaving Edward to follow later. He did not return for dinner and everyone supposed the navvy was still working. Lucy wondered how Myles was feeling. He must be exhausted. She prayed he would not be humiliated. At eleven o'clock, when the ladies decided to retire, Edward had still not returned.

She was sitting in the parlour working on her sketch the following morning when he entered the room. He stood over her, looking at what she was doing. 'You draw well,' he said. 'The navvy in his true environment—in the dirt.'

She looked up at him, wondering if there was more behind the comment than appeared on the surface. 'Good morning, Mr Gorridge. I trust you slept well.'

'Like a top.' He laughed. 'Don't you want to know what happened yesterday after you all left?'

'No, I have no interest in your childish games.'

'Oh, Lucy, you are a poor liar. Why, if you have no interest, are you drawing it?'

'It is the work that interests me.'

'And that is going on apace.' He laughed. 'Quicker since yesterday. They are all vying with each other to see who can shift the most muck. There's earth flying all over the place. Come for a ride and see.'

'No.' He still had not said if he had won the wager and she would not ask him.

'Oh, come on. We will see if he has recovered.'

'Recovered? What is the matter with him?' She did not need to ask whom he meant.

'He was so exhausted his men had to carry him to the beer shop. They have one on every site, you know, and the whole twenty guineas went on ale for every man on the works.'

'By that, I assume you were obliged to pay up.'

'Yes, more's the pity. But that is all he won.'

'I did not know there was anything else at stake.'

'There certainly was and that is most decidedly mine and well he knows it.' He ran his finger down the sketch, tracing the outline of Myles's body. She had had trouble getting it right and wanted to dash his finger away. 'All that muscle. Do you like muscles in a man, Lucy? Is that why you are so taken with the navvy?'

'Taken with him? I don't know what you mean.'

'Don't you? Don't you have little fantasies about him, wondering what it would be like to be held in his great, muscular arms? Have you ever been held in his arms, Lucy?'

'Don't be silly.'

'Am I? I think perhaps you have.'

'Whatever gave you that ridiculous idea?' she snapped, but she could feel her face growing warm.

'I have seen the way he looks at you. There is a lustful gleam in his eye that says he would like to bed the Earl's daughter and put another notch on his bedpost. I hope the Earl's daughter is not foolish enough to be taken in by him. It would end in tears, Lucy.'

She had already shed enough tears to fill a lake, but she would never admit that to anyone, particularly not to him. 'I wish you would cease this conversation,' she said. 'It is offensive.'

He leaned forward and twisted one of her ringlets round his finger. 'I am only trying to warn you. For your own good.'

'I do not need to be warned.'

'Good. I am glad we understand each other.'

'Do we?'

'I certainly hope so. I suppose you want it put formally in the time-honoured way.' He dropped on to one knee beside her chair and grabbed her hands. 'Lady Lucinda Vernley, will you do me the honour of consenting to be my wife?'

Although she was supposed to be expecting it, the manner of it shocked her and she could only stare at him.

'Don't look so taken aback, Lucy. It can hardly be a surprise to you.'

'I don't know what to say.'

'Say yes, of course. That's the usual thing. Then we go and announce it and everyone congratulates us and my friends call me a lucky dog, and all your friends tell you how they envy you.'

Not a word about being in love, of feelings, certainly no passion. 'I thought... No, it doesn't matter. I do not think I can say yes.'

'Why not?' He got to his feet again. 'Oh, you are going to

keep me dangling for a while to test my mettle. Well, no matter, I can wait. But what your papa will say, I do not know.'

'I am sure he will say I am wise to think about it carefully before making a decision.'

'What is there to think about? You know me and my family and my prospects and you know that both families are in favour of the match.'

'But are you?'

'Of course, or I would not have asked you. So what do you say? A spring wedding?'

'Please give me a little more time, Mr Gorridge. I need to be sure.'

'Very well. But I suggest you forget all about him.' And he pointed to the sketch. 'He'll never amount to anything. Are you sure you will not ride out with me?'

'Not today, thank you.' She could not go on working with him looking over her shoulder. She collected everything together and stood up. 'I have to think. We shall, no doubt, meet at dinner.' And with that she swept from the room.

She went up to her room and put her sketching things in the drawer where they belonged, then she put on her cloak and bonnet and slipped from the house. She would not go riding, but she would go for a walk. She did not want company. Her head was buzzing. She could not marry Edward Gorridge, she simply could not. She had begun by liking him well enough, but now not even that was true. He *was* a cold fish and the prospect of spending the rest of her life with him was appalling. But turning him down was going to cause the most terrible battle. Was she strong enough for it?

Her feet took her, without any conscious thought, into the

village where she entered the church. Here she might find solace. It was cold in there and she drew her cloak closer about her. It was only as she walked down the aisle that she saw the vicar talking to Myles. It was too late to turn back.

'Lucinda,' the reverend called out. 'Good morning to you.'

'Good morning, sir.' She tried not to look at Myles, but could not help herself. His presence demanded attention. He was dressed in a brown suit of clothes which were not the common garb of the navvy, but neither were they the fashionable attire of a gentleman, but something in between. His smile betrayed his pleasure at seeing her.

'Good morning, Lady Lucinda.'

Now what was she to do? Her mother had forbidden her to speak to him again, but she could not ignore him. Besides, they had a chaperon. 'Mr Moorcroft.'

'Mr Moorcroft is here to arrange for me to minister to his men while they are working in the area,' the vicar explained. 'Some of them would like to attend church with their families on Sunday, but I understand the Earl has forbidden them to come to the village. Do you think he might make an exception for churchgoers?'

She forced herself to pay attention. 'I do not know. You must ask him, but perhaps your congregation might object.'

'Surely not? They are Christian folk and should welcome other Christians in their midst.'

'What about you, Lady Lucinda?' Myles asked. 'Would you object?'

She turned towards him. 'Of course not, but I cannot speak for the rest of my family.'

'Ah, there's the rub,' he said, addressing the parson. 'Not all are as tolerant as Lady Lucinda.'

'Then tolerance shall be the theme of my sermon. I shall

go up to the Hall and request an interview with my cousin. He could surely lift the ban for Sundays.'

Myles laughed. 'He will say mischief can be done as easily on a Sunday as any other day.'

'Then I must persuade him that is not the case. Will you come with me? It will help if you can give him some reassurance.'

'No, Reverend, I think he is more likely to give way if he thinks the idea was entirely yours and you are only thinking about saving men's souls.'

'Lucinda?' the reverend asked. 'What do you think?'

'I think Mr Moorcroft is right.'

'Then I will go now. Lucinda, did you come to see me? Is there something I can do for you?'

'No, I came for quiet meditation and to check on the hassocks. I noticed last Sunday that some need repairing and I thought I might organise that.'

'Bless you for that.' He strode off down the aisle on his errand, quite forgetting that he should not have left Lucy alone with Mr Moorcroft.

'Lucy.' Myles reached for her hand. 'How good it is to see you here. I noticed you on the hill yesterday. Were you there to watch the fun?'

'Please leave. I have been forbidden to speak to you.'

'I see.' He paused, realising the obstacles to his happiness were every bit as high as he had imagined. 'But you haven't been forbidden to listen to me, have you?' He smiled suddenly. 'A nod will do.'

She nodded, managing to find a brief smile. She was sure that listening to him or being in his company was part of the stricture and she should have walked away. But she could not. She could not walk away from him, would never be able to turn her back on him. Georgie's description of being in love came back to her and she knew without a shadow of a doubt she loved this man.

'Good. Come, let us sit down. I want to talk to you.' He led her by the hand into a pew and drew her down beside him.

She was glad to sit; she was shaking so much her legs were buckling under her. She looked into his dear face and was overcome with sadness.

'Don't look so sorrowful,' he said, noticing a tear bright on her lashes. 'It breaks my heart. You must have realised I love you and that will never change, but I need to know if you love me.' He smiled again and took both her hands in his. They were hard and calloused, but he was gentle and she hardly noticed. 'A nod will do. Please nod. My future happiness depends on it.'

She nodded and then the need to say something overcame her scruples. 'It is impossible, you know it is.'

'Impossible for you to love me or impossible that I love you and want you for my wife? I assure you that I do.'

'Oh, Myles! I… Can you really mean it?'

'Of course I mean it. I am not in the habit of telling young ladies I love them. In fact, it is the first time I have ever done so.'

'Oh, Myles,' she said again, unable to express the tumbled emotions that beset her: joy, hope, despair in equal measure.

'Well?'

She made a feeble attempt to laugh. 'Yours is the second proposal I have had today.'

'Damn! I am too late. You have accepted him.'

'No, I said I needed time to think about it.'

'Do you need to think about it?'

'No, only about how I can say no without giving offence, not only to him but to Papa and Mama and his parents.'

'You won't let that weigh with you, will you? It is your life, your happiness.' He paused and ran a finger down her cheek, making her shiver. 'And mine, too. I cannot contemplate life without you. Say you will make me the happiest man in the world. Say you will marry me.'

'How can I? My father would never agree.'

'I seem to remember you saying that about him allowing the railway on his land and yet here we are. We shall have to persuade him.'

'How? Myles, how?'

'I don't know. I must give it some thought.' He wondered whether to ask her if she would consider defying her father, but knew that was too much to ask. She would not risk being cut off from the rest of her family and he knew that was not the way for them to be happy. 'I suppose I had better start by throwing off the navvy and behaving like a gentleman.'

'Oh, Myles, you must not change your way for my sake. You are you and it is the you that you are whom I love.'

He put his arms about her and hugged her to him. 'You are amazing. Do you know what I said to my father? I said I wanted you to love me for the man I am and not for what I have or might become. And you do, don't you, my darling?'

'Oh, yes, but I am so afraid of the storm.'

'We will weather it together.'

'I am afraid of living in a hut, too. I should not manage, I know I should not.'

'Live in a hut, Lucy? Oh, my darling, you surely did not think I would ask that of you? You shall have the best of everything. I am successful at what I do. As for my prospects, you know I am my father's heir and will in due course come into a large engineering concern, a woollen mill and the railway business—not the sort of wealth your father approves

of, but you would never want for anything. As for my ante-
cedents, my mother is the daughter of Viscount Porson and
that title goes back several generations. You will not be
marrying a navvy, my love.'

'I wouldn't care. I love the navvy, too. I would be proud
to be a navvy's wife.'

He smiled. 'Bless you for that.' He tipped her face up and
kissed the tip of her nose, then her forehead and each cheek
and then her lips. He was so gentle, so considerate, and she
knew he would stop instantly if she asked him to, but she did
not ask it. She clung to him in a kind of desperation, wanting
to savour every moment, knowing it would not come again.
What he was suggesting was the stuff of dreams and she did
not want to wake up.

'We won't say anything yet,' he murmured. 'Wait until
we've finished this section of railway and are off Luffenham
land. Then I'll ask my mother to invite the Countess for tea
or something like that. We'll try and get your mother on our
side for a start.'

'I don't think she dare defy Papa. It was she who forbade
me to speak to you.'

'Ah, but she only knows the navvy in me and believes all
the stories she has heard about how navvies behave.'

'They are not true?'

'Oh, undoubtedly some of them are. I could tell you some
shocking tales, but it doesn't happen on Moorcroft lines
because my father knows what it's like to be a labouring man
and so he treats his workers like human beings and they repay
him with loyalty and affection. It is something I strive for
myself, which is why I learned to be a navvy. With a few ex-
ceptions, our men are hardworking, no drunker than most, and
we encourage them to marry the women they live with. If

some of them are allowed to come to church on Sunday, perhaps your mama will see the good side of them.'

'Oh, so it was your idea to bring them to church. They did not think of it themselves.'

'They did, but I saw the advantages, especially as the reverend was enthusiastic. He went among them yesterday, having a word here and a word there, so you may put the idea down to him.'

'What did happen yesterday? I gather you won your wager.'

'Yes, easily.'

'Easily? Mr Gorridge said your friends had to carry you, that you were too exhausted to stand.'

He laughed. 'They carried me shoulder high, cheering. And they cheered even more when I gave them the wager money to celebrate.' He paused and grinned ruefully. 'That's not to say I didn't have an ache here and there through being out of condition, but Gorridge knew nothing of that.'

'Good for you. I am proud of you.'

'Thank you, sweetheart. Now, much as I would like to keep you here, I think you had better go home before someone comes looking for you, especially if the Reverend lets out that he left us together.' He stood up and held out his hand. She took it and together they walked back to the door.

'You know,' he said. 'When you came into the church just now and I turned and watched you coming down the aisle, I imagined I was standing there watching you come down to join me for our wedding. I thought about how beautiful you would look in your wedding gown and how gloriously happy I would be. And how, half an hour later, we should be leaving the church arm-in-arm as husband and wife, with everyone throwing rose petals and wishing us well.'

His words brought her back to the seemingly unsolvable problem of her parents' implacable opposition. And there was also Viscount Gorridge's 'consideration,' whatever that was. 'Papa and Mama would not be among them,' she said. 'And you will have made an enemy of Mr Gorridge. When he told me you had won the wager, he said that was all you had won.'

'I know, he said the same thing to me. You must think my love a poor thing if I am put off by things like that.'

'I do not know what he will say when I turn him down.'

'You are not afraid of him, are you?'

'No, I do not think so, but I hate dissension. I shall be in disgrace.'

'When is he going home?'

'The day after tomorrow, but they are all coming back for Christmas and the hunt.'

'Then tell him you will give him his answer then. The Luffenham section of line should be finished by then and the navvies gone.'

'And you along with them.'

'Yes, but I shall not be far away. When the storm breaks, if it breaks, and you need me, I will come.'

They stood a moment in the porch, knowing they would have to release each other and go their separate ways. He kissed her. 'Be patient, my love, all will be well.'

She moved away from him, still holding his hand, reluctant to let go. He squeezed her fingers. 'Go on, sweetheart. My love goes with you.'

She stood on tiptoe to kiss his cheek and then turned and hurried away. She dare not look back, because if she did she would run back to him and he was right—they must have patience.

* * *

Slowly he turned and fetched Trojan from the Plough where he had left him and set off back to the navvy camp. There were one or two things he needed to check on before he went home, but he was in a buoyant mood. Lucy loved him and he loved her and he could not see that anything could stand in their way for long. He would talk to his mother, enlist her help. Surely the Countess would not be so uncivil as to refuse her admittance if his mother called on her socially. After all, she was a lady born and bred, daughter of a viscount.

At the camp he spoke to O'Malley about the next day's work and then walked forward along the line of the railway, checking the stakes and marking those trees on the edge of the copse that needed to be felled before the excavators arrived. He was turning for home when he heard the sound of a woman giggling and a man's chuckle. Guessing what they were at and not wishing to intrude, he turned away, but then he recognised the man's voice. 'You're a little fireball, aren't you, my sweet? Much better than the simpering miss I'm expected to marry. God, I shall need someone like you when that happens.'

'Why marry, then?'

'My dear papa thinks being married will settle me down and keep me on the straight and narrow.'

'I don' reckon it will, do you?'

'Not a hope while there's accommodating little ladies like you around.'

Myles heard more scuffling and then a chuckle and a giggle. Unable to contain himself, he walked towards the sound and found the two lying on the ground half-naked. He made no effort to be quiet and the girl, who was no more than fifteen, turned and gasped when she saw who it was, then endeavoured to cover herself. 'Go home, Lottie,' he said quietly.

She picked up her skirt and scuttled away and he turned to face Edward, who was grinning complacently. 'You disgust me,' he said. 'Lottie is no more than a child.'

'Oh, she's no child. She's all woman. And willing.'

'I should tell her parents and they'd have the whole camp after you.'

'But you won't, will you?' He pulled at his riding breeches and tucked in his shirt. 'Who'd believe you? And I reckon the last thing you want is trouble between the navvies and Lord Luffenham.'

'What about Lady Lucinda?'

'What's she got to do with it?'

'I was given to understand you had offered her marriage.'

'So I have. A fine wife she'll make, too, a well-bred mother for my children, but that doesn't mean I have to curtail all my pleasures.'

Myles let fly with one clenched fist. He didn't need another blow. Edward went down like a stone. He stood over him until he came round. 'That was instead of sending Lottie's father after you,' he said. 'But touch her again and you will live to rue the day.'

Edward shook his head as if to knock his brains back into place, then rubbed his chin, which was feeling decidedly sore. 'I wonder if it is Lottie you are concerned about or Lucy Vernley. I should forget her if I were you. She'll do as she is told like the good daughter she is.'

Myles raised his arm again, but decided against brawling with the man; he was quite capable of killing him. Instead he turned on his heel and strode away from temptation. But he was more determined than ever to save Lucy from the fate of being married to that lecherous bounder.

* * *

It was evident at dinner that night that Edward was very pleased with himself in spite of the bruise on his chin, which he said had been caused by a branch sticking out from a tree which he did not see while he was out riding. He did not seem to care if anyone believed him or not. He kept dropping hints about how he would soon be the happiest of men and that in a little while he would have an announcement to make. Lucy longed to contradict him, but, remembering what Myles had said, she simply smiled and said nothing, until after dinner when they were in the drawing room.

She had gone to sit in a corner near the piano, but he found her there and settled himself beside her. 'I say this for Lord Luffenham,' he said, 'you cannot fault his hospitality, but I am sure this little dinner party was meant to introduce me to friends and neighbours as a future member of the family and he must be disappointed that he has nothing to tell them.'

'He has said nothing to me.'

'No doubt he will, unless you are a good girl and stop this nonsense about having to think about it.'

'You cannot tell me you did not have to think long and hard before you proposed, Mr Gorridge. It is an important step to take and should not be undertaken lightly. I want to be sure I can live in harmony with the man I marry.'

'Why should you not live in harmony with me? I promise you I will make no great demands upon you, though of course I should expect you to fulfil your wifely duties, but other than that you can pursue your own interests. Within reason, of course. And I can be very generous, you know.'

'You say nothing of love.'

'Why, Lucy, I did not know you were one of the romantic

sort. I always took you for someone as down to earth and practical as I am, but if it is a declaration of love you want, before saying yes, then I am sure I can supply it.'

'And mean it, Mr Gorridge?'

'Of course. So, shall we make the announcement?'

'Not tonight. I will tell you my answer when you come at Christmas.'

'That's six weeks away!'

'Six weeks is not very long when you are talking about a lifetime together.'

'Lucy, how can you be so cruel? It's that navvy, isn't it? He's turned your head with his physique. But that's all he has to recommend him, you know. His grandfather made a lot of money, but that will all disappear on failing railways and Moorcroft will be left where his grandfather began, with nothing.'

She longed to contradict him, to tell him that Myles had far more than that in his favour. He was gentle and kind and protective. He was not arrogant or foolish or indolent, and he showed compassion to those beneath him. Besides, he loved her. But she could not say anything like that and, because she could not deny Myles, simply smiled and said, 'I know nothing of business, naturally, but perhaps he is more astute than you give him credit for.'

'We shall see. But let us not talk about him....'

'What are you two whispering about?' Rosemary demanded. 'Lucy, come and play some music.'

Relieved by the interruption, she went to comply.

The reverend must have been persuasive, because when Lucy went into church on Sunday, the usual congregation had swollen to include several navvies and their families, dressed as flamboyantly as ever, and, though their clothes

could not be described as pristine, some effort had been made
to be clean. Knowing that every drop of water they used had
to be brought up from the river, this was quite an achievement.
Lucy, with Edward and Dorothea at her side, followed her
parents and Lord and Lady Gorridge down the aisle, looking
about her for Myles. He was sitting at the end of a pew in front
of his own people and turned, as all the navvies did, to watch
the procession of gentry in all their finery, walking to their
own pews. Lucy caught his eye and was rewarded with a
slight smile and a tiny bow, which could have been for the
whole party, but she knew it was for her.

'What's he doing here?' Edward hissed in Lucy's ear.

'I expect, like you, he has come to worship God.'

'Hmm. Believe that, if you like.' He deliberately picked
up her hand and laid it on his arm, grinning at Myles as he
did so. She saw Myles's face darken and hoped he would
not do or say anything to upset either Edward or her
parents.

It was an effort, but Myles managed to contain himself. Everything depended on the navvies behaving well and impress-
ing the Earl with their godliness and sobriety and he included
himself in that. But, oh, how he longed to grab Lucy and
declare their love to the world. 'Patience,' he admonished
himself and turned to the front as the service began.

The parson had never had such a large congregation and
he made the most of it, preaching to them for over two hours.
It was two hours in which Lucy's emotions ranged from
despair to hope, from the sheer joy of having Myles near and
knowing he loved her, to utter misery. And beside her,
Edward, secure in his own little world of the spoiled son who
had never been denied anything he wanted, sang the hymns
and made the responses and grinned in triumph, believing he

would win. Lucy was aware of it. She wondered if, in the end, he would, that she would be forced to agree to the marriage, out of consideration for her family.

Could Myles turn things around? Judging by the stern look on her father's face, she doubted it. Who would be the most stubborn, her father and Edward or Myles and herself? She feared her own weakness. Defying her father was something she had never tried to do. Was it permissible to pray for the strength to do that? Probably not. Honour thy father and thy mother, the Bible said.

The family filed out of the church before the main body of the congregation and she passed the end of the pew where Myles stood, waiting to follow. She was so close that the warm blue cloak she wore over her dress brushed against him and his hand briefly touched hers. She looked up and saw the message of love in his eyes and was heartened.

She felt a great deal easier when, later that day, their guests departed, even though she was subjected to a lecture from her father about not accepting Edward's proposal.

'Why you have to keep him waiting, I do not know,' he told her. 'I thought it had already been decided between you and the announcement was a mere formality.'

'We had decided nothing, Papa,' she said. 'He did not propose until yesterday and I asked him for time to consider. I am not sure enough of my feelings for him to give him an immediate answer.'

'What did he say to that?'

'He agreed to wait until Christmas.'

'I don't know what the world is coming to,' he muttered. 'In my day we accepted the advice of our parents without question. Young people today have far too easy a time of it. But I tell you, child, Christmas is the latest I will suffer your delaying tactics. I shall expect to make the formal announcement at our New Year ball.'

Rosemary clapped her hands in delight. 'Oh, Papa, are we to have a ball?'

'If it is the only way to get your sister to the altar, then we will.'

'And may we have new gowns?'

'More gowns? Haven't you got a wardrobe full already?'

'Nothing suitable for Lucy's engagement ball.'

Lucy remained silent. She prayed that everything would come right in the end, and if there was a ball it was to announce her engagement to Myles, not Edward, but she had no great expectation of her prayer being granted.

Two weeks later Georgina wrote with the happy news that she was expecting a child. 'We are both thrilled,' she wrote. 'But I have been dreadfully sick every morning and that has made me very tired. Gerry is busy with his clients and I am feeling a little down. Do you think your family can spare you to keep me company for a week or two? Do try to persuade them. I want to hear all your news....'

Remembering the scolding she had had from the Earl the last time she stayed with Georgie, Lucy did not hold out much hope that she would be allowed to go, but her father saw it as a way of separating her from the navvies. It wasn't Myles he meant because he assumed she had obeyed him and not spoken to him again, but the children. She had extended her good works among the village children to include those at the navvy camp, taking them food and toys, slates and chalks for their lessons. Although her mother agreed because she was soft-hearted where children were concerned, Lucy was never allowed to go alone. Either Miss Bannister, Sarah or Rosemary accompanied her, none of whom relished going among the navvies. They made her stay on the edge of the encampment and have the children come to her, which they did, as soon as they saw her riding down the hill with her basket of good things on her pommel.

Occasionally she glimpsed Myles; sometimes she was close enough to bid him good day, but with her eagle-eyed chaperons watching and listening they could not talk. More often than not he was not at the works, but on business elsewhere. It was frustrating and heart-rending and all the time Christmas was drawing closer, when the Gorridges would once more descend upon them. Seeing Georgina again would be a welcome diversion before the struggle to come, always assuming Myles had not changed his mind about her. It would break her heart if he did, but it would not make any difference to her determination not to marry Edward Gorridge. Georgie was the only person she could talk to about that.

The weather was cold and dismal the day she travelled, but Georgina had a warm fire and an even warmer welcome for her. 'It is good to see you,' she said when Lucy had been to her room to wash and change and had returned to the drawing room. 'I want to hear all about everything. I dare not write and ask about Mr Moorcroft in my letters.'

'I am glad you did not. If Mama asked to see them, I could not refuse to show them to her and there would have been a dreadful row.'

'You can tell me all about it over dinner. Gerry is dining out, but of course, in my condition, it was not appropriate for me to accompany him....'

'Your condition!' Lucy laughed, following her friend into the dining room. 'You are as slim as ever.'

'If I am it is because I have been so sick, but I am better now and beginning to grow fat.'

'Do you mind?'

'No, not at all. It means I will soon be a mother and I can't wait.'

Lucy smiled. 'You are happy, then?'

'Oh, wonderfully. Being married to the man you love is the most glorious, the most uplifting thing in the world, as you will find out when it happens to you.'

'I do not think it will.'

'Oh, dear, that doesn't sound good. You must tell me all about it.'

A maid served them with soup, followed by crown of lamb and then a delicious lemon pudding. Lucy was in no hurry to embark upon her story; it was not easy to find the words to begin and she decided to wait until the meal was over and she and Georgie retired to the drawing room.

When her tale was eventually told, as they sat one on either side of a roaring fire toasting their toes, Georgina was all sympathy for her friend's predicament, but advised her to stick to her guns. 'It would be different if you wanted to marry a real navvy,' she said.

'He is a real navvy.'

'Yes, but he's a great deal more than that, isn't he?'

'Oh, much, much more.'

'Then your task is to make your papa see it.'

'I do not think he will. He despises Lord Moorcroft for being a self-made man and not a gentleman, but it is not so much that but that he is determined I shall marry Mr Gorridge—'

'Whom you like well enough. Isn't that what you said?'

'Maybe I did, but that was when I did not know him very well. I had only seen the polished side of him he displayed to the world. The more I see of him, the more I know I cannot marry him.'

'Then you must be blunt and tell your father so. Get him used to the idea of your not marrying Mr Gorridge before you spring Mr Moorcroft on him.'

Lucy laughed. It was the first genuine laugh she had managed in weeks. 'Georgie, you are so clever and so wise.'

Georgina did not reply to this flattery because the sound of the door knocker came to their ears. 'Who can that be at this time of night?' Georgina murmured as she got up and left the room. The maid had been told she could have the rest of the evening off and there was no one to answer the door. Lucy heard voices and then Georgie came back. 'Lucy, we have a visitor.' And she stood to one side to allow Myles to enter the room.

Lucy sprang to her feet, so flustered she did not know what to do, what to say, whether to retreat or run forward. 'Myles!'

'I'll just go and check the maid hasn't left any candles burning,' Georgie said. The door clicked shut and they were alone.

He held out his arms and she ran into them with a little cry of joy. He kissed her tenderly and drew her down beside him on the sofa. 'How have you been?' he asked. 'Has anything changed?'

'Nothing. I am to give Mr Gorridge his answer at Christmas. What about you?'

'I am still as much in love with you as ever and always will be, to the end of my days.'

'How did you know I would be here?'

'I met Lady Brotherton in the town a fortnight ago when I was here on business and we had a little talk.' He laughed. 'She is a gem, isn't she? It was her idea to invite you here so that we could have a little time together.'

'Myles, what are we going to do? Papa says he will not put up with my delaying tactics beyond Christmas and he is giving a ball, when he hopes… Oh, Myles, I am in despair.'

'Take heart,' he said. 'We will prevail.' He sounded more optimistic than he felt, but one thing he was sure of, he would not stand by and see her married to Gorridge. What he wanted to avoid, if it was at all possible, was carrying her off against her parents' wishes, even if Lucy herself agreed to it. He did not want to subject her to the misery a rift with her family would cause. Some other way had to be found.

'Do you know what Georgie said? She said I ought to get Papa used to the idea of me not marrying Mr Gorridge before I told him I wanted to marry you.'

'Your friend is a wise lady.'

'And a naughty one for leaving us unchaperoned.'

'Not naughty, sympathetic. While you are staying with her, we can see each other often. It will give us strength for what lies ahead.'

'Papa knew I had seen you last time I came to Peterborough. Mr Gorridge saw us talking at the meeting and told him. He was very angry. If he finds out we have met and talked again, I dare not think what he will do. I do not know why he is so adamant I must marry Mr Gorridge. I think, perhaps, he has made some financial arrangement with the Viscount, though what it is I do not know. Mr Gorridge says he will take me without a dowry, so what is going on?'

'I do not know, sweetheart.' He was tempted to tell her about Gorridge and Lottie and what he had overheard, but decided not to; such a tactic was not worthy of him and he was not at all sure that the Earl would consider it reason enough to withdraw his support of the man and it was the Earl he had to convince.

She looked up at him and smiled. 'Will you mind about the dowry?'

'Oh, my love, how can you ask that? I would not care if you did not have a penny.'

'It might come to that, you know. If I defy Papa, he will cut me off and forbid my mother and my sisters ever to speak to me again.'

'I will not ask that of you. It will not answer.'

His words did little to cheer her, but before she could ask him what alternative there was, there was a little tap at the door and Georgina put her head round it. 'May I come in?'

Startled, Lucy pulled herself away from him and turned to Georgie, trying to smile. Her friend should not have engineered the visit and certainly she should not have deliberately left them alone, but she had meant it for the best. 'Of course. We cannot keep you from your own drawing room.'

The visit ended with mundane conversation mostly between Myles and Georgina. Lucy marvelled that he could sound so normal when her own emotions were overflowing and she could hardly speak without choking. She was afraid that he would rather lose her than risk her father's wrath. And then what would she do?

Chapter Eight

'They're here!' Johnny called out. 'There's a carriage coming up the drive. And another one behind it.' He scrambled from his perch on a chair by the nursery window and dashed downstairs to find his mother, ignoring Miss Bannister's cries for him to come back. 'Mama, they're here!' he shouted, skittering along the shiny marble in the hall towards the drawing room.

He flew into the room to find his mother and sisters sitting round the fire, decorously awaiting the arrival of their guests. 'Johnny, do calm down,' the Countess said. 'It is unbecoming to dash about like a common potboy. Besides, you should not be here. Go back to the nursery until you are sent for. You may come down for a few minutes after tea to greet our guests. Now, run along and take the back stairs.' The door knocker was heard as he disappeared down the corridor. The Countess rose, ready to receive the first of the guests.

Lucy had returned from Peterborough to find her mother in the throes of preparing for the accommodation of the twenty guests who were expected on the afternoon of Christmas Eve, which meant opening up unused bedrooms, finding bed linen, organising the cleaning and polishing, arranging flowers, as well as the all-important menus. The Earl was concerned only with the horses and dogs for the hunt and making sure there was plenty of game for those who preferred the shoot. Rosemary and Esme talked of nothing but the company they were expecting, the clothes they would wear, the entertainments and parties, the hunt which Papa had promised them they might join, the secret gifts they had bought and those they hoped to receive from a generous papa. And the New Year ball. That was to be the highlight. Lucy could not join in their enthusiasm. Her whole being was concentrated on how she was going to refuse Edward Gorridge without causing the most terrible row. And it would happen while the guests were in the house because he would be one of them and expecting his answer. The Earl was heard to mutter about what it was all going to cost and expressing the hope that it would all be worthwhile in the end, which did nothing to make her feel any better.

She helped her mother as was expected of her, but then, unable to sit still, would go out walking or riding, filling in the time until the guests arrived, thinking about Myles, wondering what he was doing, wishing she could be with him. She had met him every day while she had been staying with Georgina, always in secret, in case they were seen.

During that time she had learned more about him, about his family and his home and his plans for the future, plans that included her, for he said he could not contemplate life without her. They had talked and kissed and talked again and the bond that was their love for each other was tightened and strengthened so that it seemed nothing could break it. Parting on the last day had been sorrowful in the extreme and, since she had been home, she could think of nothing but when they might be together again. But the longer they were apart and the longer she was under the influence of her parents, the more she despaired. Myles had said he would not sever her from her family, but what alternative was there? She could not, would not, marry Edward Gorridge and that alone was enough to cause a huge rift without the added misdemeanour of falling in love with someone her father considered unsuitable.

Now the guests were arriving and she braced herself for what was to come. How she wished Myles was one of the party because he would not let her bear the burden alone, but he was not welcome and she did not see how he ever would be. He was no doubt at home with his family at Goodthorpe Manor, enjoying a convivial time. Would he be thinking of her? He had said he would be.

She rose as Viscount and Lady Gorridge were announced, followed by Edward and Dorothea. There were greetings all round and Lucy managed to keep a smile of welcome on her face, but the grinning Edward unnerved her. 'My dear Lucy,' he said, taking her hand and suddenly leaning forward to plant a kiss on her cheek. 'You look delightful in that blue. It matches your eyes.'

She did not know what to say and felt herself growing hot. How could she ever have contemplated marrying him? He was repulsive. His smile was oily and his eyes darted everywhere as if afraid to look her in the eye. His hand, still grasping hers, was clammy. If anyone mentioned marriage she would keep silent no longer. She would announce, loud and clear, that she would not marry him. The storm was going to happen anyway and she might just as well get it over and done with.

'It is bitterly cold out,' Lady Gorridge said, approaching

the fire. 'We had rugs and hot bricks in the carriage, but they did little except take the chill off. But as I said to Gorridge, Lady Luffenham will have made sure there are good fires in all the rooms—not one to stint is Lord Luffenham.'

'Yes, I had the fires lit in your rooms early this morning,' the Countess told her. 'If they need making up, do not hesitate to ring for a maid. Do you think it will snow?'

'It is certainly cold enough,' Lord Gorridge put in. 'If it does, it will drift. The wind is in the east.'

'I hope it won't spoil the hunt,' Rosemary put in.

'It'll take more than a few flakes of snow to do that,' Edward told her. 'I am looking forward to it.' He glanced in Lucy's direction. 'Especially if I have the charming company of Lady Lucinda.'

'I do not care to hunt,' she said.

'Oh, but you must. I insist. The day will be quite spoiled if you do not come.'

Why did she think he was insincere? If Myles had said that, she would have been glowing with pleasure, but because it was Edward, whose eyes held no warmth, she was repelled.

'Oh, let us leave her at home,' Rosemary said dismissively. 'She can keep Mama and Johnny company.'

More guests arrived, each exclaiming about the bitterness of the weather. Mrs Ashbury even mentioned that she was not sure they should have made the journey. It made Lucy think of the children at the railway works. Were they warm and well fed? Were the men still working? Since returning from Peterborough three weeks before she had not dared go down there herself, though she had sent one of the grooms over with food, especially milk for the babies, on several occasions. The navvies were making a huge cutting, Andrew told her when he returned, and the landscape was hardly recognisable. The ground had been levelled and lines had been laid almost the whole way across the side of the hill. Soon they would be gone from Luffenham land and moving on to Gorridge land, where they were going to build a bridge to take the line over the river. She asked if he had seen Mr Moorcroft and was told he had been spotted at the head of the cutting, but he wasn't digging like the men. 'I don' reckon he'll do any more o' that,' the lad said. 'A'er all, he's a gen'leman, ain't he?'

'Yes, Andrew, he is a gentleman.'

After dinner, which was prolonged and lavish, the whole company played parlour games and sang together and then danced on the marble floor of the hall. It was all very convivial and Lucy managed to pretend to be enjoying herself, though the shadow of that proposal hung over her.

The next morning everyone arrived at the breakfast table at different times and she did not see Edward until it was time to go to church at half past ten. Everyone attended, dressed warmly because it was still bitterly cold. Lucy wore a red flannel petticoat as well as her usual two cambric ones, and a wool dress in a cornflower blue topped with a dark-blue cloak. Her curls were framed by a soft velvet hat and she carried a matching muff.

The church, bedecked with greenery, was packed, not only with the Hall's guests and the villagers, but a crowd of navvies. All were dressed in their best and on their best behaviour. Lucy, walking up the aisle beside Edward, was surprised to see Myles among them; she would have expected him to attend church with his family and yet he had chosen to come to Luffenham. Her heart lifted and she gave him a joyful smile, which he returned with a broad grin that spoke volumes. He was here, not beside her exactly, but it was the next best thing. His presence gave her courage and hope.

'He can't keep away, can he?' Edward murmured, as they passed him. 'And leering at you as usual. I've a good mind to send him packing.'

'No, don't do that, Mr Gorridge, it is Christmas, after all, and he is doing no harm. I should hate a disturbance in church.'

'Yes, you are right.' He stood aside to let her enter the pew, and then followed her. 'There are better places to settle our differences.'

'I thought they had all been resolved.'

'That, my dear Lucy, is up to you.'

She did not like the sound of that, but was given no time to comment because the Rector, followed by the choir, entered the church at that moment and the service began. Lucy took part automatically while her mind ranged freely. Myles was just behind her on the other side of the aisle and she could almost feel his presence, so strong were the ties that bound them. He was watching her, she knew, but she dare not do anything to let him know she appreciated it. Oh, how she longed to turn away from the man at her side and run to him! If thoughts had wings and could find their target, he must know what she was thinking. 'Myles, what are we going to do?' she asked herself, while singing 'Adeste Fideles' in a clear soprano.

She knelt and prayed, stood and sang, sat and listened to Cousin Cedric intoning the sermon and, when it was all over, turned to make her way out of church behind her parents and Lord and Lady Gorridge. Myles was kneeling at the end of the pew he had occupied, apparently praying. She positioned herself so that she passed very close to him. She felt his hand reach out for hers and put a slip of paper into it. 'Happy Christmas, my love,' he murmured. She closed her fingers over the missive and put her hand into her muff. It had a little pocket for a handkerchief inside it and she slipped the note into that before withdrawing her hand.

She looked about her, but no one seemed to have heard his words or seen what had happened. She smiled. 'Mr Moorcroft, how nice to see so many of your people here this morning. I wish you all a happy Christmas.' She spoke clearly, not whispering. After all, she was only being polite. And then she moved on.

On her return home she hurried up to her room, ostensibly to remove her outdoor clothes, but as soon as she was alone, she shut the door and sat on her bed to read what Myles had written. *My Dearest Dear, I cannot resist coming to church to see your sweet face even if I cannot speak to you. This is written in the hope that there will be an opportunity to pass it to you. I beg to remind you of everything we said to each other in Peterborough and that nothing in the world will alter my love for you, unless it be to make it stronger, and you must hold on to that no matter what. With God's help, a way will be found to overcome all obstacles and we shall be together at last and then nothing and no one will ever part us again. Until then, be strong, my love, and do nothing, promise nothing. Your ever-loving, ever-faithful M.*

She sat for several minutes with tears streaming unchecked down her cheeks. He still loved her, he still thought a way could be found out of their dilemma and she trusted him, but he was a man, used to his independence. Did he realise what it was like for her? Did he understand how torn she was? Not between him and Edward, that was no contest, but between her love for him and her love for her family? Did he know how hard it was for her to stand up to her father, whom she had always revered as someone who was never wrong? Until she met Myles she had always obeyed him. If he said such and such was so, then in her mind it was so. If he said she should marry someone he had chosen, she would not have questioned the right of it. A whole lifetime's teaching was being overturned because she had fallen in love with Myles Moorcroft.

'Lucy, what are you doing in there?' Rosemary's voice called to her. She just had time to scrub at her eyes and push the letter under her pillow before the door opened and her sister came into the room. 'Goodness, you are still wearing your cloak. I don't know what's the matter with you, Lucy. You always seem to be daydreaming. It's being in love, I suppose.'

'What do you know of it?' Lucy asked sharply.

'Nothing, but what else could it be? Mr Gorridge is going round with a grin on his face from ear to ear, so I suppose you have given him his answer and we shall soon be congratulating you.'

'I haven't given him an answer.'

'Well, he doesn't really need one, does he? No one in their senses would turn down the chance to be mistress of Linwood Park one day.'

'Then I must be out of my senses.'

'Lucy!' Rosie sat down beside her. 'You are never going to refuse him.'

'Why not? I do not love him.'

'What is that to the point? Love is nothing weighed against Linwood Park, not to mention a handsome man who will give you everything you could wish for.'

'I wish to be in love with the man I marry.'

'Lucy, Lucy, do not be a ninny. You can't back out now. Everyone is expecting an announcement. Whatever has got into you? It must be nerves. Mama will give you something for them.'

'Don't you dare say anything to her. Don't say a word to anyone. I have to deal with it in my own way.'

'I do not envy you. There will be an unholy row, you know that, don't you? Lord Gorridge has promised Papa shares in the railway if you marry his son. I heard him telling Mama. He said they would pay huge dividends. He is already out of humour because you have kept Mr Gorridge waiting.'

'So that is the consideration! I am to be sold just like a horse or a cow.'

'What does it matter if everyone is happy.'

'I am not. I am most unhappy.'

'Why, Lucy? Have you developed a *tendre* for someone else?' She looked hard into Lucy's face. 'You have, haven't you? Who is it? Someone you met in London?'

'No.'

'It's never that navvy! Oh, Lucy, tell me it isn't the navvy.'

'It's none of your business, and if you breathe a word I shall murder you, I really will.'

'It is the navvy! Papa will hit the roof. You know what he thinks about Lord Moorcroft and his son. Lucy, how can you have fallen for that man? He is uncouth.'

'He is not! Rosie, you know nothing about it, so please do not say anything at all, or we shall have a serious falling-out.'

Rosemary put her arm round Lucy's shoulders. 'I am sorry, Lucy, really I am, but I do not think you should cross Papa. It will upset the whole household. It won't be so bad being married to Mr Gorridge, will it?'

'It will be dreadful and I can't do it. Rosie, please support me, I beg of you. One day, when you fall in love yourself, you will understand.'

'If falling in love brings a body to such a sorry state, I think I will give it a miss,' Rosemary said firmly. 'But if I can help, I will, but don't expect me to defy Papa, because I can't do it.'

'I don't expect you to. Just lend me a shoulder to cry on.'

Rosemary chuckled. 'I'll do that, but I think you've done enough weeping for one day, so take off that cloak and come downstairs. I heard the dinner gong ages ago and we shall be in trouble for being late.'

They went downstairs together and somehow, having unburdened herself a little, Lucy felt better and managed to endure the meal with her customary smile. The food was sumptuous, the best that money could buy, and lasted a long time.

It was late afternoon by the time they adjourned to the drawing room to exchange gifts. The Earl had provided something for every guest and the presents Lord and Lady Gorridge had brought were the height of extravagance. Jewellery, perfumes, embroidered canvas and cottons, books and toys for the children. Edward gave Rosemary and Esme pearl brooches and Johnny a sled, which made the boy long for snow. He said he was keeping Lucy's gift for later and winked at the company, who all laughed. All Lucy could manage was a weak smile.

The rest of the day was one of jollity, eating and drinking and playing party games. Lucy was always paired with Edward while their respective parents looked hopeful, but the day ended without their hopes being realised. Only her father voiced his disappointment and that was when she was bidding him goodnight after everyone else had gone up to their rooms. He had asked her to stay behind because he wanted to speak to her and she obeyed with some trepidation, guessing what was coming.

'Have you given Gorridge his answer?'

'No, Papa, it hasn't been mentioned. There has been no opportunity.'

'You should have made the opportunity. Well, I will tell you this, my girl, if you do not come to me with some positive news by the day of the ball, I shall make the announcement notwithstanding.'

She gasped. 'Papa, you wouldn't? Supposing he has changed his mind and does not ask me again?'

'He doesn't need to. You have only to see him and hear him to know he is expecting you to say yes. Nor is he such a fool as to go against parental wishes.'

'Why does Viscount Gorridge wish it so much?'

'Do you need to ask? You are the daughter of an earl, a good-looking chit and an asset to any young man. And what could be better than two great houses united by marriage? Now, go to bed and think of what I have said. And remember this—I can, and will, make life very uncomfortable for you if you cross me.' He waved his hand in dismissal.

She curtsied and left him. Alone in her room, she realised she had let slip the opportunity to tell him she meant to refuse Mr Gorridge. But would he have accepted her decision? She doubted it. He might even lock her in her room until she came to her senses—is that what he had meant about making life uncomfortable? If he did that, how was she to let Myles know what was happening? She reached under her pillow, drew Myles's letter out and read it over and over again, until she fell into an exhausted sleep.

* * *

The next morning was still bitterly cold and the lawns and bare branches were bedecked with frost, but the sun was shining. Everyone was up early to get ready for the Boxing Day hunt, but Lucy was downstairs before them, dressed in an old velvet riding habit that was warmer than her new one. She ate her breakfast in the kitchen as she liked to do and asked Mrs Lavender to provide a basket of food to take to the village children, along with a few presents, such as warm scarves and gloves she had collected for them. She did it every year and her mother approved, so there was no need to hide what she was doing. This year, she had extra goodies intended for the navvy children.

Putting a riding cloak over her habit, she set off on Midge, but instead of returning home after she had seen all the deserving village families, she passed the Hall gates and turned to the path that led behind the house and up on to the hill. Perhaps Myles would be there. She longed to see him again; he would prop up her courage and give her the strength to refuse Mr Gorridge's proposal and face the wrath of her father. On the other hand, she knew he had planned to spend Christmas at home with his family and no doubt had returned to them immediately after church the day before.

She paused a moment at the top of the rise to look down on the scene below her. It was very different from what it had been two months before. The hutted encampment was an established feature, the new railway line gleamed in the sun. There were trucks half-filled, but no one was at work and there was no sign of Myles. There were children running about, making for a large hut that Matty O'Malley had pointed out as the place they went to for lessons. They were poorly clad for such bitter weather and she was glad she had raided the trunk in the attics where the clothes she and her sisters and brother had worn as children had been stored away.

She urged her horse down the slope. Having no chaperon to hold her back, she rode right into the encampment before dismounting. Some of the children saw her and ran to greet her. She stooped to speak to them all; when she straightened up, she found herself face-to-face with Myles. He was smiling broadly. 'Lucy, what brings you here?'

She was smiling herself, mostly with relief that she would be able to tell him of her father's ultimatum. Stolen moments together were few and far between and, though they had an audience of several dozen children, it was as if they were alone. They searched each other's faces for signs of change and were both relieved to find nothing but love mirrored on the other's features, though he noticed she looked more than usually troubled. 'Has something happened?'

She looked round at the children all clamouring to tell her their news and decided it was not the time to voice her woes. 'No, nothing has happened. I came to give a few things to the children.' She indicated the basket on her pommel.

'Then you are doubly welcome. But should you be here?'

'I am on a charitable errand and it is Christmas after all, the season of goodwill. I am sure Mama would not forbid me to help the children in such bitter weather. I thought they might appreciate some warm clothes. I have a few toys, spinning tops, rag dolls, penny whistles, things like that.'

He lifted the basket down. 'Then come into the warm before you freeze to death. You can give them to the children yourself and help us to celebrate Christmas.' He turned to the children. 'What do you say, my friends? Shall we invite Lady Lucinda to our party?'

'Yes! Yes!' they chorused. Two of them dragged on her hands and propelled her towards the hut they had been making for when she arrived. Myles followed, carrying the basket.

Inside there was a huge fire in the stove and the room was decorated with greenery and coloured bunting. The middle of the floor had been cleared and some navvy women supervised a table on one side of it, which groaned with food: pies and chicken legs, roast potatoes and fruit. 'Coals to Newcastle,' Lucy murmured.

'Did you think they would be in want?' Myles asked.

'No, for I know the men are well paid, but one hears such tales of them having to wait weeks for their pay and—'.

'Not on Moorcroft lines, Lucy, surely you knew that.'

'Yes, I knew it.' She smiled. 'I expect I just wanted an excuse to visit, though I didn't think you would be here.'

He laughed. 'I came on the same errand as you, trying to brighten their Christmas festivities with coals and vegetables to make hot soup, considering the weather is so cold. Let me introduce you to the ladies. Mrs O'Malley, Mrs Greenock, Mrs Bates. Lady Lucinda has come to help us entertain the children,' he told them.

They curtsied, looking uncomfortable. Lucy felt she must do something to put them at their ease. She smiled and turned to the children. 'Have you ever played charades?'

They looked blankly at her so, watched by an amused Myles, she explained how the game was played, using children's rhymes as examples. 'If you want to dress up, I've brought some dressing-up clothes,' she said, pointing to her basket. They might be offended by charity, but if the clothes were part of the game, they would enjoy wearing them and she could always leave them behind when she left.

Myles, watching her, was filled with tenderness towards

her. She was so good with the children, establishing a rapport with them that other ladies of her rank could not have managed in a thousand years because they did not know how to unbend, to meet the children on their own terms. He joined in the fun and they laughed a great deal as the game progressed, but he could not rid himself of the idea that something was worrying her and could not wait to find out what it was.

The opportunity came when she suddenly realised she had been away from home almost three hours and it was time she left. He helped her on with her cloak and accompanied her to where one of his men had been looking after Midge. Taking the reins, he led the animal while she walked beside him.

'Lucy, did you read my note?'

'Yes, many, many times. I have it by heart.'

'I have talked to my mother. She is going to call on Lady Luffenham in the New Year.' He did not add that she was surprisingly reluctant.

'I fear it will be too late.'

'Too late?' He grabbed her hand and turned her to face him. 'You don't mean you have accepted Gorridge?'

'No. I have until New Year's Eve to do so.'

'Lucy, you aren't going to, are you?' He searched her face and noted the tears glistening on her lashes. 'Please say you won't do anything so foolish. He is not the man for you.'

'It won't make much difference what I say. Papa says he'll announce the engagement anyway.'

'How can a father who is supposed to love his daughter do anything so cruel?'

'He doesn't think he is cruel, he thinks he is doing it for

my own good because I don't know my own mind. He says he will make life very uncomfortable for me if I refuse.'

'We've got to get you out of it. I'll talk to Gorridge, persuade him to withdraw his offer.' Just because he had decided not to tell Lucy about Lottie, did not mean he could not use that to try to persuade Gorridge to forget about marrying Lucy. It was a faint hope, but worth a try.

She gave a cracked laugh. 'He is more obedient than I am. He will never go against his father.'

'But I must try that first. The alternative is to take you away from there.'

'Elope, you mean? You said you would not do that.'

'I would if there was no other help for it.'

'But where would we go? What would we do? We can't hide for ever and Papa is bound to come after us. Myles, oh, Myles, I think this must be goodbye.'

'No.'

'Yes. It is for the best.' She had suddenly realised the consequences if they eloped. Not only would she be ostracised by society, so would he. His business would suffer. His plans for his future, of being even more successful than his father, of bettering the lot of the working man, of his campaign to educate the children of itinerant workers, would all collapse around him because no one of any note would ever listen to anything he had to say. And it would break his mother's heart. She could not ask that sacrifice of him.

'You don't mean it. Lucy, you cannot mean it. All the plans we made, our love for each other, cannot count for nothing.'

She swallowed hard. 'They do not count for nothing, Myles. I shall always think of you with great affection, but that is not enough for me to abandon my family.'

'Lucy!' He grabbed her by the shoulders, too frustrated to be gentle. 'I do not believe you. You've been got at.'

'No, Myles. It is my decision. Please let me go.'

He dropped his hands and watched as she scrambled up into the saddle and cantered off. He stood watching her disappear over the brow of the hill, too numb to think clearly. For a big, hardened man, he was as near to tears as he was ever likely to be. He kicked savagely at a stone and watched it roll all the way down the hill to the encampment. Then he sank to the ground, put his head in his hands and groaned aloud. He was still there when the hunt came hallooing over the brow of the hill after the fox. The hounds chased their quarry into the navvy encampment, scattering screaming children, barking dogs and burly men and wreaking havoc among the huts.

Lucy rode home in abject misery. Love was beautiful and sweet, but when it could never be declared, never consummated, it was nothing but the bitterest heartbreak. But she had had to say what she did, for his dear sake. She could not ask him to cut himself off from his family any more than she liked the idea of being ostracised by her own. They might brazen it out for a while, but the tension would make itself felt in the end and they would find themselves quarrelling. And there would be no escape from what they had done. Myles had known that, which was why he had not protested more strongly.

She hardly knew the direction Midge was taking; the mare clopped at a steady walk, finding her own way home. She handed her over to a groom and went indoors and up to her room without encountering her mother, who would undoubtedly ask her where she had been. She changed out of her habit into a day gown of amber grosgrain but, unwilling to go down and join the rest of the ladies who had not gone hunting, she sat on the window seat, gazing out across the park.

Over the hill behind the trees, Myles would still be supervising the children's games. There would be a great deal of laughter and when the party was over he would go home to Goodthorpe Manor. Until today she had thought there might be hope that one day she might go there with him and meet his family. What would they think of her decision? Would they be angry with her for leading him on to expect more than she was prepared to give, or would they shrug their shoulders and say perhaps it was for the best? She had done it for his sake, not her own, but they would not know that, would they?

The sound of horses alerted her to the fact that the huntsmen were returning and soon the yard was filled with yapping, bloodied dogs and muddied, sweating horses. Viscount Gorridge was holding a fox's brush aloft in triumph. All looked satisfied with a good day's hunting. The grooms ran forward to take charge of the horses and it was then Lucy saw Myles ride into the yard. What was he doing here? Surely he had not come to tackle her father over her decision? She leaned forward and opened the casement in the hope of hearing what was said.

The Earl was waving his crop at Myles. 'What are you doing here, Moorcroft? I thought I told you to keep away.'

'I came to speak to you, my lord.'

'I have nothing to say to you. The rules for your navvies were laid down weeks ago and nothing has changed. So what do you want?'

Lucy held her breath, but when Myles spoke it had nothing to do with her at all. She was not sure whether to be relieved or disappointed. 'My lord, your dogs and huntsmen ran the fox over the navvy encampment and did a great deal of damage, not to mention frightening the women and children half to death.'

'I cannot direct the fox where to run and where he runs the dogs will follow. If you were any sort of a gentleman you would know that.' The Earl dismounted and handed his horse over to a groom.

'My lord, the navvies are extremely upset. If you could compensate them and ask the hunt to avoid the works in future, it would be appreciated.'

'I will do no such thing. The hunt goes where the fox goes, everyone knows that. You could always complain to Reynard.' He laughed at his own joke. 'Or you could, if he was still in the land of the living.'

'My lord, it was wanton destruction and the huntsmen did nothing to control the dogs. They seemed to find it a great joke.' Lucy could see by the set of Myles's jaw that he was finding it an effort to be polite, but if her father continued to hold him in such obvious contempt, she doubted if he would stay cool much longer.

'I was told the work would be finished by Christmas,' the Earl said. 'If you had completed it on time the navvies would not have been there to get in the way of the hunt.'

'I am afraid bad weather has held us up for a few days,' Myles said.

'Then that is your bad fortune.'

'I do not think my men will think of it like that, my lord. They are incensed and were only prevented from marching here to put their own case by my promising to speak to you. If I cannot take them the reassurance they need, I cannot answer for their actions.'

'You had better. It's what you are there for, to keep the peace.'

'Peace, my lord, needs both sides to agree to it.'

Any last vestige of hope died in Lucy's breast when she heard that. Myles must have accepted her decision or he would not have been so outspoken. He had stopped trying to be the gentleman and reverted to the navvy. He was fighting for his men and his railway; his love for her and hers for him had been pushed to one side, buried out of sight.

'I have nothing more to say to you, Moorcroft,' she heard her father say. 'Go back to your fellows and wallow in the dirt with them. And if you so much as set foot on my domain again, I will set the dogs on you. Is that clear?'

'Crystal clear, my lord, but I hope you do not live to regret it.' He turned on his heel and walked back to his horse. He glanced up at the house as he did so, but he did not see Lucy because she had closed the window and retreated into her room. The effort Myles had made to keep the peace between navvies and villagers and not to alienate her father now counted for nothing. There would be open warfare.

She heard Rosemary come up the stairs and enter her room and went to join her. Her sister's habit was covered in mud and there were streaks of blood down her cheeks, but she was glowing with elation. 'I was in at the kill,' she told Lucy. 'It was magnificent. You should have been there.'

'I am glad I was not. What was that all about in the yard, just now? What happened at the navvy camp?'

'Oh, that!' She spoke dismissively. 'Reynard was a wily old devil, a big dog fox. He led us a merry dance right up into the hills and along the ridge and then he doubled back and dashed down into the valley. We thought we had him cornered down by the bridge, but he suddenly darted over it and ran into the navvy camp. The hounds chased him round and round and then he went into one of the huts. There were a lot of children in there and they ran about screaming and making things worse. Papa told them to keep quiet and they would come to no harm, but they kept running round making a real din and that upset the dogs. They didn't know which way to turn, but then the fox made a break for it and they were on to him.'

'The children witnessed it?'

'Yes, couldn't be helped, could it? They were there, the fox was there and so were the dogs. Anyway, those urchins are hardened little devils, I can't see it would do them any harm. It wouldn't worry Johnny.'

'How can you be so unfeeling, Rosie? Many of those children are not used to country ways. No doubt they thought it was barbaric.'

'Don't be silly, Lucy, they are barbarians themselves.'

'They are children, Rosie. Was M—Mr Moorcroft with them?'

'I didn't see him. He must have turned up after we left. He's shot his bolt now, you know. With Papa, I mean. Coming here and threatening Papa in front of everyone. You can forget any idea of being allowed to marry him.'

'I already have. We have decided to part.'

'Very sensible of you, though it puzzles me how you can have any sort of conversation with him.'

'He is quite easy to talk to.'

'No, I meant when do you have the opportunity? Have you been over there today?'

'Yes.'

'Good God! You might have been there when we rode in.'

'But thankfully I wasn't.'

'Amen to that. Papa would have had apoplexy. So, have you decided to accept Mr Gorridge, after all?'

'No, I have decided to remain single.'

Rosemary laughed. 'You will change your mind as soon as you get over this obsession with the navvy.'

'No, I will not.'

'Not change your mind or not get over the navvy?'

'Both.'

'We shall see.'

Lucy decided not to argue. Her sister would never understand. 'You had better hurry and change. I thought I heard the first gong.'

'Wait for me. We'll go down together.'

The men were still talking about the chase when everyone gathered about the dinner table. It transpired that Edward had found himself separated from the hunt and he was highly amused when the tale was told to him. 'I wish I had been there to see the fun,' he said. 'But I was miles away on the other bank, chasing a vixen. Pretty little thing she was, too, but she went to earth.' He grinned as he spoke as if at some amusing memory. 'How much damage was done? It won't delay the finishing of the line, will it? Our shareholders won't be at all pleased if that happens and they miss their dividends.'

'It wasn't the line so much as the encampment,' his father told him. 'I wasn't up with the leaders and only arrived after it was all over. But some of the shanties were destroyed and others had their stoves pulled over and were set on fire. Without ready water to hand it was difficult to extinguish the flames. I imagine the contents of those huts were entirely consumed. A few of their dogs were injured, scrapping with the hounds, and I saw a couple of dead cats and goodness knows how many chickens.'

'Oh, how dreadful,' the Countess exclaimed. 'Those poor children will be without homes in this dreadful weather.'

Her husband looked sharply at her. 'There are huts in plenty down there. They can move in with others. It is hardly my fault the fox decided to run there. He is no more used to seeing habitation on that hill than we are. Thank goodness they will soon be gone.'

'Was Moorcroft down there?' Edward asked.

'No, not at the time, but he had the temerity to come up here and demand compensation. I sent him away with a flea in his ear.'

'I am not sure that was a wise thing to do,' Viscount Gorridge said. 'The navvies won't stand for it.'

'I don't know what they think they can do about it,' the Earl said. A good day's hunting with everyone calling him a jolly good Master and praising his hospitality had soured and he was irritable.

'They can go on what they call a randy. If they get themselves stirred up enough, they are quite capable of marching up here and destroying everything in their path. They might even break the windows and set fire to the house.'

'Oh, surely not,' Lady Gorridge exclaimed.

'Oh, I assure they could,' her husband insisted. 'I have seen the result of some of their randies on other lines. The destruction done to the encampment here is nothing to what they might do.'

'Mr Moorcroft would never allow it,' Lucy said quietly.

Her father turned sharply towards her. 'What do you know of it, miss?'

'Nothing except that he has always kept his word about the navvies. They have caused us no trouble and many of them come to church. They are peaceful folk.'

'That is because until now they have not been roused to anger,' Lord Gorridge said. 'Luffenham, I strongly advise you to pay their compensation if you don't want to have to barricade yourself in the house.'

'Barricade myself in! I never heard of anything so ridiculous.'

'It's war!' Edward said gleefully. 'Now we shall see who is the stronger man.'

His father turned angrily on him. 'I'll thank you not to make such foolish remarks, Edward. You are frightening the ladies. Whatever there is between you and Moorcroft, I advise you to forget it.'

Edward looked at Lucy. 'What do you say, Lady Lucinda, should I forget it?'

'Yes,' she said. 'I am sure Mr Moorcroft feels no ill will towards you.'

'Wisely said, my lady,' Lord Gorridge said. 'I hope that you will always be a steadying influence on this headstrong son of mine.'

Lucy felt her face flood with colour. His lordship, like his son, was assuming she was going to marry Edward. She was not. Just because she had told Myles she would not run away with him, did not mean she would marry Edward Gorridge. 'I…' She paused. She could not reject him in front of a roomful of people, it would hardly be courteous, and so the words she had formed on her tongue were not uttered. But she would have to seize the first opportunity to make her feelings known.

'Oh, I do hope this won't make any difference to the ball,' Rosemary put in. 'Papa, you are not going to cancel it, are you?'

'Certainly not! I am not going to let a rabble spoil my plans.'

Lucy's heart sank. She hardly heard the rest of the conversation as dinner was concluded and the ladies retired, leaving the men still talking about the day's events and Lord

Gorridge continuing to exhort her father to pay the navvies some compensation.

The ladies, too, discussed the matter over the tea cups. They were all afraid and several said they would like to go home out of danger. The Countess reassured them that they were quite safe, but even she did not sound sure. Nor was Lucy sure. Myles was angry, she knew that, and disappointed with her, and perhaps he would not try too hard to prevent his workers from making trouble. She must do something to prevent it. But what? How much pin money did she have? Her father had given her several guineas to spend in Peterborough, but she had not needed them, and she had a few pieces of jewellery. Would the navvies accept that? She could pretend it came from her father. But would it be enough? And would they believe her?

Pleading a headache, she excused herself and went to bed. She did not want to be in the drawing room when the gentlemen joined the ladies. She could not sit and listen to more arguments and Edward being so sure of himself and of her. And she hated his obvious delight at the damage to the encampment. The poor children! She was incensed on their behalf and would not be able to keep silent if the men persisted in talking about it. If that was the way the navvies were treated wherever they went, then it was hardly surprising they rebelled against it and earned the reputation they had. Tomorrow something must be done to resolve all the issues: Edward's proposal and the threat from the navvies.

Chapter Nine

Lucy had been right about Myles being angry and disappointed. His men were angry, too, and their wives incensed and worst of all, the children were frightened and many of them in tears. Their lovely party had been spoiled, their dogs mauled and their kittens trampled to death. Two of the huts had been completely destroyed by fire and windows broken in several others. He felt guilty and in some measure responsible. If he had not gone part of the way with Lucy he would have been on the site when the fox arrived and he might have been able to divert it before the dogs were on to it.

O'Malley, who was especially roused because Matty had been knocked over and had a nasty bruise on her face, was all for marching on Luffenham Hall and avenging the outrage. 'We'll serve him as he served us,' he said, and was met with a chorus of agreement.

Myles, still feeling the effects of Lucy's rejection, had been angry enough to agree with him, but then common sense prevailed and he had undertaken to go and ask for compensation. Perhaps his lordship would see reason. But reason was the last thing the Earl had wanted to see, that and the thorn in his flesh that was Myles Moorcroft. Myles rode back to camp with his spirits at their lowest ebb. His plans had been ground into the dirt. The girl he loved had rejected him because she was afraid of her father and the work was behind schedule, not by much, but enough to prevent the line moving off Luffenham land before the New Year, which was the target he had set himself when Lucy had said she must give Gorridge his answer by then. It would go even further behind while the men rebuilt their homes. And, to cap it all, the sky looked full of snow. He did not want to throw his problems into his father's lap, but he needed his advice.

On arriving back at the camp he told O'Malley the Earl was considering their request and not to do anything foolish or his lordship might change his mind. He told him to send a wagon back down the line and pick up a load of wood and glass to make new huts and whatever furniture they needed and have the account sent to him.

'Why should you pay?' O'Malley demanded. 'Tweren't your doin'.'

'Lord Luffenham will recompense me,' he lied.

'For the young lady's sake, we'll hold fire,' one of the others said. 'But if 'e ain't paid up and given us an apology by tomorrow a'ernoon, he'll larn not to trifle with us. We ain't his minions.'

He could ask no more of them and rode home.

Home was a haven. It was a solid mansion in grounds of about twelve acres, which had been almost derelict when Lord Moorcroft bought it, but he had had it repaired and re-furbished and now it reflected Lady Moorcroft's exquisite taste. It was not especially large, not outdated like Luffenham Hall, nor as ostentatious as Linwood Park, but comfortable and befitting a man of Lord Moorcroft's wealth. He had realised early on that railways would make travel so easy that business men who had once had to live close to their mills and factories could enjoy living in the clean air of the country and still go to work in the towns every day. Goodthorpe Manor was midway between his engineering works at Peterborough and his mills in Leicester. And once the new line was completed, travel between the two would only be a matter of an hour or two.

His mother had been concerned by her son's long absence. 'I expected you back hours ago,' she said when he arrived, chilled to the marrow in spite of a warm riding cloak. 'What has happened? You look all in. You haven't been excavating again, have you?'

'No, Mama, there's been no work on the site today. I gave the men a holiday. Give me time to change and I'll tell you all about it.'

'Yes, do change, Myles. I hate to see you in those working clothes. It is not at all necessary.'

'But practical when I am on site, Mama.' He had this conversation whenever he dressed in working clothes. His mother disapproved and his father simply laughed and told her not to keep nagging the boy. As for his paternal grandmother, who preferred to live in the town where she had lived all her life, she was firmly rooted in her past and could see nothing wrong with cord trousers and fustian jackets so long as they were clean, though she was very proud of him when he took the trouble to dress like a gentleman. 'Give me ten minutes.'

Ten minutes later he came down to discover they had waited dinner for him and he was hungry. 'Now, lad, there's something amiss, am I in the right?' his father asked when they had been served and were tucking in to a succulent steak and ale pie.

'I'm afraid there is. It's trouble with Lord Luffenham.' He went on to tell them about the children's party and the invasion by the hunt and the navvies' determination to exact revenge. 'The only way I could stop them was to ride over and ask for compensation for them. Lord Luffenham would not even listen. I told the men he was considering it, but I don't think they believed me. They know Lord Luffenham as well as I do.' He paused. 'Why does the he dislike me so much? As far as I know I have done nothing to harm him.'

'Except covet his daughter.'

'He knows nothing of that. Lucy will not tell him. She is so afraid of him, she says she won't see me again.'

'Oh, dear,' his mother said. 'Do you think she means it?'

'I think so. I had hoped I might persuade Lord Luffenham to look favourably on a match, but after today, I know that is a vain hope. I have made an implacable enemy of him.'

'Not your fault, boy,' his father said. 'Mine.'

'Yours?'

'Yes. It goes back a long way.' He looked at his wife. 'Shall I tell him?'

She nodded. Myles looked from one to the other and waited.

'It was when we were young,' his lordship said. 'I was making my way in the world and doing well for myself, enough to break into some social circles, but not all. There was, and I suppose always will be, a core of old-fashioned gentry who cannot abide to see a man getting rich by the sweat of his brow. They set great store by breeding and in-herited wealth and I had neither. It did not matter to your mother. I met her at a charity ball where the upper crust allow themselves to mix with us lesser mortals. The long and the short of it was that we fell in love. The trouble was that she was being courted by John Luffenham. I knew John—Viscount Vernley he was then, because the old Earl was still alive—and he did not take kindly to being rejected. Everyone put pressure to bear on your mother until we were both in despair, but fortunately Viscount Porson was a loving and generous father and in the end agreed to have me for a son-in-law and Luffenham had to accept it. He married the present Countess a year or two later, and as far as I know the marriage has been a successful one.'

'Then he has no reason to complain.'

'Old grudges die hard, Myles. Since then we have prospered and he has not, mostly because of poor investments, and he cannot forgive me. He was never very astute and he won't give up his extravagant lifestyle in order to retrench.'

'No wonder you were reluctant to call on Lady Luffenham when I suggested it, Mama.'

'Oh, I do not think Lady Luffenham knows anything of it,' she said. 'I was afraid I might come across John. I had hoped he might have forgotten what had happened all those years ago, but his recent behaviour towards you and your papa has convinced me that he hasn't. I would have done it for you. I will still go, if you think it will help.'

'No, my dear, I will not have you humiliated,' her husband said. 'You will stay out of it.'

'Yes, Mama,' Myles agreed. 'I shall have to think of something else. I could be patient and wait for things to calm down, but for the fact the Earl is determined to announce Lucy's engagement to Edward Gorridge at the New Year ball he is holding and I do not know if she is strong enough to stand up to him.'

'Why is he so keen on the match with Gorridge?' her ladyship asked.

'I don't know.'

'Viscount Gorridge is as rich as Croesus and anxious to settle his son,' Henry explained. 'The lad is a great trial to him. He has been obliged to pay off so many pregnant servants the whole county will soon be populated by young Gorridges, none of whom will be acknowledged. And there have been one or two in the upper echelons of society too and that has all had to be hushed up....'

'Good God!' Myles was appalled. 'I caught him with one of the girls from the works a few weeks ago, but I never dreamed it was as bad as that. I've got to do something and quickly. I offered to take Lucy away with or without her father's consent, but she would not hear of it.'

'No, of course she wouldn't,' his mother said. 'It would be social suicide for both of you. I think you should settle this business of the damage to the works first, then we shall have to put our heads together to persuade Lord Luffenham to change his mind.'

'Pay the compensation yourself,' his father advised him. 'Tell the men Luffenham stumped up after all. That way you'll restore peace. How long before you move off Luffenham land?'

'Another ten days, if the weather holds.'

'Then hold your fire until then. If the little lady is worth her mettle, she will wait for you.'

It was sound advice; as he could do nothing that night in any case, he spent the rest of the evening going over the railway accounts and planning the last stage of the line to Leicester, which had given him so much heartache and yet so much happiness, meeting Lucy and realising there could be no other wife for him. She was everything to him. Without her he did not see how he could go on living and breathing, working and sleeping. She had said goodbye. She hadn't meant it, had she?

Lucy had meant it, though it had broken her heart to say it. Before the trouble between the navvies and the hunt, she had hoped to reconcile her father to the idea that she wanted to marry Myles, but now she knew he would never counte-nance it. In a way it was a pity she could not be more like Rosemary and not care so much. But she did care—she cared so much her head and heart ached. Her mother, realising that all was not well with her eldest daughter, came to her room and sat on the edge of her bed, stroking her brow.

'Lucy, dearest, you must not take everything so much to heart. Papa will relent and pay for the damage. We shall be in no danger.'

She gave a cracked laugh. 'I am in no danger from the navvies, Mama. They like me.'

'Because you take them food and warm clothing?'

'Yes.'

'Lucy, I am sorry for the children down there, I truly am, and if we can do anything to make them more comfortable, then it is our Christian duty to do so. But matters have gone too far now.'

'I have never said this before, nor ever even thought it, but I think Papa is wrong.'

'You must not question your father, Lucy.'

'I can't help it. When I think of those poor children sur-rounded by a whole pack of hounds I want to scream at him for being so unfeeling. I wonder what he would have done if I had been down there or Johnny. He would have called the hounds off then, wouldn't he?'

'That's different.'

'No, it isn't, it is exactly the same. And I was down there half an hour before.'

'Lucy!'

'Yes, Mama, I was. I was playing games with the children. They were having a Christmas party. Mr Moorcroft organised it for them. And before you ask, I did speak to him. We talked a long time.'

'Lucy, I am appalled that you should have so far forgotten your duty of obedience.'

'I didn't forget it and I tried to obey, but Mr Moorcroft is a true gentleman and I could not be uncivil to him, could I? I cannot understand what Papa has against him.'

'No doubt he has a very good reason for it and we must not question it.' She stood up and straightened the cover where she had been sitting. 'Now I must go back to our guests. Try to sleep, Lucy, and try not to worry. The workmen's children are very resilient. They will come to no harm.'

'They have to be,' Lucy murmured as the door shut on her mother.

Not only was the Earl not going to shut everyone up in the house for fear of attacks, he was going to take the hunt out again. 'We'll go up on the abbey hill for a change,' he said at breakfast time. 'Edward said he saw a vixen there yesterday. We'll try to run her down.'

'I am afraid my wife insists on being taken home,' Mr Ashbury told him. 'And to tell the truth, I feel inclined to go. The sky is leaden and I think it will snow before long and we do not want to risk being cut off from home if the roads become impassable.'

Several other guests, who had a distance to travel, agreed

with him and there was a flurry of activity as bags were packed and carriages sent for.

By mid-morning, only Lord and Lady Gorridge and Edward remained. Lucy wished heartily that they would go, too, but there was no hope of that while Edward still waited for his answer. She was afraid that if the roads did become impassable, they would be at Luffenham for days, even weeks. And how could she endure it?

'Well, are we going hunting that vixen or not?' Edward asked, as the first few flakes of snow drifted down.

The Earl was reluctant to forgo his day's hunting. It was a matter of honour to him to fulfil his promise to his remaining guests and so he set off with Lord Gorridge, Edward and Rosemary, and two of the grooms to swell their numbers. Lucy waited until they had gone and her mother and Lady Gorridge were gossiping in the morning parlour beside a large fire, before changing into her old habit and wrapping herself in her warm cloak and making her way out to the stables.

Only Andrew was there, sweeping the yard. Already his coat was dotted with wet snowflakes. 'My lady, the men went half an hour ago, you'll never catch them now. And you oughtn't to go out alone. You never know what them there navvies will get up to.'

'I shall be quite safe, Andrew. I am not going far. Just a little gallop to give Midge some exercise. If the snow becomes very thick in the next day or two, she won't be taken out at all.'

Reluctantly he saddled the mare and helped Lucy to mount. She rode out of the yard and made her way along a path that went past the kitchen garden and the glasshouses, where the gardener tended the tropical flowers and fruit her mother liked so much, to a gate in the rear wall of the grounds. From there it was an easy ride up to the crest of the hill and then down to the navvy encampment. In a bag on her pommel were two cold roast chickens and some bread hot from the oven. It also contained a purse in which she had put every penny she possessed and some jewellery she had not worn for some time, which she intended to give to Mrs O'Malley. She had no idea what it was worth, but hoped the gesture was enough to appease the men.

The men should have been back at work, but it was obvious to Lucy, when she topped the rise, that no work was being done, except repairing and rebuilding the huts. The wagons stood empty on the rails, the horses were tethered in a line, stamping and snorting, their breath like steam in the cold air. She sat watching it for a moment before descending, going carefully because the snow was making the slope treacherous. She was met by Myles, who had been in one of the huts fixing the windows when he saw her.

She had come back! She had changed her mind and it was not goodbye after all. He hurried to help her dismount. 'Lucy, you should not have come in this weather, but, oh, how glad I am to see you.'

The sight of his dear face, lit with pleasure, made her feel weak as a kitten. She almost said she would stay with him for ever and never go back, but then she remembered the reasons why she had told him they must part and they had not changed. She stiffened her spine and faced him, head held high. 'I came to see if I could help…'

'Bless you for that, but there was no need. The men will soon have the huts rebuilt and we can start work again. That is, if the weather lets us.' He looked up at the sky. It was black all round. 'I had hoped to be off Luffenham land in a week or so.'

'I brought this.' She delved into the basket on her saddle and fetched out her purse. 'It's not much, but it might forestall the men marching on my home.' She took his hand and tipped the contents into his palm.

He stared down at the handful of coins, the small ruby necklace, two or three brooches, some pearls and matching eardrops easily contained in his big hand and then looked into her face. It was colourless, except for two bright pink spots on her cheeks. Her lovely green eyes had lost their lustre and betrayed her determination. She had not come to tell him she had changed her mind, but to stop his men attacking the Hall. And with a pittance. 'Oh, Lucy, the men will not take these from you.'

'Is it not enough? I was afraid it wouldn't be.'

He did not know what to say. He loved her all the more for trying. 'It is more than enough, but they will not take it from you. They like you. They would never harm a hair of your head.'

'But you threatened Papa. I heard you myself in the stable yard.'

He had not known she was anywhere in the vicinity, but it would not have made any difference if he had. At the time he was too angry to think clearly. His anger had not been directed at her, but at her father. He was still fuming. 'I am sorry for that, but the men have been placated for the moment and, for your sake, they will do nothing.'

'Has my father paid them compensation after all?'

'Let us say they have been compensated.' He accepted the food, but put the trinkets back in her purse and tucked it into the bag on her saddle. 'Now please, Lucy, let me take you home. If it snows any harder, the path will be obliterated and you could wander about the hill all day.'

'Midge knows her way home.'

'Nevertheless I will come with you. At least until we are in sight of the Hall.' He beckoned to one of the men to bring his horse and then helped her into the saddle, wrapping her cloak as closely round her as he could. 'Come, sweetheart, let's get you home.'

'The weather is bad for the work, isn't it?' she said as they rode. It wasn't what she wanted to say. She wanted to tell him how much she still loved him, how she wished things could be different, how she would follow him to the ends of the earth, through snow or rain or baking heat, and would defy anyone to part them, but that was weakness, she told herself, and she had to be strong.

'Yes, if it goes on for any length of time it could delay the completion of the line and that is bad for the shareholders, who cannot see a return on their money until the line is in operation.' It wasn't what he wanted to talk about, either. He wanted to beg her to change her mind and agree to marry him no matter the opposition, but his mother had agreed that Lucy was right and, dammit, he knew they were right.

'Does that mean you will lose over it?'

'No, Moorcroft's can stand the loss of a few days, but I fear it might be the ruin of other companies where the finance is not so rock solid and the navvies not so loyal.'

'They are loyal because you treat them well.'

'It pays in the long run.'

'And their loyalty will not let them go against you and march on the Hall, no matter what my father has done.'

'I sincerely hope so.' He paused and added softly, 'It is not the only hope I have.'

She had to take a great gulp of air into her lungs before

she could make herself speak. 'Please don't. It will only make it harder.'

'Then will you promise me one thing? Will you promise me you will not accept Gorridge? While you are free, I shall continue to hope.'

'I promise I will not accept Mr Gorridge,' she said. 'But that is not grounds for hope and I wish you would not. I only came today to assure myself the children took no harm yesterday and to offer what recompense I could.'

'Lucy, how can you say that? If you are trying to pretend you no longer love me, you are making a poor job of it. I must hope. Without it I have nothing. Hope was the last thing in Pandora's box when everything else flew out, wasn't it?'

'So the legend goes.'

'Well, then…'

'Here is the gate into the back garden. I shall certainly not get lost now. Go back, Mr Moorcroft, before you are caught out by the snow. Go home to your family.' She did not wait for him to say goodbye, but spurred her mare through the gate, which she had left open for her return.

He sat and watched her go, unwilling to turn away. How could she have been so unkind, putting her nose in the air and calling him Mr Moorcroft as if he were a stranger and not the love of her life? He knew the reason well enough. She was as unhappy as he was and trying to hide it. He listened to the clip-clop of her mare's hooves on the gravel path. How long would he go on hoping? Would her father ever soften? He appeared as hard and cold as the ice on the water butt.

Lucy was passing along the path beside the glasshouses when she heard a strange scrabbling noise that brought her back to where she was with a jolt. Surely the fox had not been driven to take shelter in one of the hothouses? If it had and the hounds caught its scent, they could wreak havoc among the gardeners' precious plants, just as they had the navvy encampment. And her father would not treat the matter so lightly.

There was no one about; most of the garden staff had been given a holiday. She dismounted and walked to the door of the glasshouse from which the noise had come, intending, if it was the fox, to drive it out into the open. The warmth hit her as she opened the door and stepped inside, searching around for whatever it was that had made the sound. There it was again. She peered round the side of a small handcart used for moving pots and plants about the garden, and the sight that met her made her cry out in horror.

Edward was lying on top of a young girl on a bed of straw and both were completely naked. Their clothes were scattered everywhere. He looked up from what he was doing and, seeing her, rolled off the girl and sat up. Lucy averted her eyes; she had never seen a naked man before.

'Home, Lottie,' he said.

The girl scrambled into her clothes and squeezed past Lucy, who also turned to leave, but he rose and grabbed her arm. She tried to pull herself away from him. 'Let me go,' she said. 'You disgust me.'

'What's so disgusting? It's what men and women do. Surely you knew that?'

'I don't want to talk about it. Let go of my arm. I never want to see you again.'

'Oh, Lucy, don't be such a prude. I was only amusing myself while you made up your mind to marry me. She means nothing to me.'

'Then that makes your behaviour all the more despicable. If you think I will marry you after this, you are sadly mistaken.'

'Oh, but I think you will.' He forced her round to face him. She shut her eyes and struggled to free herself. He laughed. 'Open your eyes, Lucy, and look at me.'

She refused. He put his hands round her face, forcing her to look at him and then he kissed her full on the lips, a savage and bruising kiss that made her feel sick. She struggled, but he held her fast with one hand while trying to lift her skirt with the other. She kicked out. He gripped her tighter. 'You will marry me because after I have done with you, no one else will have you. It's time you came out of your stiff corset and learned a little of what life is all about.'

'I cannot think why you are so keen to marry me if you hold me in such contempt.'

'It's not me that's so keen, it's my dear papa. Bought you for me, he has. Wants me to settle down and be a good boy.' He laughed harshly.

'I will not be bought. Now let me go at once.' She renewed her struggle and heard her skirt rip.

He laughed. 'We might as well have it right off,' he said, tearing at it.

'Let me go. I can't go home with my clothes all torn.'

'Why not? We'll say the big navvy did it and I rescued you from a fate worse than death. Oh, your papa will have the time of his life driving the navvies off his land. Moorcroft will be ruined.'

'Of course he won't. I won't be party to such a vicious scheme. I shall tell everyone the truth.'

He was not going to let her go and she was desperate. Her struggle up to then had been silent except for the words she hissed at him, but now she let out a piercing scream. He clamped his hand over her mouth and wrestled her to the floor. 'Shut up, you little fool, do you want the world in here to witness your deflowering? Or has that already happened?'

With his hand over her mouth, she could not breathe. Feeling sick and desperate, she struggled, kicking and clawing, but he was heavy on her and she could not throw him off. He laughed and lifted her skirts, fumbling with her underwear. And then suddenly he was gone from her. She gulped a huge breath and opened her eyes. Myles was standing over her and Edward lay in a heap a little way off. She sat up, gasping and sobbing, and tried to gather her clothes about her.

Myles fell to his knees and put his arm about her. 'It's all right, love, I'm here now.'

'What a pretty picture!' Edward's voice was scathing. 'Pity you're too late, Moorcroft. She's mine.'

Myles was sickened. He looked at Lucy. 'Lucy, did he…? Did he…?'

She shook her head, unable to do more than sob, but her distress was such that she could not speak.

'I waited to see you safely home and heard you cry out.'

'Yes, how did that come about, Moorcroft? You're banned from coming anywhere near the house. Spying on us, were you? Tickle your fancy, did it?'

Myles turned to him. 'Get out, Gorridge. Leave now or I won't answer for my actions.' He helped Lucy to her feet and tried to draw her torn skirt about her. 'Run indoors, my love. I'll take Midge to the stables. Tell your mother what happened. We'll talk later.'

Nodding, she wrapped her cloak about her and darted outside, into the snow, but she hardly noticed it as she sped down the path and in at the kitchen door. Mrs Lavender, who was rolling pastry at the table, gasped when she saw her.

'Miss Lucy, whatever happened to you?' Lucy was sobbing too much to answer, but the cook stopped her from running through into the main part of the house where she might be seen by anyone. 'Sally-Ann, fetch Lady Luffenham and then tell Sarah to bring some fresh clothes for Lady Lucinda. Now, Miss Lucy, you sit down by the fire and compose yourself and I will fetch you a tot of brandy.'

Lucy obeyed. She was numb with shock. She stared into the flames, feeling sick and ashamed, ashamed because of what Edward had done, ashamed because of what Myles had seen. It must have given him a great disgust of her, though he had hidden it well.

'Lucy, what has happened?' Her mother breezed into the room, but stopped when she saw the state her daughter was in. 'Oh, my darling child.' She squatted down beside Lucy and put her arms about her shoulders. It was obvious that she had not fallen from her horse nor had an accident. The way her clothes were torn and her bruised lips told their own story. 'Who did this to you?'

'Mr Gorridge.'

'Edward Gorridge! You are sure it was him? Did you see him plainly?'

'See him!' Lucy's laugh was a hysterical cackle. 'I saw every inch of him. He was naked as the day he was born and he… he… Mama, he tried to…to rape me.'

'Are you sure? You did not misunderstand?'

'Of course I am sure. Do you think I would make something like that up?'

Cook handed her ladyship a glass of brandy and she helped Lucy to drink it. 'Now, Sarah is here with a dress for you to put on. Then we'll go up to your room and you shall tell me what happened.'

Lucy stood up and the torn dress was taken from her and a clean one slipped over her head. Then the Countess and Sarah helped her up to her room, taking the back stairs so they did not meet Lady Gorridge, who might have wandered out of the drawing room. They were followed by Sally-Ann with a jug of hot water.

'Ain't surprised,' Sally-Ann whispered to Sarah. 'Andrew told me he'd seen that Mr Gorridge with one o' them navvy girls more'n once. Shouldn't be let anywhere near Miss Lucy, 'e shouldn't.'

'Shh,' Sarah admonished her.

Once in her room, Lucy was washed and placed into a nightgown and put to bed. Her mother sat on the edge and took her hand. 'Now, Lucy, I want you to be strong and tell me exactly what happened. Your father must know about this.'

Falteringly Lucy explained exactly what had occurred. The Countess was horrified. 'To think we have made him welcome and encouraged him to offer for you,' she said.

'Mama, I don't want to marry him.'

'No, of course you do not. And you won't, I can promise you that.' She paused. 'But I am mystified by the appearance of Mr Moorcroft. What was he doing here? Had he come to repeat his threats?'

'No, Mama. He didn't mean them, anyway. But I am thankful that he was nearby. I should never have got away if he hadn't heard me scream.'

Sarah was busy tidying the clothes Lucy had taken off. 'This habit can't be mended,' she said, holding the ripped garment up to examine it.

'No, but I'll take it. I will show it to his lordship.' Her ladyship paused. 'Sarah, there is no need to speak of this to anyone, you understand?'

'Of course, my lady. But…' She hesitated.

'But what, Sarah?'

'Mr Gorridge. He tried it on with me once. I was in his room, helping Kitty to make his bed, and when Kitty went out to fetch clean towels, he grabbed me. I only got away 'cos Kitty came back. And I'm not the only one. Now none of the female staff will go into his room alone.'

'Why didn't you report it?'

'Who'd have believed me?'

The Countess acknowledged the truth of this. 'We'll leave Lucy to rest now, but when the men come back from the hunt, you will tell Lord Luffenham what you have told me. He will deal with it.'

'Mama, I do not think I can come down to dinner,' Lucy put in.

'No, I shall say you are not well and offer your excuses. Now go to sleep, if you can, and everything will be dealt with. That man will not stay another night under this roof and I do not care what excuses he makes or what inducement Lord Gorridge offers.'

'Papa…'

'Leave your papa to me.' It was said with a conviction that surprised Lucy—she had never heard her mother so determined before.

'And you will thank M—Mr Moorcroft, won't you?'

'We shall see.' The Countess bent to kiss her and then left the room, ushering Sarah out before her.

Myles took Midge to the stables and handed him over to a stable hand, who was concerned about what had happened to the horse's rider, especially as Lady Lucinda had left a bag on the saddle that she would normally have taken indoors with her.

Myles told him that Lady Lucinda had been very cold and had asked him to bring Midge back. He suggested the boy should deliver the bag into Lady Lucinda's hand himself. The boy didn't seem satisfied, but young lads did not question the big navvy.

Myles's thoughts, as he left, were all on Lucy. Poor darling, it had been a dreadful ordeal and he hoped she would not be scarred by the experience and afraid to let anyone near her again. If what Gorridge had done spoiled her for someone who really did love her and would be gentle and tender in his lovemaking, it would be a terrible tragedy. His only consolation was that he did not think even the Earl would now insist on her marrying Gorridge. Unless, of course, her ladyship chose not to tell him. Or perhaps Lucy had crept into the house without being seen and would say nothing to anyone. Oh, he hoped she would not do that. She should not have to suffer alone.

He was on his way to collect Trojan when the Countess came out of the kitchen door and approached him. 'Mr Moorcroft, will you come inside a moment?'

'Yes, my lady.'

He followed her through the kitchen to a small parlour where she turned to face him. 'Mr Moorcroft, we are all in your debt. I have just left Lucy—'

'Is she all right?' His voice betrayed his concern.

'She is resting. It was a terrible thing to happen, but, thanks to your prompt action, she was saved the worst humiliation. I believe she will recover, given time.'

'Thank God.'

'That was said with a great deal of feeling, Mr Moorcroft.' She was smiling and he realised how much like her Lucy was. The same smile animated her face, the same bright eyes and sympathetic nature softened her features. Did the Earl realise how lucky he was to have found her after his early disappointment? 'Am I right in guessing you are very fond of my daughter?'

'I love her more than life. I would marry her tomorrow, but she will not go against her papa's wishes and he seems determined to make an enemy of me.'

'Mr Moorcroft, am I to assume that you have talked to her about it?'

'Yes.'

'You should not have done that. She is a carefully nurtured young lady, not used to dealing with men....'

'I know that. We have done no more than talk a little. I am not Edward Gorridge, my lady.'

'No. I realise that, but the manner of your meeting was, let us say, unconventional, and you have perhaps aroused feelings in her she does not understand nor know how to cope with.'

'The manner of our meeting was in God's hands, my lady. I did not choose it and neither did she. I would have liked nothing more than to have met her in what you might consider more conventional surroundings, but that was not granted to us, nor would it have been considering Lord Luffenham's antipathy towards my family.'

'No doubt he has his reasons for that.'

He smiled, wondering if she knew what they were. 'No doubt.' He paused and then went on, determined to make his point. 'My lady, my whole concern is for Lady Lucinda's happiness. I would sacrifice anything for that, go away, never speak to her again, if that is the only way, so long as she is not forced to marry Gorridge.'

'I do not think that will happen now. Lucy does not wish

it and who can blame her? And I will fight to my last breath to stop it. But that doesn't mean Lord Luffenham will look more kindly on you as a son-in-law. That, I am afraid, will take time. And Lucy needs time, too, to recover from today's ordeal.'

'I understand.'

'Go now, before Lord Luffenham comes back, and, if you can possibly stop your navvies exacting revenge over the invasion of their camp, it will go some way to help.'

'They will do nothing. I recompensed them and implied Lord Luffenham would repay me, so they are satisfied. And I have given them their usual pay while they rebuild their homes. With luck they will all be snug again by this evening and out of the bad weather.'

'Good. Do they have adequate fuel, food and warm clothes?'

'Yes, my lady.'

'Good. I should hate to think of them in need.' Instead of calling for a servant to see him out, she accompanied him herself back through the kitchen and opened the door for him. A flurry of snow landed on the mat. 'Oh, dear, it is getting worse. Do hurry home.'

He did not need that advice. As he left the house, the snow was flying straight into his face and already it was heaping itself up against trees and buildings. But he was warm inside. Hope had not died after all.

Lucy, sitting in the window seat in her bedroom, unable to rest, saw him come round the side of the house and walk along the path that led to the kitchen garden and the glasshouses, where presumably he had left his horse. He did not look back and did not see her.

She stayed where she was, too numbed to think clearly, until the huntsmen returned, cantering into the stable yard covered in snow. They did not spend long in the yard after handing over their horses, but hurried into the house by a door that led to the gun room. Here they took off their boots, hats and the heavy cloaks that had protected their hunting pink and kept them warm. They were noisy and cheerful and the Earl was calling loudly for cognac to warm them. A little later she heard them troop into the hall and come upstairs to their rooms to change. She heard Rosemary's voice, talking about an incident in the hunt that had amused her, and then Edward's laugh.

He had come back with them. She opened her door a crack and saw him speak to Rosemary before continuing down the corridor to his own room. Rosie turned and saw Lucy and walked over to her. Her eyes were sparkling with excitement, her cheeks rosy and her hair wet. 'Oh, Lucy, you should have been with us. It was so exhilarating.'

'Did you find the vixen?'

'No, Mr Gorridge was not with us so we had no idea where he had seen her. He met us as we were coming back. He told us he had heard the navvies were going to cause trouble, so he rode over to the camp to reason with them. He said he had managed to calm them down, but what with that and everyone going home and the bad weather, Papa has cancelled the ball. It is too bad. I was looking forward to it.'

'There will be other balls.'

'Yes, but it was supposed to be your engagement ball. Everything will go very flat now with just the Gorridges here.' She did not seem to notice that Lucy was not dressed or that she had little to say.

'Perhaps they will leave, too.' Oh, she hoped they would! She could not bear to be under the same roof as Edward Gorridge. She was astonished that he should be behaving as if nothing had happened, as if he were still welcome. And pretending that it was he who was responsible for keeping the peace with the navvies was the last straw. She began to wonder how he would excuse himself when tackled over the insult to her.

'Why should they? Viscount Gorridge is Papa's especial friend and you have yet to announce your engagement to Mr Gorridge.'

'That isn't going to happen.'

'You meant it, then? You really are going to refuse him.'

'I have already done so.'

'Does Papa know that?'

'He will, when Mama tells him.'

'Oh, dear, I wouldn't like to be in your shoes. It will put Papa in a terrible mood.'

'I can't help that.'

'You haven't told anyone about the navvy, have you?'

'There is nothing to tell.'

'Thank goodness for that. There's no sense in making Papa angrier than ever. I'm going to change for dinner. And you had better do the same unless you want to be in even greater disgrace.' She went off to her own room, leaving Lucy to go back to bed, but rest was impossible. She paced the floor, listening to people coming and going in the corridor as they came up to change for dinner. She did not think her parents were among them. She imagined Mr Gorridge being asked to go to the library, which was almost certainly where her father would interview him. Lord Gorridge, too, perhaps. It was very quiet. And then she heard raised voices and a door bang and the next minute Sarah was sent to fetch her.

'Mr Gorridge isn't with my father, is he?' she asked.

'No. He returned to his room. Lord and Lady Luffenham are alone.'

Sarah helped her dress and tidied her hair, and with some trepidation, but even more determination, Lucy went down to the library.

Her father was still dressed in riding breeches, but had changed his boots for slippers. Her mother was sitting on an upright chair near the hearth. She smiled encouragingly, though she did not speak.

'Lucinda, what's all this about young Gorridge?' the Earl demanded.

'He tried to rape me, Papa.'

'Nonsense, you don't know what rape is. He says all he did was try to steal a kiss and that you misunderstood his intentions and panicked.'

'I know the meaning of the term perfectly well, Papa. He wanted to steal more than a kiss—it was my maidenhood he was after. He tore my clothes and said some vile, disgusting things.' She tried to sound calm and reasonable, but having to recount the episode was making her tremble uncontrollably. Her mother rose and came over to take her hand. It gave her the courage to go on. 'I found him lying with a young girl in one of the hothouses. He was completely naked.'

'Good Lord!' Edward had obviously not seen fit to tell him that and it gave him pause for thought. 'Is this true?'

'Yes, Papa, it is.'

'Who was she? One of the servants?'

'No, not one of ours.' She thought she had recognised the girl as one from the navvy camp, but decided not to tell him that. 'She ran away and he turned on me.'

'This is astonishing. Incredible. Edward Gorridge has been represented to me as all that is admirable in a young gentleman—clean-living, chivalrous, affectionate, a worthy husband for my daughter. If your mama had not been so sure herself, I would have said you imagined it.' He obviously did not want to believe that he could have been so thoroughly taken in.

'I did not imagine it, Papa. It was a very real and very frightening experience.'

'Did he…?' He paused, struggling to put his fear into words. 'Did he touch you? Intimately, I mean.'

'No, though it was not for want of trying. Papa, I know it will displease you, but I cannot marry him. I never want to see him or speak to him again.'

He stood looking at her, his affection for her doing battle with the knowledge that, if he sent Gorridge away, he would lose the financial support he had been counting on from the Viscount. There was also the problem that if Gorridge had really had his way with her, they would have to marry. 'Do you swear you are telling the truth?'

'Yes, I swear it.'

He turned on his heel without another word. Lucy stood in the middle of the room, trembling like a leaf. Did he believe her? Did he know that it was Myles who had saved her? If he did, she doubted if he would swallow his pride sufficiently to admit his obligation. But that was not important now. What was important was what he would do about Edward Gorridge. Would he ask him to leave? If he did, there would be a terrible row between him and Lord Gorridge and if, as had been hinted to her, Papa depended on the Viscount's good will to help him out financially, then she had really put the cat among the pigeons.

'Come, dear,' the Countess said gently. 'It is all over. Mr Gorridge will be asked to leave. What do you want to do now?'

'Go back to my room, please, Mama.'

She returned to her room and sat down heavily on the bed, facing the window. Already the snow was piling up on the outside window sill. Supposing the weather was too bad for anyone to travel and they had to stay until the snow had gone? It might be weeks. It might be weeks without seeing Myles. He had said they would talk later, but when and how? And what was there to talk about? She did not want to go over what had happened again. She was entirely innocent, but she still felt shame and revulsion, unable to face anyone. He must feel that, too, and might even think she had encouraged that dreadful man. Mr Gorridge had told him he had arrived too late. Would he believe it? And if he didn't, could he bear to look at her again? He had always buoyed her with hope, but now hope had gone.

Chapter Ten

~~~~~~~~~~~~~~~~~~~~~~~~

Lucy was woken next morning from a troubled sleep of exhaustion to find sunshine streaming into her window. She left the bed and went to look out. The snow was deep, crisp and white. Across the lawns and park it lay undisturbed, undulating with the land over which it lay. It balanced itself on the bare branches of the trees, dotted each berry on a holly bush near her window, hung on to the stable roof and covered the stable yard where the hands were busy with brooms sweeping it away. Andrew stood beside the water trough, breaking the ice with a mallet. A solitary robin, its breast a splash of red, sat on the pump, watching him with bright, alert eyes. More staff were using shovels to clear the drive.

She shivered and turned to go back to bed, but a sound halted her in her tracks and she returned to the window. Viscount Gorridge's carriage was being brought round to the front. Behind it, a groom led Edward's horse, saddled and ready to go. Lucy moved round from the side window to the one at the front, where she could look down on the roof of the carriage as it halted beside the front door. The four horses that drew it snorted and pranced, their breath steaming in the cold air. A footman ran out with hot bricks and blankets, which he put inside, while another loaded luggage into the boot. Viscount Gorridge escorted his weeping wife out to the carriage and they both disappeared inside it. Nothing happened for a minute or two and Lucy imagined they were debating whether it was safe to proceed. Then she saw Edward leave the house. His riding coat was covered by a thick cloak, which enveloped him almost completely. He stopped beside his horse and turned back to look up at the house. Catching sight of her at the window, he made an elaborate bow, kissed his fingers to her and sprang into the saddle. And then he was gone, cantering down the newly cleared drive. The carriage followed more slowly.

Lucy breathed a sigh of relief and turned back into the room. Her father had believed her and stood by her and the menace was gone, but had he gone for good? That gesture before he left had not been one of remorse, or even embarrassment, and it had unnerved her. Did he think it was only a minor setback to his plans and he would be back? Oh, she prayed he would not. All that was left for her now was to be the dutiful daughter and do nothing to make Papa regret his decision. Life must go on as normally as possible and she must try not to think of Myles, but how could she not? He was in her head and in her heart, part of her. She imagined him with the navvies in their encampment and wondered how the children were faring in the bitter cold. She pictured him at home with his parents, dressed as befitted a gentleman, not in the rough clothes of the navvy. Would he tell them what had happened to her? Perhaps. Perhaps not. He might have decided to forget her after seeing her so compromised. Mr Gorridge's mocking words came back to her: *Pity you're too late, Moorcroft. She's mine.*

She turned as Sarah came into the room, bearing a breakfast tray. 'They've gone, Miss Lucy.'

'Yes, I saw them from the window.'

'There was a terrible row last night. Did you hear it?'

'No.' She had heard raised voices, her father's and Viscount Gorridge's and Edward's hollow laugh, but had been unable to make out anything of what was said.

'Viscount Gorridge was shouting at his son. Called him all sorts of names, telling him he'd let him down and he couldn't trust him an inch, and Mr Gorridge was shouting back and saying it wasn't his fault, that you flaunted yourself in front of him and tempted him. And Lady Gorridge was crying fit to bust. We could hear them from the servants' hall, being his lordship had the room directly overhead.'

'You didn't say anything about what happened to the other servants?'

'No, how could you think I would? But it didn't take a genius to work out that something terrible had happened and it involved you. Anyhow, we're all glad they've gone.'

'So am I.'

'Your mama says if you want to stay in bed today, you may, and she will have a fire lit for you.' A fire in the children's bedrooms was something the Earl deprecated, unless they were ill. Did he imagine she was ill?

'No, I will get up,' she said. 'I must try to put this behind me and behave as if nothing out of the ordinary happened. Where is my mother?'

'In the morning room, writing to everyone cancelling the ball. Not that I think anyone would come, anyway, the weather being what it is. Master Johnny is with her, plaguing her to let him take his new sled out.'

* * *

Lucy ate her breakfast and then Sarah helped her to dress in the warmest clothes she could find: red flannel petticoat, two more of cotton, a thick wool skirt, two shifts and a velvet jacket, which matched the burgundy of the skirt, and black button boots. She would take Johnny out with his sled.

Rosemary and Esme had the same idea, for Lucy found them dressed to go out in warm clothes, woolly hats and colourful scarves and gloves. Johnny, similarly clad, was dancing about them impatiently. 'Oh, good, here is Lucy,' he said. 'We are going to build a snowman on the front lawn,' he told her, grabbing her hand. 'Come on, before the snow melts.'

'I don't think it is going to do that,' Lucy said. She was smiling. Johnny's enthusiasm was catching and a little strenuous exercise in the open air was just what she needed. She tried not to think of the Gorridge carriage ploughing its way though the snow to reach Gorryham.

They ran outside and began rolling the snow into two balls, fashioning a snowman's body from a big one and his head from a smaller one. He was given a carrot for a nose and another was cut in the shape of a smiling mouth into which they stuck an old clay pipe. Two lumps of coal made his eyes and some straw inside an old hat was put on his head. Johnny was ecstatic. He had seen snow before, but never in such quantity, and he danced round the snowman and then began making snowballs and flinging them all over the place. Soon a real fight was in progress with Johnny squealing and the girls shouting and laughing. After the tensions of the last two weeks, it was medicine for Lucy's soul.

While they played, some of the outdoor staff, having little else to do, set off to prepare a suitable hill for tobogganing. The one they selected as being the smoothest, with no protruding rocks to upset the sled and with an incline that would give a good run, but not be so steep as to be dangerous, was the one behind the house that led to the rise from which Lucy had first seen Myles. He would not be there now, of course, but at home in Goodthorpe Manor.

They plodded almost to the top and, while Andrew took the first run down to make sure it was safe for Johnny, Lucy climbed a little farther to look down into the valley on the other side. It was blanketed by snow. She could hardly make out where the railway line was, except that one or two empty wagons stood waiting for the work to be resumed. The huts were covered in snow and it was piled up against their walls, but paths had been cleared between them and smoke rose on the air from their chimneys. Someone had built a huge campfire and they were roasting a pig on it. A noisy group of children were sliding on frozen, hard-packed snow; others were building a snowman. Children, whatever their rank, rich or poor, did that whenever there was snow, she thought, and they did not seem to feel the cold.

'Can we go and talk to them?' Johnny was standing beside her, watching them.

'No, sweetheart, the slope is too steep.' She turned away. 'And besides, I thought you wanted to ride on your sled. Andrew is bringing it back for you.'

'I could ride it down there.'

'No, Johnny. The men have made you a run down this way. Look how smooth it is. Shall I come down with you?'

They settled themselves on the sled and propelled themselves downwards. Johnny shrieked with delight and could not wait to drag the sled back up to the top and go down again, this time with Esme. After that it was Rosemary's turn, and then they did it all again. With each run the snow became packed harder and the speed at which they hurtled down increased.

Miss Bannister, who had accompanied them, became fearful and insisted that the servants put fresh snow down. It was while they were doing this that the Earl and Countess arrived.

'My goodness, I have never seen Johnny so animated,' his father said. 'I hope he isn't overexciting himself.'

'Papa! Mama! Come and see me go down.'

The Countess put her hand to her mouth as he hurtled down the slope and tumbled off at the end, rolling in the heap of soft snow at the bottom. He was soon on his feet and plodding back to them, dragging the toboggan. 'Did you see me? Did you?' he called out before he reached them.

'Yes, we saw.' His father smiled. 'How strong is that thing?'

'It's well made, Papa,' Lucy told him. 'Andrew and some of the other men tested it.'

'Right,' he said, sitting on it. 'Come on, son, let's go down together.'

Johnny seated himself in front of his father and off they went. The Countess smiled indulgently at them and then turned to draw Lucy away from the others. 'How are you, sweetheart?'

'I'm fine, Mama. None the worse, but I'm glad Mr Gorridge has gone. I was afraid Papa did not believe me.'

'Lucy, we brought you up to tell the truth and he knew you would not lie. He only wanted to be sure there was no possibility that you had misunderstood the situation. I showed him your torn dress and told him what I had seen, which helped to convince him. He ordered Mr Gorridge out of the house and when the Viscount heard of it, he was all apologies and said he and Lady Gorridge would go, too, though Papa said it was not necessary, it was snowing too hard for the carriage to leave, but Edward could go and stay in the village because he would not entertain him in the house a second longer.'

'But he was here this morning. I saw him from the window.'

'Yes, his mother begged that he be allowed to stay the night and Papa realised it would not do for half the village to be wondering why he did not sleep at the house.'

'Does Papa know it was Mr Moorcroft who saved me?'

'I did not intend to tell him. I thought it better that he did not know Mr Moorcroft had been up at the house again, but unfortunately Mr Gorridge made some scathing remark about him, which I will not repeat, and so I could not remain silent.'

'I can guess. He said I had already been spoiled by the navvy.'

'Yes.'

'What did Papa say?'

'He was very, very angry.'

'With me?'

'No, of course not, with Edward Gorridge.' She put a gloved hand on Lucy's arm. 'I beg you not to say anything more of it to your father. He might acknowledge his debt to Mr Moorcroft, but it will take time for him to come round to agreeing he was perhaps wrong to condemn the man out of hand.'

'What about you, Mama?'

'Lucy, child, all I want is your happiness and the happiness of everyone else in the family, including your papa, but it cannot be had with everyone at each other's throats and so I told Mr Moorcroft and he agreed with me.'

'You spoke to him?'

'Yes, in the yard, after he had taken Midge back to the stables. I wanted to thank him. But, Lucy, there must be a time of calm, a time for the navvies to finish their work and move on, you do understand that?'

'Yes, Mama, I want it, too.'

'Good, now here they come back. We will enjoy this time together and put everything else behind us.'

A few more runs were made, then, as the sky darkened, they returned home warm and glowing and ready for a good dinner.

It was the next morning that Johnny was missed. Miss Bannister came downstairs looking for him. 'The young rascal is hiding,' she said, when the Countess and Lucy said they had not seen him. 'He did not want to do the Latin exercise I set him and could not sit still. It was all the excitement of yesterday, I suppose. I only turned my back on him for a moment and he disappeared.'

'He can't have gone out,' the Countess said. 'We'll search the house.'

The house was old and rambling and there were many nooks and crannies where a six-year-old could hide and, even with the help of the indoor servants, it took some time to establish that Johnny was not indoors.

The stables and outbuildings were searched next and by now everyone was becoming very worried and the Earl had to be told. More fruitless searching and calling the boy's name followed, but it was not until Lucy thought to look in the coach house where the sled had been put away the day before that she discovered it was missing, and realised where her brother was.

'He must have taken it up to the hill,' Lucy said when she reported it to her father, who had gone up into the hayloft above the stables to search there for himself.

He fairly flew down the ladder. 'Someone saddle my horse,' he shouted and rushed indoors to put on his riding boots and a big waterproof cape.

'I'm coming, too, Papa.' Lucy ran indoors to change into her habit and cloak while Andrew saddled Midge. By the time that was done, her father, too impatient to wait for her, had gone. She set off after him. More snow had fallen in the night and would have obliterated the run and on the hills. It was easy to lose one's way when everything looked a uniform white. Johnny might be anywhere, fallen down a hole, into a drift, anything. Two pairs of eyes were better than one.

The snow started again in earnest before she had gone very far. It obliterated everything except Midge and even her thick coat was soon spotted with white flakes. She was a sturdy little mare and plodded slowly onwards and upwards. Lucy shouted Johnny's name over and over again, but there was only an eerie silence. No birds sang, no sheep bleated, not even a dog barking disturbed the silent world of the snow. Even the sound of the river, which could usually be heard from some distance away, had been stilled under ice. Not only could she see no sign of her brother, no footmarks, no sign of a toboggan, she could not see her father, who was undoubtedly some way ahead of her and on a bigger horse. Again and again she shouted while Midge floundered in drifts that came up to her stomach.

She considered turning back, but the thought of her little brother being out in this wilderness of white kept her going. He would die if he were not found and rescued soon. She floundered about, calling his name, making little headway, wondering why she had not caught up with her father. The snow seemed to be coming from every direction, now in her face, now behind her, now to the side. When she came upon disturbed snow, which looked as though a horse had been that way not long before, she thought she had found her father and shouted again, calling his name alternately with Johnny's. When there was no answer, she realised it wasn't her father's horse that had made the marks, but her own, and she had been going round in circles. Only two or three miles from home and she was lost.

Luffenham Hall was a substantial building. Its chimneys must be spewing smoke, but she could see nothing and had no idea of its direction, except that it must be downhill. In any case, there were roads in the valley and she ought to be able to find those. But could she abandon her search? If Johnny was lying buried in snow only a few yards from where she gave up and turned back, she would never forgive herself. She called again and again in more and more desperation, urging Midge to keep going, though the little mare was all but exhausted. Supposing Johnny had found his own way home hours ago and was sitting cosily by the fire, being scolded by their mother for frightening them so? Supposing someone had simply moved the sled and he had not come out at all? Supposing her father had found him and taken him home, not realising she was also out on the hill? She realised how foolish she had been and urged Midge to turn about and start making her way downhill.

'Home, Midge,' she said. 'You know the way.'

The mare seemed unable to obey. She resisted the pressure on her mouth to turn round, floundered in a drift that threatened to swallow both horse and rider and then slipped. The next second, they were both down in the snow. Lucy had the presence of mind to roll out of the way of the mare's flailing hooves and then sat up. She had lost her crop and her hat and sat shaking her head before getting to her knees and trying to stand. She had landed in a drift that was almost up to her waist, but she could see that Midge was on her feet and where she stood was not nearly so deep. Lucy struggled to reach her, but the mare had been frightened and was cold and missing her warm stable. She set off at a canter and was soon lost to sight. Lucy was on foot, alone on the hill.

She felt like bursting into tears, but there was no time for that. Floundering in wet snow that dragged at her clothes and froze her feet and fingers until she could not feel them, she struggled in what she thought was the direction of home. Johnny had been lost and might be dead, and she was lost and might also soon be dead. Because of her foolishness one tragedy could be turned into two. Poor Mama, poor Papa. But she wasn't dead yet. She floundered on, talking aloud to herself to keep up her spirits.

The fire crackled and blazed as the footman put more logs on the library fire and withdrew. Myles sat toasting his toes on the fender and sipping a glass of brandy, which his father had poured for him. 'It's going to put us weeks behind,' Myles told him, continuing the conversation that they had begun over dinner which, true to his roots, Henry liked to take in the middle of the day. Only when they had guests was it served in the early evening.

'Can't be helped. The weather is something we cannot control. There isn't a penalty for delay in the contract, is there?'

'Not for acts of God. It's just as well the snow came to our aid, because you could not call an invasion by the hunt an act of God and the men would not resume work on the line until they had rebuilt their homes.'

'They've done that now, haven't they?'

'Yes. I was vastly overcharged for the wood. The men naturally went to the nearest supplier and that was a sawmill in Peterborough, which I discovered afterwards was owned by Viscount Gorridge. Not that I could have done anything about it. The need was urgent and I could not have kept the men hanging about while I found a cheaper source.'

'I doubt Gorridge takes much interest in it so long as his rent is paid. He wouldn't have known you were in the market for wood.'

'I suppose not, but I still don't like dealing with him.'

'You have to deal with all manner of men in business, Myles. It doesn't mean you have to like them.'

'Oh, I've nothing against the Viscount, except that he tried to foist his no-good son on to Lucy, knowing what he was like.'

'She won't be forced to marry him now, will she?' his mother asked. She had been working on some embroidery and taking no part in the conversation, but had evidently been listening.

'Lady Luffenham said not, but I am not sure how much influence she has with Lord Luffenham.'

'Enough, I think,' his father put in. 'No man worth his salt would allow his daughter to be molested like that and not do something about it.'

'Poor child,' her ladyship said, dropping her sewing in her lap and looking at her son. She felt for him, felt for both the young people, and she could not believe that John Vernley could be so stubborn.

Myles smiled at her. That she had not had a daughter was a source of disappointment to her, though she rarely mentioned it, but it did mean that she was wont to befriend and mother any young girl who seemed to need it and contributed to several charities that helped girls either by finding them schools, homes or jobs. Several had ended up in her own household. 'Yes, Mama. I wish I knew what was happening over there. I would like to think Edward Gorridge has been banished, but he might have been allowed to stay because of the weather. The roads are impassable. Goodness knows when they will be cleared.'

'At least the snow has stopped,' his mother said. 'I do believe the sky is brightening.'

Myles rose and walked over to the window. The long drive from the road to the house had been cleared by the outside staff, but it was piled high on either side. A weak sun was trying to break through the clouds, making every bush and plant look as if it were bedecked by a myriad of tiny ice diamonds. His found himself thinking of Lucy at Luffenham Hall, perhaps looking from her window on to a similar scene. Was she well? Was she being sympathetically treated? Was she thinking of him and wishing, as he was, that they could be together? How long must he stay away? The Countess had given him hope, but his impatience was making him fidgety.

'I'm going over to the line.'

'Myles, whatever for?' His mother was dismayed.

'It is pay day and I have never missed a pay day yet.' He had realised that the next day was the last of the month, indeed of the year, and it set him wondering what 1845 would bring. There was to have been a ball at Luffenham Hall, but he doubted it would take place now. He tried to imagine what might be happening there, but all he could picture was Lucy being mauled by that fiend and it made his blood boil. He could not sit still.

'The men will understand this once,' his father said. 'And what have they got to spend it on, except the grog shop?'

'There's a tommy shop as well as a grog shop on the site,' Myles said, a fact his father knew quite well. A tommy shop was a store where the navvies and their families could purchase provisions with tommy tickets, which were issued in advance of their pay. On some sites they were badly run and the men charged so much for inferior quality goods that, when it came to pay day, they did not have enough to cover their debts and so had to ask for more tickets. It put them permanently under an obligation to the tommy-shop keeper, who made a handsome living out of them. Myles would not allow that. He put his own man in charge, made sure the meat was of good quality, the flour free of weevils and all the other goods were fresh, and he personally controlled what was charged for it. 'The women will want to buy food.'

'They were roasting a pig yesterday,' his father said. 'They are not hungry.'

'Myles, don't go,' his mother pleaded. 'You will never get through the snow.'

'I'll ride along the road to the crossing and then make my way up the line,' he said. 'If it really is impassable, I can always turn back.'

'Must you?'

'Yes. Something tells me I ought to be there. I don't know what, but I feel uneasy.'

'Then wrap up warmly and take a flask with you.'

He smiled indulgently at her and bent to kiss her cheek. 'Yes, Mama. I'll be back before dark.'

He left his parents by their warm fire, changed into the warmest clothes he could find—thick cord breeches, woollen jacket, top coat and a big riding cape—put the navvies' pay in a bag and went and saddled Trojan. He felt better being on the move.

He rode down to the road that led from Peterborough to Leicester and which, until the railway was completed, was still the main artery between the towns. A stretch of it had been cleared by the inmates of a nearby workhouse the day before, but even as he turned along it, it began to snow again and he wondered how long it would remain clear. It did not take him long to reach the turning for the minor road that led to Luffenham. This was a different matter. On parts of it the snow was not deep, but on others, the wind had whipped it into drifts and it was only when Trojan floundered that he was able to tell one from the other. He wondered if it had been such a good idea to come, but something, an inner voice, drove him on.

He did not ride the whole way into Luffenham, but turned off at the level crossing and rode along the track, thankful for his thoroughness when he had surveyed it. He knew every bump and hollow, every tree and bush along the way, almost every blade of grass, except there was no grass to be seen. Everywhere was eerily quiet; there was no sound except for Trojan's blowing as he struggled manfully on. Even the wind was silent as it whipped up the snow and blew it in clouds across the landscape, stinging his face. He could hardly see where he was going, but he knew he could not be far off the encampment.

A sudden flurry and visibility returned. It was then he noticed a movement on the hill the other side of the river. It was probably an animal, a sheep or even a fox, struggling through snow that threatened to envelop it. He reined in to watch, trying to make out what it was, but then a squall obliterated the hill and he could see it no longer. He went on, wondering if he ought to investigate; he hated to think that an animal was injured and in pain when he could put it out of its misery, but he was disinclined to struggle up the steep slope.

A keening sound came to him, the sound an animal might make if it was injured, and he stopped to listen. At first he could not hear it, and then it came again more clearly. It sounded human. 'There's nothing for it, old fellow,' he said to his horse. 'We'll have to go and investigate.'

He rode Trojan across the river bridge, but the horse was

exhausted and Myles did not want to force him up the steep slope. He tethered him to the bridge and set off on foot, falling into snow and getting up to go on. The sound had stopped. Whatever it was must have either recovered and moved off or had died. He decided to go back, but before he did so, he stood and shouted. 'Is anyone there?' There was no answer.

'A fox,' he said to himself, but he shouted again to make sure and this time there was a weak answering call. There was someone there! He redoubled his efforts. 'I'm coming,' he shouted. 'Keep calling.'

The sound was weak and several times it stopped; he could not be sure he was moving in the right direction. He was right on top of her before he saw her. She was lying in a snowdrift, almost covered. 'Lucy! My God! Lucy!' He fell on to his knees beside her and gathered her into his arms. 'I'm here now. You're safe.' He stripped off his cloak and wrapped it round her and then he picked her up and carried her semi-conscious body back through his own footprints to where he had left Trojan. He tried talking soothingly to her as he went, but the struggle was making him breathless and he had to concentrate on not pitching both of them into the snow. Occasionally she moaned softly, which was the only indication he had that she was still alive.

He was a very strong man and able to carry someone of Lucy's weight with ease, but in such conditions, and desperate as he was to reach warmth and safety, it seemed to take for ever to reach his horse. Even then his problems were not over. He could not put Lucy on the stallion's back because she could not support herself and he could not mount with her in his arms. He put Trojan's reins over his shoulder and the horse followed as he continued on foot. The railway had moved on and was now beyond the bridge and higher up the slope, but here it was sheltered from the wind and the snow had not drifted so badly. He was able to move a little more quickly. As soon as he came within sight of the camp, he was seen and Adam came running to meet him.

'Fetch your father,' Myles said. 'Hurry.'

The boy obeyed and Pat was soon running towards him. 'What's happened? What have you got there?'

'Lady Lucinda. I found her in the snow.'

'Is she alive?'

'Yes. Just.'

'Bring her into our hut. Kathy will look after her.'

Lucy was carried into the hut and all the other occupants, half a dozen men who lodged with them, were sent out to find other huts where they would be welcomed and find a spot by a fire. 'Leave her with me,' Kathy O'Malley told Myles. 'I'll see to her.'

He put his burden into a chair beside the stove and stood looking down at her, reluctant to leave her. Her eyes were closed. There was not a vestige of colour in her face; even her lips were white. It was only the slight fluttering of her chest that told him she was still in the land of the living. He could not imagine why she would leave the house in such weather, let alone come so far. Unless… Surely to God nothing terrible had happened at Luffenham Hall and she had felt compelled to flee? What was her father thinking of? And her mother? Where was Gorridge? He was on tenterhooks until he could ask her himself.

'Go on,' Kathy said. 'I need to strip her clothes off and I can't do that with you there. Go to the grog shop. You look as though you could do with a drink. You, too, Pat. I'll call you when you can come back.'

'She'll be all right, won't she?' Myles was still hesitating.

'God willing. Now shoo.' She waved her hand at him and he turned and followed Pat out of the hut.

'How did you find her?' Pat asked, as they sat beside the stove in the grog shop, with a double tot of rum each.

'I was on my way here, when I saw something struggling in the snow up on the other hill. Then I heard a cry and went to investigate. She was almost buried. If anything happens to her…' He dare not go on, could not bear to think of a world without Lucy.

'It won't. Kathy is a wonder when it comes to upsets and disasters and looking after sick people. She'll know what to do.'

'Yes, I know. I nearly didn't come. Thank God I did.'

'Why did you? Think we'd be working, did you? Or worried we might go and raid Luffenham Hall if you didn't keep an eye on us?'

Myles grinned. 'You gave me your word you wouldn't and I accepted that. Nor did I expect you to be working. But it's pay day.'

'Good Lord, you didn't venture out just to bring us our pay, did you?'

'I've never missed a pay day yet.'

'Not like some. I've known men wait three months for their pay and living on tommy tickets the whole while. We know you'd not keep us waiting, Mr Moorcroft, you needn't have worried.'

'In the circumstances, it was as well I did.'

'Amen to that. What do you suppose she was doing up there?'

'I don't know.'

'What are you going to do now? When she comes round, I mean.' He glanced out of the window. 'It's snowing harder than ever. You'll never be able to take her home.'

'No, we'll have to make her comfortable here. Will your wife mind?'

''Course not, Mr Moorcroft. We all like the little lady. And she is a lady, too.'

'Yes.'

They were silent for a moment or two, contemplating the snow driving against the window. If it had come earlier, Myles would never have set out and Lucy would still be lying out there on the hill and she could not have survived many more minutes. He shuddered to think what a close call it had been. Had she been missed at the Hall? Were they even now searching for her?

He looked up as Adam burst into the hut. 'Ma says you can come back now.'

Myles went at a run.

Lucy had been stripped of her clothes, put into a flannelette nightdress of Kathy's and tucked into a bed in a section of the hut which had been curtained off with a sheet of canvas. The pot-bellied stove in the centre of the room had been stoked up and glowed almost red with heat. Kathy was stirring soup in a big black pot on the top of it. When Myles arrived, she nodded in the direction of the curtain. 'She's thawing out nicely.' It was said with a smile.

He pushed aside the makeshift curtain, dropped on to his knees beside Lucy and took her hand. She was restless and kept flinging her head from side to side and mumbling something he could not understand. 'Lucy,' he said. 'It's me. Open your eyes, sweetheart, let me see you smile.'

Her head thrashed. 'Johnny. Johnny,' she mumbled.

'That's all she's said,' Kathy put in. 'Seems to be worrying her.'

'It's her brother's name.'

'James Middleton is looking after a bratling his daughter found wandering down by the bridge early this morning. He's no bigger than a sixpence and says he's called John and comes from the big house. Chirpy little fellow he is, but Mary said they couldn't do anything about taking him back to his parents until the snow cleared.'

'I'll wager it's Lucy's brother,' he said, remembering that Lottie Middleton was the girl he had found with Edward Gorridge. 'But what was he doing out alone? He's never left unguarded for a second. Baby of the family he is, doted on by the whole household. If it is him, every spare man in the county will be out looking for him. Unless they think he is safely with Lucy at someone else's house.'

'No one has been here looking for either of them,' Kathy said. 'And mayhap it's as well they haven't. Lord Luffenham would find some way of blaming us for his disappearance, you may be sure. I think Lottie is expecting a reward for his safe return.'

Myles grinned wryly. 'No doubt she is, but his sister has risked her life looking for him and she won't rest until she knows he is safe, so we'll have him fetched here. We'll talk about rewards later.'

'I'll go.' Pat was standing in the doorway, unwilling to intrude, though it was his bed Lucy occupied.

'Thanks.' He turned back to Lucy and took her hand again, rubbing it gently to warm it. She had a little more colour and he fervently thanked God he had found her in time. 'Lucy, wake up.'

Her eyes flickered open. 'Myles. What are you doing here?' She stared up at the wooden ceiling and the canvas curtain, a puzzled frown on her face. 'Where am I?'

'In one of the huts. You are safe now. As soon as you are ready you shall have some hot soup.'

'How did you find me?' she asked, managing a weak smile. 'I had been shouting for ages, but I couldn't make anyone hear and I was lost. I thought I knew the hills, but I just didn't know which way to turn. Oh, Myles, if you hadn't found me...'

'I think God guided my footsteps. I was at home and something told me I was needed here. I couldn't rest until I came. I saw something dark in the snow and then I heard you cry out. What were you doing out in such weather?'

'Looking for Johnny. He managed to slip out of the house very early and when we found his sled was missing, we guessed he had taken it to ride down the hill like he did yesterday. We all went out looking for him, Papa, the servants, everyone, but I missed my way. Then Midge stumbled in a drift and threw me. Did you see her?'

'No, she probably went home.'

'Oh, if she goes home without me, they will be worried to death. I must go.' She struggled to sit up. 'And I have to tell them I couldn't find Johnny. Oh, I cannot bear to think of him lying in the snow like I did. Perhaps he's been found, perhaps he's safely at home all the time. I have to go.'

He pushed her gently back on to the bed. 'Johnny's safe, Lucy. It's you we're worried about.'

'Safe? Are you sure? How do you know?'

Her answer came in the shape of Johnny himself, who tore into the room and flung himself on the bed beside her. He was dressed in a borrowed fustian jacket and cord trousers that were so big they had to be held up with string. 'Lucy, Lucy, you came. I knew you would. I've had such adventures, but now I want to go home.'

Lucy hugged him to her, while tears of relief and exhaustion ran down her cheeks. 'Oh, Johnny, thank God. I thought you were lost. Why, why did you go out alone?'

'I wanted to go tobogganing again and Mr Gorridge said he knew a much better place.'

'Mr Gorridge!' The exclamation came from Myles and Lucy simultaneously.

'Yes, he said if I met him at the back of the stables with my sled, he'd take me. He said not to tell anyone or they would all want to come and it was a secret place.'

Lucy looked up at Myles, a puzzled frown on her brow. 'I don't understand.'

'Then what happened?' Myles prompted.

'We went a long way up a hill, but it was snowing so hard and I didn't want to go any farther. He called me a baby and he said babies didn't deserve to be given sleds if they didn't have the stomach to use them. He sat me on it and gave it a push. It was very steep and I went down very fast and then I fell off. I called out, but no one came. Then the lady came and brought me here.'

Lucy looked from her brother to Myles. 'He abandoned him,' she said. 'Why would he do that? He must have known Johnny could not survive out there on his own.'

Myles said nothing, but it was not difficult to guess the man's motives. Without Johnny, the Earl would have no heir and Gorridge evidently had not given up on the idea of marrying Lucy and inheriting Luffenham Hall as well as Linwood Park. The greed, callousness and sheer conceit of the man was unparalleled. But what had Lottie Middleton to do with it? Was she in league with Gorridge, or was it simply a coincidence that she was the one to find him? Was it ransom rather than reward she was thinking of? He should have sent her from the site the first time he had caught her with Gorridge, but James was a good worker and he had a wife and other children to care for and he couldn't have condemned them all because Lottie fell for the blandishments of the so-called gentleman.

'You are safe now and your sister needs to rest, young man,' he said, picking the boy off the bed and standing him on the floor. 'She has been very brave coming out in the snow to look for you, but you can't go home for a little while, not until the snows stops and Lady Lucinda is stronger.'

'But, Myles…' she protested.

'No,' he said firmly. 'When the snow stops and someone can get through, I will send a message to say you and the young master are safe and well, but going now is out of the question.'

Kathy brought a bowl of soup and a spoon and Myles took it from her and sat on the side of the bed, intending to feed Lucy from it. 'I can manage,' she told him.

He smiled. 'Perhaps you can, but it will give me pleasure to see you take every drop. It's good soup, I can vouch for that. There's many a time I've had Kathy's soup warming my insides.'

Kathy put her arm about Johnny's shoulders. 'Come, young master, let's leave your sister to enjoy her dinner. You come with me and I'll find something tasty for you.' She led him away and dropped the curtain behind her.

'It is good,' Lucy said, tasting the first mouthful.

'You are not to speak until it's all gone.' He smiled and popped a second spoonful into her mouth. He wanted to know exactly what had happened at the Hall after he left, why Gorridge was still about the place, but he could wait. She was here with him, and though their surroundings were not what he would have wished for her it could not be helped; at least Kathy, unlike many of the navvy women, was clean and respectful and her home kept as spotless as was possible given the conditions under which the navvies lived.

'Now, my darling,' he said, when she had finished and he had set the bowl and spoon on the floor. 'I want to know everything.'

'I told you, I was looking for Johnny and Midge threw me. It wasn't her fault, poor thing…'

'I did not mean that and you know it.' He hitched himself closer to her and took both her hands in his. 'I want to know what happened after you left me last time. What happened to Gorridge?' He checked suddenly. 'I don't think you will be going to any ball this evening.'

'I wouldn't have, anyway. Papa cancelled it. There was an awful row and he sent Mr Gorridge away and Viscount and Lady Gorridge said they would go, too, only there was so much snow, they couldn't leave until yesterday morning. I watched them go. Poor Lady Gorridge was distraught.'

'Obviously Gorridge did not go far.'

'He must have stayed in the village. Why? Did he mean to harm Johnny? What can he have against him?'

'Revenge, perhaps. If he was sent away…'

'But surely if it was vengeance he wanted, he would have taken it on me, not my brother.'

'Are you quite sure he doesn't expect to be allowed back to Luffenham Hall to marry you?'

'If he does, he will be disappointed. I will never consent.'

'So, there is to be no marriage.'

She smiled. 'Not to Mr Gorridge.'

'Ah, you think there might be one to someone else?'

She twisted her head to smile up at him. 'If he were to ask me.'

He smiled and bent to put his lips to hers. 'Has your father relented?'

'I pray that he will.'

'I hope so. But it isn't a case of off with the old and on with the new, is it? Your mama said that we had to give it time. His lordship will not suddenly turn round and say he approves of me.'

'No, but your people saved Johnny's life and you saved mine.'

'Do you think that will have any bearing on the matter? I do not think so. I am still a brute of a navvy who aspires to be a gentleman, an upstart in his eyes. He would most definitely think so if he could see us now. Here I am, almost in bed with you, and you are wearing nothing but… What is it?'

'Mrs O'Malley's nightgown. It's much too big for me.'

'So I noticed.' She looked down to see that the garment had fallen off one shoulder and the top of a rosy breast was visible. Hurriedly she pulled the neckline back into place.

'Why are you being so negative, Myles?'

'I am being realistic. It was you who insisted on saying goodbye.'

'I know.' She sighed. 'I could see no way forward and it broke my heart. But if I have to say I was in bed with you, then I will.'

'Don't tempt me, Lucy.' He smiled, but moved a little away from her, knowing how easy it would be to give way. 'What do you think that would do to your reputation as a virtuous young lady, or to my good name? Navvy or gentleman, I value my honour.'

'I know you do. I was only teasing.'

'Teasing or not, the sooner we get you out of this compromising situation, the better.'

'You said the snow was too thick to get through.'

'To Luffenham, yes, but Goodthorpe Manor is nearer and the terrain easier to traverse. We will have the railway line to guide us back to the road and once we are on the main road, the snow shouldn't be so bad. It had been cleared when I came along it earlier.'

'Goodthorpe Manor. Will your parents welcome us?'

'Of course they will.' The only problem as far as he could see was not with his parents, but how to transport her and her brother. It was clear she was not strong enough to walk or even ride. He might have to wait until the morning and what would her father say to that? He would be for ever condemned. Lucy might have been teasing, but the world would see a young, aristocratic lady staying among labourers whose reputation for depravity was legendary. All the excuses in the world would not save her reputation. He bent to kiss her and picked up the empty soup bowl. 'Try to get some sleep.'

Johnny, who was on the floor playing five stones with Adam, looked up as Myles came into the room. 'Has Lucy finished her dinner?'

'Yes, son, and now she is resting. Be a good boy and don't disturb her.'

'Aren't we going home?'

'Not today, Johnny. We can't get through the snow. As soon as I can I will send a message to Luffenham Hall to let them know where you are. You don't mind that, do you?'

'No, I don't mind. I like it here. There are so many other boys to play with. I wish I hadn't lost my sled. We could have had some rides.'

'We'll find it when the snow has gone.'

He went outside. The snow had stopped falling and a watery sun was trying to break through the clouds, but the afternoon was well advanced and darkness would fall rapidly once the sun sank below the crest of the hill. It was all very well to say he would take them to Goodthorpe Manor, but how? Trojan could not carry all three, even if Lucy was strong enough to ride. She needed a carriage. But there was no carriage on a navvy site. He looked about him for inspiration. The snow was deep, the line of the track barely visible. An empty bogey stood on the rails, covered in snow. An old cart, its shafts pointing skyward, had been abandoned beside one of the huts. The trouble was that however many horses he hitched to it, they would never be able to pull it through the snow. The cart would fall to pieces first. He smiled suddenly and went to find Pat, who had gone back to the grog shop where it was warm. 'Call the men together, Pat. I'll give them their wages. After that I've a job for them to do.'

He had a couple of hundred navvies with nothing to do under his command, navvies accustomed to shifting tons of earth every day—moving a few tons of snow would be nothing to them. He sat at a table in the grog shop and gave each man his wages. When all had been paid and most had used some of their wages to pay off their tommy-ticket debts and had a tankard of ale in their hands, he went outside and stood on the bogey to address them.

'Most of you know that Lady Lucinda Vernley is in Pat's shanty, recovering from being caught out in the snow. She is weak and shaken by her ordeal and I want to take her home.'

'Ain't Kathy O'Malley's place good enough for 'er, then?' someone shouted.

'Of course it is, but she's taking up Pat's bed. Can't have that, can we?'

'You ain't goin' to share it with 'er, then?' another called out and they all laughed.

He grinned. 'What do you think Lord Luffenham would say to that?'

There were several more ribald comments, which he ignored. They were all good natured because there wasn't one among them that had not been affected by Lucy's kindness. 'I'll give double pay to those of you prepared to clear the rails of snow back to the crossing on the lane.'

'That's all of three miles. We'll not be done by dark and if it snows again…'

'Then we must hope that it does not. Will you at least attempt it?'

'Oh, aye, for double pay we'll try anything.'

'Off you go, then. Pat…you, George Munster and Will Williams, come with me. I've another job for you.'

The men dispersed and were soon busy with their shovels. Some of the children, thinking it was a great joke, found smaller spades and went to help, Johnny among them. Myles went over to the cart and examined it carefully. 'Seems stout enough.'

'What are you going to do with it?' Pat asked.

'Put in on the bogey to make a railway carriage. We'll harness a couple of horses to the bogey and, once the line is clear, we'll run it back to the crossing.'

'Then what?'

'We'll take the cart off and harness the horses to that. They ought to be able to manage it along the road as far as Goodthorpe Manor.'

'I hope you know what you're doing, Mr Moorcroft,' Will said. 'If they can't get through, you'll hev took the lady out of a warm bed for nothing.'

'He's right,' Pat put in. 'And I don't begrudge her my bed.'

'I know you don't, Pat, but it's the way she's been raised. She is in what gentlefolk would call a compromising situation and they would not believe she had not been taken advantage of while she was here.'

'Then gentlefolk are bloody hypocrites, beggin' your pardon, sir. It ain't her fault. Nor your'n, neither.'

'No, it isn't,' he said, with a wry smile. 'But there's also your lodgers to consider. They can't come back to your shanty while she is there and where else would they sleep? Most of the huts are full.'

Pat shrugged his shoulders. 'Have it your own way, but if you think we'll let you go the rest of the way on your own, you can think again, Mr Moorcroft. You'll have an escort all the way.'

Myles smiled. 'For double pay, no doubt.'

'They'd do it for no pay at all, but seeing you've offered…' And he laughed.

They dragged the cart to the line and managed to run it up some planks on to the flat bed of the bogey, where they tied it securely with strong rope. Then Myles rigged up a canvas top, begged some blankets and hot bricks and went back to O'Malley's hut, while the others fetched two strong horses, used to pulling wagons full of soil, and harnessed them to the bogey.

Lucy was sitting by the fire on a stool by the fire, talking to Kathy. She was wearing her own clothes. They looked bedraggled, but at least they were dry and decent. She looked up as Myles came in. He was smiling. 'My lady, your carriage awaits.' He swept her an elaborate bow.

She got up and went to him. 'How have you managed that?'

'Come and see.' He wrapped a blanket round her and picked her up as if she weighed no more than a feather.

Lucy looked back at Kathy from the safety of his arms. 'Thank you, Mrs O'Malley. I shan't forget your kindness.'

'You're welcome, my lady. God bless you.'

Myles strode out with her in his arms and deposited her in the cart, calling to her brother as he went. 'Come on, Johnny, you're going for a ride.' The boy gave his spade to Adam and ran to climb up beside his sister. Myles put the hot bricks at their feet and wrapped them in more blankets. They were rough and worn, not what they were used to, but they would keep the pair of them warm. Pat, Will and George climbed up on the bogey to make sure the cart did not slip and Myles mounted Trojan. The rest of the men were some way ahead, clearing the rails. He had taken a terrible gamble, but would it work?

Chapter Eleven

⁓⁓⁓⁓⁓⁓

They reached the crossing without mishap. From here, they had to go for a mile or two along a narrow lane and then on to the main road, which he hoped was still clear. Another couple of miles and they would be at the gates of Goodthorpe Manor and he knew the servants would have kept the drive free of drifting snow.

Lucy and Johnny climbed down while the cart was taken off the bogey and the horses harnessed to it. With so many willing hands it was soon done, but standing waiting took its toll of Lucy and she began to shiver uncontrollably, although Johnny was so excited he danced up and down and did not appear to feel the cold. As soon as the cart was ready, Myles helped them both back on to it, made sure they were well wrapped up and climbed up on the cross plank to drive it. Pat led Trojan. They were strong horses and used to much heavier loads, but the last snowstorm had piled the snow up into fresh drifts and it was hard going. The navvies refused to return to the camp, but continued clearing a passage all the way to Goodthorpe Manor gates. By then it was dark, but he had the lights of the house to guide him.

'You'll manage now,' Pat said, hitching Trojan on to the back of the cart.

'Yes. You have my gratitude. If the weather holds, I'll be back at the works tomorrow with your extra pay.'

'No need, Mr Moorcroft, no need at all.'

Lucy leaned forward. 'Thank you,' she said. 'Say thank you to everyone for me.' It seemed inadequate for what they had done, but she meant to make sure her father acknowledged his debt to them. She would make him understand their bad reputation was undeserved. They turned and marched off back down the road they had so willingly and so nobly cleared.

The door opened as they reached the front door and a footman stood in a pool of light, uncertain whether this was a visitor he ought to welcome or send packing. Myles jumped down and called to him. 'It's me, Craske, come and help.'

He carried Lucy into the house, followed by the footman carrying Johnny, who was now very cold. His teeth were chattering and his bravado had long since vanished.

'Goodness, Myles, what have you got there?' Lady Moorcroft had come out from the drawing room to find her son carrying a large bundle and the footman with another.

'Lady Lucinda Vernley, Mama, and her brother, Viscount Vernley. They have been caught out in the snow and need warm beds and hot food, soup or something like that. Can you organise it?'

Her ladyship hurried forward and lifted the blanket aside to look at Lucy's pale face. 'I'm sorry to be such a bother,' Lucy said, shivering uncontrollably.

'Oh, you poor mite. Take her up to my room, Myles. There's a fire in there. Put the boy on the sofa in my dressing room until I can have somewhere made ready for him.' She turned back towards the room from which she had just emerged. 'Harriet, you are needed.'

In no time at all, her ladyship had taken control and Lucy was put into a warm bed, given a hot drink laced with brandy, and, murmuring her thanks, was soon asleep. Her ladyship returned to the drawing room where Myles, having changed his clothes, was sipping a glass of cognac with his father.

'Now,' she said, seating herself by the fire. 'Explain this strange visitation, if you please.'

He gave them a graphic account of what had happened. 'I couldn't leave her with the navvies and I couldn't risk trying to take her back to Luffenham Hall,' he said. 'The road to the village must be one of the worst in the county and it's considerably farther than coming here, not to say more hilly. I hoped you would not mind.'

'Of course I do not mind. I have been looking forward to meeting the young lady, you know that, but not in such extraordinary circumstances! I wonder what Lord Luffenham will have to say.'

'I hope he will be grateful and realise I acted for the best.'

'He must be worried to death.'

'No doubt he is, but I cannot feel much sympathy for him. None of this need have happened. If he had not been so stubborn over Gorridge...'

'He never did like being crossed,' she said. 'But it was the way he was brought up, to consider his position as heir to an earldom before anything. His parents taught him that his rank meant he had God-given rights over his family and his people and that no one should say him nay. I think I was the first person to frustrate him and he did not like it. I expect his daughter has caused him more soul-searching. You ought to feel sorry for him. If not for him, then for Lady Luffenham.'

'I feel for her. She is a gentle, caring lady and she loves Lucy, but she dare not go against her husband. As soon as I can, I will go to Luffenham and tell them what happened.'

'Yes, you must, but I don't know when that will be. There is no sign of the weather breaking and it will be days before the roads are cleared.'

'I'll go back to the works and walk from there. There must be some snow shoes lying about somewhere. If not, I'll fashion some.'

'It'll be hard going, son,' his father put in.

'But short of sprouting wings and flying, what else can I do?'

'If you must, you must,' his mother said, knowing she could not change his mind and sympathising with the Countess, whom she had never met. If she had had a daughter lost in such dreadful weather, she would have been out of her mind by now.

Dinner had been kept back against Myles's return, but now the butler came to tell them it was served and they moved into the dining room, still talking about Lucy and Johnny, the weather and when it was likely to break so that building the railway line could continue. Myles had the added worry of wondering where Edward Gorridge was and what other mischief he might be planning. Whatever it was, he must be thwarted and Lucy freed from his attentions forever.

Poor darling! What a time of it she had had, but how courageous she had been. He could not forget the sight of her frozen in the snow, with her white face and still body, almost like a corpse. His heart had almost stopped at the sight of her. He thanked God that he had been able to save her. Surely, surely that proved they were destined to be together?

Lucy, exhausted and properly warm for the first time since leaving home, slept until the following morning. She woke to find herself in a huge feather bed in a pretty bedroom with the sun peeping in at the window. Lady Moorcroft was sitting in a chair drawn up to the bedside. Her ladyship was a little plump, with bright blue eyes, pink cheeks and hair that had once been fair, but was now tinged with grey. She wore a morning dress of green grosgrain, decorated in bands of black and turquoise. 'Good morning, my dear,' she said, smiling in such a friendly fashion that Lucy found herself smiling, too. 'I trust you slept well.'

'Oh, yes. I am most grateful to you for taking me in. I must have looked like a bundle of rags when I arrived. And Johnny not much better. I am afraid I was so cold and exhausted I did not thank you properly at the time.'

'No thanks are necessary, Lucy. I may call you Lucy, mayn't I? Or do you prefer Lucinda?'

'Lucy, please. I am only called Lucinda when Papa or Miss Bannister are being severe with me.'

Her ladyship smiled. 'I shall not be severe with you. I have been looking forward to meeting you for some time. Myles has told us all about you.'

'Oh, dear, what has he said?'

'Nothing but good, I assure you. He loves you and I can see why. You are truly beautiful. But I believe there is more to you than that and today we shall get to know each other.'

'I should like that, but I am worried about my parents. They must think I have perished in the snow and Johnny, too. Poor Mama will be distraught.'

'Yes, I am quite sure she is, but Myles has gone to see them.'

'He can get through?' she queried. 'Does that mean the roads are open?'

'No, I do not think so. The snow has stopped, but there has

been so much of it, it will take some time to clear it all away. Myles has ridden as far as the works and means to go the rest of the way on snow shoes. Wonderful things for walking on snow, they are.'

'Oh, I pray he does not get lost, too. When the wind whips up the snow, it blinds you. You can't see a hand in front of your face and on the hill where there as so few landmarks… I shall not rest until he returns.'

'Nor I, my dear, but he is a strong man, used to hard work, and he is accustomed to walking for miles across country when he is surveying a route for a railway. And I believe he is going to take Mr O'Malley to bear him company. We must be patient.'

'Did he tell you what happened, how I came to be out?'

'Yes, Lucy, he did, and very brave you were to go looking for your brother like that. I am sure I should not have had the courage.'

'I did not know it then, but Johnny was lured from the house by Mr Gorridge. I cannot understand why he should do it. It would not change anything and, but for the navvies, Johnny would have died. It does not bear thinking about.'

'Then do not think about it.' A knock at the door interrupted her and a maid came in carrying a tray. 'Good. Here is your breakfast. Eat it up and then we will find some clothes for you. I am afraid your habit is ruined.'

'It was only an old one. I wore it because it is warmer than my new one.' She accepted the tray on to her lap. There was bread and butter, two coddled eggs, some grapes and a pot of fresh coffee. 'Thank you.' She paused. 'Lady Moorcroft, where is my brother?'

'Oh, he has been up and about for ages, exploring the house and the stables. He ate a hearty breakfast downstairs with me and seems none the worse for his experience. Little boys are very resilient, you know.'

'I hope he is not being a nuisance.'

'Good gracious, no. He's a fetching little chap and very comical in those funny clothes. Unfortunately I haven't any boy's clothes that will fit him. It is many years since Myles was that size.' She paused and gave a light laugh. 'If he ever was that small. It seems impossible to believe now, he is grown so big.'

'He is, isn't he? But he's so gentle and kind and patient. But I fear I have tried his patience to the limit.'

Her ladyship put a hand on Lucy's arm. 'It is good that you did.'

'Why?'

'Oh, he would have carried you off and caused no end of a scandal if you had not had a wise head on your shoulders. Starting off your life together in that fashion would not have led to lasting happiness.'

'I am sorry to say it, but Papa is so against Myles. I do not understand why. I cannot see there is anything wrong with earning an honest living.'

Her ladyship smiled. 'It has nothing to do with that, my dear, that is only an excuse. The real reason goes back much further than that. Now finish your breakfast, while I see what I can find for you to wear. We will talk some more later.' She patted Lucy's hand and left the room.

She did not shut the door and Lucy realised it was a connecting room. She could hear doors being opened and closed and the rustle of silk and murmured voices. The maid was in there, too, and they were selecting garments. Lucy smiled. She was much taller and slimmer than her ladyship and she doubted anything of hers would fit. She looked about her; the room was furnished with cupboards and chests of drawers in a pale, delicate wood. The curtains and carpet were pink and the bed linen cream. The dressing table bore hair brushes and bottles and jars; some porcelain ornaments were arranged on the chest. It was a lovely room and, Lucy guessed, her ladyship's own and not a guest room. How privileged it made her feel!

She left the bed and padded across to the window. It looked out on a gravel drive from which every vestige of snow had been cleared, though it still lay like a white carpet over the lawns and flower beds. Beyond the boundary, the hills were covered in snow; it sparkled in the sunlight, pretty but deceptively dangerous. Her thoughts flew to Myles, trudging through it to tell her parents she and her brother were safe. How would her father receive him? And would Mr Gorridge be there?

Comfortable as she was and welcoming and hospitable as Lady Moorcroft was, she wished she were beside him, showing her father and the world in general that there never could be anyone else but Myles for her. She loved him, she loved everything about him: his fine physique, his handsome looks, his voice, which could rise to address a crowd or drop to whisper sweet nonsense for her ears alone. She loved his courage and his compassion, his ability to inspire loyalty and respect. He was a good man and anyone who could not see that must be blind. Lady Moorcroft had hinted she knew the reason her father was so against him, so perhaps she might learn something in the course of the day. But would it help?

Lady Moorcroft came back into the room, bearing an armful of clothes. 'Nothing I have will fit,' she said. 'It will have to be something of Harriet's, she is more your size. You don't mind, do you?'

'Of course I do not mind. Yesterday I was wearing a coarse cotton nightdress belonging to Mrs O'Malley and grateful for it. And I am grateful to you and to Harriet.' She smiled at the maid, who had followed her mistress into the room to help her to dress.

Half an hour later, clad in a dove-grey taffeta gown trimmed with white braid, which was a little too short so that it showed her trim ankles, she was conducted on a tour of the house. Although nothing like as large as Luffenham Hall, it was obviously the home of a wealthy man, and it was furnished in exquisite taste. Lucy loved it. When they went up to the nursery suite and the schoolroom, they found Johnny sitting at a scratched wooden table, completely absorbed in a book about railways.

He looked up when they entered, his face split by a broad smile. 'Lucy, Lucy, you are awake at last. I've been up for ages. I have been out to the stables and down the drive to the road to see how much snow there is and Cook made some gingerbread for me. And now I'm reading Mr Moorcroft's book. It's full of drawings of railway engines and cuttings and vi…' He struggled over the word. 'Viaducts. I am going to be a railway engineer when I grow up.'

'You have to study hard for that, Johnny,' Lucy said, wondering what her parents would make of his strange ambition. Johnny was destined to be the sixth Earl of Luffenham and that did not accord with railway engineering. Poor little chap had much to learn about his destiny. Myles had told her he had not found it easy to be two men in one, and, if Johnny pursued that kind of life, he would find it even harder. Oh, where was Myles? Had he arrived?

Myles was approaching Luffenham Hall, dragging Johnny's sled, which he had found upended in the snow near the bridge. If Gorridge had sent the child hurtling down that bit of slope, no wonder he was frightened. It was dangerously steep with the river at the bottom. He could have crashed down and gone through the ice and might never have been found. The evil intent of the man was obvious. Lucy would not believe it and he supposed the Earl would not believe it, either, and there was no point in saying anything about it. But if he ever met the man again…

His thoughts were brought to an abrupt end when the front door of the Hall burst open and the Earl stood on the step, carrying a sporting gun. 'I thought I told you not to come here again. And what are you doing with that sled? If you have harmed a hair of my son's head…'

'He is unharmed,' Myles said evenly. 'And I found the sled at the bottom of the slope by the river bridge this morning.' He paused as Lady Luffenham came and stood beside her husband. Her ladyship looked pale and exhausted and her eyes were red with weeping.

'Where is he, then? What have you done with him?'

'He is safe and well, my lord. But are you not also interested in the fate of your daughter?'

'If she has seen fit to run away with you, then she is no daughter of mine. She can live among the navvies if that is what she prefers.'

Myles exploded with fury. 'How can you be so uncaring of a daughter who has always been loving and obedient? She has not run away with me. As you see, I am here. I do not run away from my responsibilities. I came in good faith to tell you she was found more dead than alive yesterday afternoon—'

'Where is she?' the Countess broke in, pushing past her husband to reach Myles. 'Is she safe? Is she hurt?'

'My lady, she is well, but it was touch and go for a time.

I took her to Goodthorpe Manor. It was impossible, given the weather, to bring her home here, and my mother is looking after her.'

'Then come into the house. We cannot talk on the step. John,' she addressed her husband, 'Mr Moorcroft has good news and I wish to thank him.'

Almost reluctantly the Earl stood to one side to allow Myles to enter, where he stood, wiping his boots on the mat.

'Let me take your cloak,' her ladyship said, determined to make up for her husband's surliness by looking after their visitor. She handed his cloak to the footman. 'Watkins, refreshments for the gentleman in the drawing room, please.'

He went to obey and Myles followed her ladyship into the drawing room, a huge room where a poor fire gave off little heat. He was glad he had decided to wear proper riding clothes with a cravat and buckskin breeches tucked in to good boots and not the fustian coat and cord trousers of the navvy, even though they would have been warmer. At least the Earl and Countess could not fault his attire. The Countess bade him be seated and he folded his long frame into a chair. The Earl stood with his back to the fire, blocking out its meagre heat. 'Well, Moorcroft, let us hear what you have to say.'

Myles told his tale in a straightforward manner, though he was at pains to emphasise Lady Lucinda's courage in going to look for her brother in such atrocious weather and how cold and ill she was when he found her. His account made the Countess gasp with shock, though she did not interrupt. 'I took her to the navvy encampment, which was near at hand, and the wife of my foreman dried her clothes and gave her some hot soup to warm her,' Myles told them. 'I could not bring her here. The roads were blocked and she could not have walked over the snow, so I decided to take them both to my home. It was easier to move along the railway and I knew my mother would welcome them.' He could not resist making that point.

'You did the right thing, Mr Moorcroft, and we are most grateful to you,' the Countess said. 'Isn't that so, my lord?'

'Yes. Much obliged to you.' It was a huge concession on the part of the Earl and Myles let his breath out in relief, unaware until then that he had been holding it.

'We were at our wits' end,' the Countess put in. 'Everyone was searching for Johnny, and then when Lucy also went missing and her horse came home alone and covered in snow, we were in despair. We continued to search for them, but we were afraid…' She almost choked. 'We had almost resigned ourselves to the worst. You don't know how relieved and happy I am and how grateful we are.'

'My lady, it was a miracle I found her. I had not intended to go to the works yesterday, but changed my mind.'

'Thank God you did.'

'Lucinda found Johnny?' the Earl asked.

'No, it was one of the navvy women. He had tumbled off his sled very close to the river.'

'The river!' exclaimed the Countess. 'How did he manage to get that far? No wonder we could not find him.'

'Was he enticed away?' the Earl demanded. 'Is that what you have come to tell us, that he will be returned for a ransom? I wouldn't put it past those men you employ to think of some mischief like that. You can go back and tell them—' He stopped suddenly when the Countess rose quickly and put her hand on his arm.

Myles was so angry that the Earl could jump to that conclusion that he changed his mind about saying nothing of Gorridge. 'No, my lord, it was not one of my men and I resent the implication. You need to look closer to home for the culprit.'

'One of the servants. Tell me his name and I will make sure he never works in a civilised household again.'

'Not a servant. If you wish to know who it was, I suggest you ask Mr Gorridge.'

'Edward! But he has been helping us to look for the boy. And Lucy, too, when we realised she was also missing. He was most concerned for their safety.'

'I thought he and his parents had decided to return home,' Myles said.

'He came back. He said he had a premonition he might be needed and wished... Oh, never mind that. I am not of a mind to believe he would do anything so foolhardy. He knew how thick the snow was.'

'You have only to ask your son, my lord.'

'What did Johnny tell you?' the Countess asked.

Myles repeated briefly what the boy had told him. 'My lady, I fear the gentleman is not the friend of the family you thought him to be.'

'I never did think that,' her ladyship said firmly. 'And after that business in the glasshouses... I wondered why he came back when his parents seemed to have managed to get home, but he was so plausible and said he had heard that Johnny was lost and hoped we would allow him to help in the search. Do you mean to say he knew where Johnny was all the time?'

'I believe he imagined he had perished.'

'But why? What did he hope to gain?'

'A reward, perhaps? A ransom? Lady Lucinda as a wife? An inheritance? Who knows what was going on in his head.'

Both his listeners were thoughtful, dwelling on these possibilities. It was the Countess who spoke first. 'Mr Moorcroft,

I cannot express my gratitude enough. We are in Mr Moorcroft's debt, are we not, my lord?'

'Yes,' the Earl admitted. 'But I shall not feel happy until I have my son and daughter safely back under this roof.'

'I understand that,' Myles said. 'But the roads are still impassable, particularly the lane from Luffenham village to the high road. As soon as the way is open, you are welcome to come to Goodthorpe Manor and fetch them yourself. I know my mother would welcome a visit from you.' He took a letter from his pocket. 'She has written to you, my lady, thinking that you might appreciate some reassurance from her that Lady Lucinda and Master Johnny are being well looked after and inviting you to visit us.'

Nothing was said while her ladyship perused the short note, which she afterwards handed to her husband. Myles noted that the Earl's hand shook as he took it. He was not as unfeeling as he liked to pretend. 'Much appreciated,' he told Myles, giving it back to his wife.

'Yes, now that we know Lucy and Johnny are safe, we can relax and invite you to stay here tonight,' the Countess added. 'I will write to Lady Moorcroft and thank her myself and give the note to you to take with you tomorrow.'

'I thank you, my lady, but there is still some daylight left and I would like to return home. I am sure you understand— my mother will worry until I am safely back. If you could put together a change of clothes for Lady Lucinda and Master Johnny, I could take them with me. I fear the clothes they were wearing are no longer serviceable.'

She disappeared to do as he suggested and he was left alone with the Earl. Neither spoke for some time, then the Earl cleared his throat. 'I misjudged you, Moorcroft, and for that I beg your pardon. But what I cannot understand is why you insist on playing the navvy. It gives quite the wrong impression.'

'I am not playing at it, my lord. My father believes that a man should work for his bed and board and I chose to interest myself in railways. I learned the business from the bottom, working alongside the navvies and learning about the engineering side from Mr Joe Masters, who was taken on by my grandfather when he first took over the mills and has stayed with the family ever since. Now I am a major contractor on my own account.'

'What about your heritage?'

'That is my heritage, my lord. One day, and I hope it is a long way off yet, I shall be the third Baron Moorcroft, but it is not for that I should like to be remembered, but for the good I did and the railways I built.'

'And your mother…' He paused and his eyes took on a faraway look. 'What does she think of the way you conduct your life?'

Myles smiled. 'She is happy if I am happy, as most mothers would be. Besides, my father has always been the same and she is used to it.'

'I knew your mother once,' his lordship murmured, almost as if talking to himself. 'It was a long time ago. I wonder if she remembers me?'

'You would not be easy to forget, my lord.'

The Earl laughed. 'I may take that whichever way I like, eh?'

'It was meant as a compliment. But if you accept her invitation, you will find out for yourself.'

'That will be for Lady Luffenham to decide. I imagine her impatience will not allow her to sit at home and wait for Lucy and John to come back to us.'

'Did I hear my name?' The Countess had returned, followed by Sarah carrying a carpet bag.

'Yes,' the Earl said. 'We were talking about going to Good-thorpe Manor as soon as the roads are cleared. I said the decision was yours.'

'Of course we will go. So, if I were you, I should make haste and arrange for the able-bodied villagers to make a start clearing away the snow. Now, Mr Moorcroft, do you think you can manage this bag?'

'Yes, of course.' He took it from Sarah with a smile that elicited a small grin in return—he took that to mean she knew about him and Lucy. 'Perhaps you will permit me to take the sled to Master Johnny. I can tie the bag on to that and pull it over the snow.'

They agreed and her ladyship escorted him to the door herself and gave him the reply she had written to his mother. 'I shall find some way of expressing my gratitude to you, Mr Moorcroft,' she said with a smile.

'There is only one thing I want, my lady.' He accepted his cloak from the footman and swung it over his shoulders.

'I know. Have patience. At least you have broken the ice.' She gave a tinkling laugh and he grinned, understanding what she meant.

'I would have all the patience in the world if I could be sure a certain person was not lurking about.'

'If he is, he won't lurk for long, you may be sure of that. My husband is a stubborn man, Mr Moorcroft, and sometimes blind to things he does not wish to see, but I think you have opened his eyes. Once he has spoken to our son and heard the story from him, there will be no welcome here for that so-called gentleman, no welcome anywhere if the story should get out. Go now and God speed you safely home.'

He put the bag on the sled and swung off down the drive with it bumping along behind him. Pat came out of the lodge as he reached the gates. 'By gum, sir, you've been a terrible long time. I was beginning to think you'd met a nasty end.'

Myles grinned at him. 'No, all is well. Home, Pat, as fast as you like.'

Lucy was on the look out for him, so impatient she could not sit still. Was the snow so deep he was stranded? Had he reached Luffenham Hall, but was unable to return? Had her father threatened him again? Had more harsh words been said? But how could Papa not be grateful to him and ready to admit he had been wrong about him? He must surely see what a good, caring man Myles was? Her agitation made Lady Moorcroft laugh. 'Lucy, do sit down and calm yourself. You will have me as nervous as you are, if you do not.'

'I am sorry, my lady.' She settled on a sofa opposite her ladyship. 'I cannot help it.'

Her ladyship smiled. 'Myles means a great deal to you, doesn't he?'

'Everything. And it makes me so unhappy to think he and Papa are at loggerheads. It is all so silly.'

'Yes. Very silly, but you cannot blame Myles.'

'Oh, I do not. But I cannot go against my father.'

'No, of course not. You leave him to me.'

Lucy wondered what her ladyship could have to say to her father to make him change his mind, but she was too polite to ask and a few minutes later they heard the sound of a horse and Lucy flew to the widow to see Myles cantering up the drive on Trojan. He looked strange because he had something bulky strapped on behind, which made the horse's gait a little ungainly. 'He's back!' She turned back to Lady Moorcroft, her eyes alight with joy. 'He's back.'

He disappeared round the side of the house in the direction of the stables and two minutes later he was in the room. Lucy flew to him and then stopped, suddenly uncertain of herself. 'Myles.' Her smile was a little wobbly.

He stepped forward and took both her hands in his own, lifting them one by one to his lips. 'Lucy.' He smiled, looking at her over her hands still held up in his. 'How are you?'

'I'm well. What did Papa say?'

He led her back to the sofa and went to kiss his mother on her cheek. 'Has she been behaving herself, Mama? Resting and keeping warm?'

Lady Moorcroft smiled at her son, relieved to have him safely home again. 'Keeping warm, yes, but as for resting, that is another matter. If you had not come back tonight, I think she would have exploded.'

'I was anxious about you,' Lucy explained. 'You might have been lost in the snow as I was…'

'Or your papa might have shot me dead on sight.'

'Oh, no, even he would not do that when you brought him such good news. He did understand why you had brought us here and not taken us home, didn't he?'

'He could hardly not understand when some of the drifts were deep enough to bury a coach out of sight. We had a long talk about railways and the works and—'

'Myles, do not be so provoking,' his mother put in.

He laughed. 'It's true. After we had talked about Lucy and Johnny and the snow and he acknowledged he was in my debt. Our debt, I should say, because he included you in that, Mama. I have her ladyship's reply to your letter and I believe, as soon as the way is clear, they will both be here to see for themselves that their offspring are well and being looked after.' He felt in his pocket and produced the Countess's letter. 'There's one for you, too, Lucy.'

He watched as they each scanned what had been written. Lucy put her note down with a sigh. 'She is so happy to know I am safe and she hopes I will enjoy my stay here and that I will make sure Johnny behaves himself. She says she has given you some clothes for me.'

'Yes, I left the bag in the hall. There's a change for Johnny, too. Where is the young shaver, by the way? I brought his sled for him.'

'He is in his room, reading your railways books. They seem to fascinate him. He says he wants to be a railway engineer when he grows up.'

'Very laudable,' he said. 'But I don't know what his papa will say to that. He made it clear in his little talk with me that he did not approve of gentlemen dirtying their hands.'

'Oh, he has not changed his views on that, then?'

'Doesn't look like it.'

'Lady Luffenham says she and Lord Luffenham will be happy to accept our invitation as soon as it is possible to travel,' her ladyship said, folding her own letter and putting it on the table beside her. 'Now, Lucy, all is well and we can enjoy our time together and really get to know each other.'

Lucy agreed, but the thing that was uppermost in her mind was whether her father had softened enough to allow her and Myles to marry. It was what she most wanted in the world, but it did not sound as if he had. 'Myles, did…did you say anything to Papa about us?'

'Us?' he queried, pretending not to know what she meant.

'You know what I mean.'

'No. He may be glad to know you are safe and he did acknowledge that he had misjudged me and I decided that was enough to be going on with.'

'You are probably right. When he comes to fetch me, we will face him together.'

That was longer than either of them expected, because it snowed again overnight and, though the fall was not as great as on previous days, it was enough to cover the roads again. Myles, knowing that no work would be done and that the navvies were warm and well fed, did not venture out to the works. Instead he took Lucy all round the house, pointing out things of interest—ornaments his mother had collected over the years, heirlooms that came from the Porson side of the family— showed her portraits of his grandfather standing at the door of the mill beside his grandmother, others of his Porson grand- mother, upright and regal, every inch a viscountess. He talked and she talked, happy in each other's company. When it stopped snowing, they took Johnny out on his sled, helped him to make a snowman, which they dressed in an old tailcoat and a top hat, played snowballs with him and laughed a great deal. Whenever they were out of sight of anyone else, Myles would take her in his arms to kiss her and tell her how much he loved her.

It was an idyllic time, which she knew would soon have to come to an end. It worried her that she had been so happy when perhaps she had no cause to be. She was prepared to defy her father, but Myles was not. He had not even said anything to Papa when he had had the opportunity, when her father had acknowledged he was in Myles's debt and would have granted him any favour. By the time her father came to fetch her he would have had time to regret unbending even that far and be back to his old intransigence.

There was no more snow and a few days later the icicles began to drip from the eaves. The roof let slip its burden in great avalanches, which made Johnny laugh. He took a spade and insisted on helping the outdoor staff clear it away. Myles and Lucy set off down the drive to look at the state of the road. Men from the workhouse were clearing it and this time Myles thought it would stay clear. 'I'll wager Lord Luffenham has an army working at his end,' he said. 'They will be here tomorrow.'

'I want to see Mama and Papa, of course, but in a way I'm sorry. I've been so happy here.'

'I have been happy to have you here and what I want most in the world is for you to be with me all the time, for ever and ever.' He lifted her hand to put it against his cheek.

'It is what I want, too, but will Papa relent, do you think?'

'We shall soon find out. Now let us go back. You are shivering.'

He had gone to the works the following afternoon when the Luffenham carriage rolled up to the door. Johnny, who had been watching for them, rushed out to fling himself at his mother. She hugged him and kissed him and his father ruffled his hair. They went into the house with Johnny talking nineteen to the dozen about what he had been doing since he arrived at Goodthorpe Manor. He seemed to have forgotten his ordeal in the snow.

Lucy met them on the step. 'Mama!' She ran to embrace her mother and then turned to her father. 'Papa. Oh, it is good to see you both.'

The Earl did something she could not remember him ever doing before; he stooped to kiss her forehead. 'Glad to see you safe and well,' he said.

She led them indoors where Lady Moorcroft was waiting to greet them. There was a certain restraint, as if they were unsure of each other, but her ladyship's smile of welcome dispelled that and they adjourned to the drawing room where Lord Moorcroft rose from his seat beside a roaring fire, shook the Earl by the hand and added his own welcome.

'You'll stay the night?' he said after bidding them take a seat beside the fire and exchanging news about the weather and how it had affected local transport. Apparently it was worse than anyone could remember and everything had been brought to a standstill.

'Thank you,' the Earl said. He was still a little stiff.

'Myles has gone to the site to see the men get back to work,' his lordship said. 'He will be back directly.'

'We are so very, very grateful to him,' the Countess said.

'No doubt you will want to hear all about what happened to Lucy and Johnny from their own lips,' Lady Moorcroft said. 'I will show you to your rooms and you can have a little private talk with them, while I make sure all is well in the kitchen. We dine at five, if that is convenient.'

'Of course,' the Countess said, following her ladyship as she conducted them to the room they had had prepared for them. Lucy followed, with Johnny holding her hand.

Lucy was soon able to confirm everything that Myles had told them and Johnny, who could not be repressed, told them about Mr Gorridge. 'He left me,' he said, aggrieved.

The Countess hugged him. 'He is a very bad man, Johnny, but thanks to the navvies and Mr Moorcroft, you are safe and well.'

'I like Mr Moorcroft. He didn't go off and leave me. He is a good man.'

'Yes, Johnny, he is.' She looked meaningfully as her husband, who made no comment.

'Why did Mr Gorridge come back?' Lucy asked them.

'He never left the village,' her mother put in. 'I am not sure, but I think he hoped to inveigle his way back into our good books by luring Johnny away and then pretending to find him, although we did not know that at the time, of course. And when you went missing, too, he put on such a display of sorrow and remorse, we were all taken in by it.'

'But he must have known that Johnny would tell you the real story.'

'Didn't expect him to be found alive,' the Earl said.

'He must be twisted in his mind.'

'Yes, I think he is,' her mother said. 'He expected us to be grateful for bringing home a—' She stopped and looked at her son. 'No, we will not think of it.'

'Where is he now?' Lucy asked. 'I do not want to come back to Luffenham if he is there. I do not trust him.'

'He is not there,' her father assured her. 'He has fled the country.'

'Oh, poor Lady Gorridge.'

'Just goes to show it doesn't do to spoil children. Giving way to their whims and fancies leads to wayward adults.'

This statement filled Lucy with alarm. It did not bode well for her and Myles. She might have said something, but saw her mother shaking her head and desisted. 'We had better change and go downstairs,' her ladyship said. 'Lady Moorcroft will be wondering where we have got to.'

Harriet helped Lucy to dress in the white evening gown her mother had brought for her. It had a fitted bodice, huge puffed sleeves and a wide, tiered skirt, each tier trimmed with deep pink ribbon. She put pink ribbons in her hair, then went downstairs to the drawing room, where everyone was gathered, waiting for dinner to be served. Myles came back and joined them soon afterwards. He greeted her with a polite smile, shook the Earl's hand, bowed over the Countess's and seemed perfectly at ease, though Lucy, knowing him so well, noticed a slight twitch in his jaw, which told her he was nervous and anxious to do nothing and to say nothing to antagonise the Earl. It seemed all wrong to her that they could not behave naturally. Thankfully Lord Moorcroft was alive to the situation and took over the conversation and they went into the dining room apparently at ease with each other.

Under the influence of their host's generous hospitality, the Earl visibly relaxed and was soon enjoying a joke with him and talking about the railways and Lord Moorcroft's other business interests, although everyone was careful to avoid anything contentious. Lady Moorcroft was a charming hostess and she and the Countess were soon behaving like old friends and calling each other by their Christian names. Lucy looked at Myles and found him looking at her. He winked slowly, making her blush furiously. The evening ended with music when everyone contributed their party piece.

Lucy went to bed, knowing they would be going home tomorrow and she did not know when she would see Myles again. If only someone would say something! They had talked about everything under the sun except what was uppermost in her mind. Even Myles seemed to be colluding with that. He had behaved in a very polite, correct manner, as if trying to prove that he could be a gentleman when he chose. She doubted if that made any difference to her father.

Next morning, while Harriet packed her few clothes, she went down for breakfast, hoping Myles had not left for the works already and she could say goodbye to him. It was going to break her heart and she did not know how she was going to keep her misery from showing.

She was passing the drawing room door when she heard

Lady Moorcroft's voice, and what she was saying made Lucy stop and listen. 'Come down off your high horse, John Vernley, and stop being the Earl and be a father for once.'

Lucy gasped, wondering how her ladyship dared to address him like that. She did not hear her father's reply because she saw Myles coming across the hall towards her. She put her finger to her lips to tell him to be quiet and he came and stood beside her.

'You ought to be grateful to me,' her ladyship went on.

'I am. I have expressed my gratitude more than once. What more do you want?'

'I did not mean grateful for looking after Lucy and Johnny. I want no thanks for that, it was a pleasure to have them. I meant for turning you down all those years ago. If I had not you would never have met and married Lady Luffenham, would you?'

'No, of course not. I would have been married to you and Myles would be my son.'

'Oh.' She sounded taken aback. 'Would you have liked him for a son?'

'He is a fine man, a credit to you.'

'He is also his father's son, John, as little Johnny is yours. Yours and Maryanne's. She is the perfect wife for you. I should not have been so compliant, I can tell you, and my forthrightness would have had us quarrelling within a month.'

'Very probably,' he said wryly.

'Then it all worked out for the best. You would not change your family for a king's ransom, would you?'

'No, of course not. Nor my wife.'

'Then isn't it time you told them so?'

Lucy looked at Myles, who reached for her hand and smiled.

'Perhaps. But where is all this leading?'

'Can you not guess?'

'Tell me.'

'Lucy and Myles. You must know they are in love.'

'Love!'

'Yes, have you never heard of it? It is a strange condition of the heart that sometimes makes us behave irrationally, but it is ignored at our peril.'

Lucy heard her father laugh. She rarely heard him laugh, especially lately. Myles squeezed her hand and she looked up at him. He was grinning from ear to ear. 'You always did have a way with you, Hetty Porson,' the Earl said. 'You are saying you want me to consent to my daughter marrying your son?'

'Is there any reason why they should not marry?'

'He is not what I had in mind for Lucy.'

'No, you were all for forcing her to marry that charlatan Edward Gorridge. Your judgement was sadly amiss there, John.'

They did not hear her father's response because the Countess came down the stairs and they moved hurriedly away towards the breakfast room. Lucy was inclined to giggle and Myles was smiling broadly; they couldn't help it. The thought of the Earl meekly allowing himself to be scolded by Lady Moorcroft was so funny. Oh, how they hoped her words would have some effect. Lucy wondered if her father might take her to one side and talk to her, but the time for their departure came and he had said nothing and her hopes plummeted.

The carriage was brought to the door, their bags were all loaded along with Johnny's sled and there was nothing else to do but say their goodbyes. Lucy and Myles had had no chance to be alone and their farewells would have to be said in front of everyone, which meant they would consist of a handshake, a smile and a few polite words. Lucy made up her mind that, as soon as the hills were free of snow, she would ride Midge to the navvy camp. Nothing and no one would stop her from seeing the man she loved again.

Lady Moorcroft hugged Johnny and kissed Lucy and the Countess, while Lord Moorcroft shook everyone's hand. Myles came forward to say goodbye. The Earl shook his hand. That seemed to Lucy to be the end of it. It was all very well for her mother to tell her to be patient, but patience and love did sit comfortably together.

She brightened a little and sat forward when she heard her father say, 'No ban on coming to Luffenham, lad. You are welcome to come whenever you like.'

'I will do that, my lord. And very soon, because there is something very particular I want to ask you.'

Her father chuckled. 'I thought you might, but perhaps you should put your question to my daughter.'

'With your permission I will do that very thing,' Myles told him, taking Lucy's hand and helping her into the coach beside her mother. 'Soon,' he murmured. 'Very soon.'

The Earl climbed in beside them and they were away, but Lucy was crying tears of happiness. It was going to be all right. Myles was going to come to Luffenham Hall to ask her to marry him and this time it would be done formally with the agreement and good wishes of both families. And then… She sat back in her seat and allowed herself to dream.

The railway was finished and a party held to celebrate it, but that was not the only celebration that spring. Lucy and Myles were married at Luffenham church, attended by Rosemary and Esme and Johnny. When they emerged from the service, they found hundreds of cheering navvies and their families lining the road back to Luffenham Hall, where the wedding breakfast was to be held. Lucy leant from the carriage to wave to them.

'Are you happy with your navvy?' Myles asked, drawing her back beside him.

'Yes. Oh, yes.' He was impeccably dressed in dove grey with a white shirt and a mauve cravat. He could not have looked less like a navvy. 'What about you?'

'Do you need to ask? Later I will show you just how contented I am with my bride.'

Later that day, they set off in the carriage to the Lake District for a honeymoon. The railway between east and west was not yet a reality, but Lucy did not mind the slower journey. It meant they could savour the signs of spring all about them: burgeoning trees, yellow daffodils, amber gilly flowers and the song of the birds. The winter, the worst in living memory, was behind them, and they could see nothing ahead but sunshine; if the weather should turn inclement and a few tears were shed, well, that was life and they would face whatever came together.

MILLS & BOON

Historical

On sale 1st June 2007

Regency

A SCOUNDREL OF CONSEQUENCE
by Helen Dickson

William Lampard, distinguished military captain,
kept London abuzz with scandal. Against his better judgement,
he made a wager to seduce Miss Cassandra Greenwood.
But despite her provocative ways, and the impudent sway
of her skirts, he quickly realised that her innocence and
goodness put her above a mere dalliance…

Regency

AN INNOCENT COURTESAN
by Elizabeth Beacon

Caroline Besford was forced her into marriage with a
man who refused to share her bed. In making her escape,
Caro became Cleo – an untouched courtesan! Amazingly,
the husband who ignored his plain bride is now pursuing her!
But what will the Colonel do when he discovers that his
darling Cleo is his dowdy wife, Caroline?

Available at WHSmith, Tesco, ASDA, and all good bookshops
www.millsandboon.co.uk

0507/04b

MILLS & BOON

Historical

On sale 1st June 2007

Regency

THE RAKE'S PROPOSAL
by Sarah Elliott

Katherine Sutcliff would bring a scandalous secret to the
marriage bed. She needed a suitable match – so why was
she distracted by her most unsuitable attraction to the
disreputable Lord Benjamin Sinclair?

THE KING'S CHAMPION
by Catherine March

With Eleanor's reputation compromised, the King
commands her to marry. Ellie is overjoyed to be tied to her
perfect knight. But Troye is desperate to resist the emotions
she is reawakening in him…

THE HIRED HUSBAND
by Judith Stacy

Rachel Branford is intent on saving her family's name.
And handsome Mitch Kincaid may be the answer! Abandoned
in an orphanage, Mitch has struggled to gain wealth and power.
Until he finds himself tempted by Rachel's money…
then Rachel herself!

Available at WHSmith, Tesco, ASDA, and all good bookshops
www.millsandboon.co.uk

MILLS & BOON
Super
Historical

On sale 1st June 2007

ROGUE'S SALUTE
by Jennifer Blake

They are the most dangerous men in New Orleans, skilled swordsmen who play by no rules but their own – heroes to some, wicked to many, irresistible to the women they love…

At ease making life-and-death decisions between breaths, *maître d'armes* Nicholas Pasquale proposes marriage to a beautiful and desperate stranger. She's a challenge he can't resist.

Though pledged to the church since infancy, Juliette Armant must save her family in the only way possible…by marriage.

A practical arrangement, which someone is desperate to prevent. But practical turns to heady desire when a rogue's kiss unleashes the sensual woman within…

Available at WHSmith, Tesco, ASDA, and all good bookshops
www.millsandboon.co.uk

Victorian London is brought to vibrant life in this mesmeric new novel!

London, 1876

All her life, Olivia Moreland has denied her clairvoyant abilities, working instead to disprove the mediums that flock to London. But when Stephen, Lord St Leger, requests her help in investigating an alleged psychic, she can't ignore the ominous presence she feels within the walls of his ancient estate. Nor can she ignore the intimate connection she feels to Stephen, as if she has somehow known him before...

Available 20th April 2007

www.millsandboon.co.uk

FREE

2 BOOKS AND A SURPRISE GIFT!

We would like to take this opportunity to thank you for reading this Mills & Boon® book by offering you the chance to take TWO more specially selected titles from the Historical Romance™ series absolutely FREE! We're also making this offer to introduce you to the benefits of the Mills & Boon® Reader Service™—

- ★ **FREE home delivery**
- ★ **FREE gifts and competitions**
- ★ **FREE monthly Newsletter**
- ★ **Books available before they're in the shops**
- ★ **Exclusive Reader Service offers**

Accepting these FREE books and gift places you under no obligation to buy; you may cancel at any time, even after receiving your free shipment. Simply complete your details below and return the entire page to the address below. You don't even need a stamp!

YES! Please send me 2 free Historical Romance books and a surprise gift. I understand that unless you hear from me, I will receive 4 superb new titles every month for just £3.69 each, postage and packing free. I am under no obligation to purchase any books and may cancel my subscription at any time. The free books and gift will be mine to keep in any case.

H7ZEE

Ms/Mrs/Miss/Mr...Initials ....
                                                                                    BLOCK CAPITALS PLEASE

Surname ....

Address ....

....

....Postcode ....

Send this whole page to:
The Reader Service, FREEPOST CN81, Croydon, CR9 3WZ

Offer valid in UK only and is not available to current Mills & Boon Reader Service™ subscribers to this series. Overseas and Eire please write for details. We reserve the right to refuse an application and applicants must be aged 18 years or over. Only one application per household. Terms and prices subject to change without notice. Offer expires 31st July 2007. As a result of this application, you may receive offers from Harlequin Mills & Boon and other carefully selected companies. If you would prefer not to share in this opportunity please write to The Data Manager at PO Box 676, Richmond, TW9 1WU.

Mills & Boon® is a registered trademark owned by Harlequin Mills & Boon Limited.
Historical Romance™ is being used as a trademark. The Mills & Boon® Reader Service™ is being used as a trademark.